Reminding
AVERY

NEW YORK TIMES BESTSELLING AUTHOR
KAYLEE RYAN

Cover Design: Sara Eirew
Cover Photography: Sara Eirew
Editing: Hot Tree Editing
Formatting: Integrity Formatting

Chapter 1

Five years ago

Avery

"I'm heading out. I told Harley I would pick her up before the game," I yell out to my parents as I fly down the stairs.

"Hold up, Av. You got money?" Dad asks, standing and walking toward me where I now stand at the bottom of the stairs.

My father always wants to make sure I have money. Not because I'm a spoiled brat, but because he says he never wants me to be stranded. Mom confessed that it's secretly because he wants to make sure that, if I decide to participate in sexual activities and the guy's not prepared, I have the cash to cover the condoms. My then-boyfriend, Scott, who was two years older than me, and I were really close, and they feared that we might take the next step. I considered it, but I just wasn't ready. Scott was understanding and never pressured me. Turns out he was getting serviced from one of his sister's friends while they were home from college on summer break.

"Yep. I got my check in the mail today for tutoring and cashed it on the way home from school."

"You girls be safe. Curfew is midnight," he reminds me.

"You know it." I stand on my tiptoes and kiss his cheek. "Bye, Mom!" I yell out over his shoulder.

"Bye, sweetie. Have a good time. Drive safe," she says as I'm rushing out the door.

I climb into my Kia Sportage and head toward Harley's house. She and I have been best friends since she moved to town when we were in the sixth grade. We bonded over our love of school supplies. Seriously, I was obsessed and so was she. Most girls got excited about the new clothes, but not this girl; give me the pens and cool pads of paper. I'm still a sucker for school supplies, which makes it a given that my major next year at college is going to be education. I tutor three days a week after school and I love it.

When I pull into Harley's driveway, she's standing on the front porch waiting. We're both excited about tonight. Tomorrow night is the first football game of the season for our school, Montgomery High. It's a Saturday game, since the hosting school is doing a big ground-breaking ceremony at their new field tonight.

"Hey!" she says, opening the back door. She tosses her overnight bag into the back seat. "I'm so excited for this. Usually it's just a pep rally at school. Your brother is cool as hell."

My brother, Alan, is the high school football coach. He's ten years older than me. Mom and Dad were high school sweethearts and got pregnant soon after graduation. Mom had some complications and was told it was unlikely she would be able to carry another baby. They tried for years before finally giving up, accepting that they were destined to be a family of three. A few years later, I came along.

"Right? I didn't even have to suggest it. It's like he's actually cool or something." I laugh.

"That's because he is and you know it." Harley laughs along with me.

"Shh, don't let him hear you say that. His ego is big enough already." It's the truth. My brother is the high school science teacher, the football coach, and a good-looking guy: tall, dark hair, and muscular. He played football in high school and college, and always wanted to come back home and coach. Lucky for him his high school coach retired two years ago and Alan was offered the position. My parents were thrilled because he was moving back home. Now if Mom could just get him to settle down so she can have a few grandkids.

"On behalf of the entire female population of Montgomery High, let me just go on record stating that science is a hell of a lot more fun when you get to stare at his fine ass."

I can't help myself as I laugh. It's true, all the girls in our school—and even a few of the teachers, from what I've heard—drool over my brother. "So, are you going to talk to Brad tonight?"

"Who knows. One minute he acts like he's interested, and the next he's cold as ice. I don't understand him."

"He's got a lot going on. This is our senior year, and you know he has scholarships riding on this season. Cut him a little slack."

"I know, I just hate the way it makes me feel. Like he can just toss me aside and only come around when it's convenient for him."

"It's a lot of pressure. I remember when Alan was going through this, he was moody as hell."

"You were eight."

"I know that, but I also remember him being moody and mean his last year at home."

"I know you're right." She tilts her head back against the seat. "If I could just get a commitment out of him, something more permanent you know? It would ease my anxiety."

"Maybe tonight will be the night. Text him and ask him to meet us after."

Her fingers fly across the screen of her phone as we pull into the parking lot.

"He said he was getting ready to text me to tell me to wait for him."

"See," I say, tapping her arm. "Now, if he would bring Dylan with him, all would be right in the world."

"You know he will. Those two are just like us, two peas in a pod. You rarely see one without the other."

"Maybe I should rephrase that. If he would bring Dylan and he would notice me," I amend my earlier statement.

"He notices, Avery, trust me. He's just scared as hell that his coach is your older brother."

"I can't wait until college. I'll no longer be Coach Stanton's little sister."

"Yeah, even I get some reluctance just from being your best friend. Maybe that's what's holding Brad back."

"Maybe," I reply. I hate to think that because she and I are friends that guys, especially Brad, shy away from her. I know how much she likes him. "Come on, let's go grab a seat." I pull the keys from the ignition and grab my phone. We find a spot midway up the bleachers just as the band makes their way onto the field.

Harley grabs my arm. "This is our last season. Next year we'll no longer be the big fish in the little pond. College is going to be so different."

"It is. At least we're going to the same college. It would suck to go different places."

"Truth!" Harley says adamantly. "There he is." She points out on the field to where the players are now lining up beside Alan. "Oh I forgot to tell you. I have paint so we can paint their numbers on our cheeks tomorrow."

"Their numbers?" I ask her. "Whose number am I going to use?"

"Number seventeen." She grins.

Number seventeen, also known as Dylan Knight, is our quarterback. He's also Brad's best friend and hot as hell. Being Coach Stanton's little sister has placed me in the no-go zone with the football players, as well as most of the guys at this school. "I don't know about all that. That's a little forward, don't you think? I'll just wear a small warrior head." We are the Montgomery High Warriors, after all.

"Live a little, Av. You know you like him," she teases.

"He's cute, but no way is he willing to go against Alan and date me. None of the guys at this school are. I'm just going to let this year pass me by. College cannot come soon enough."

"Eep! It's going to be so much fun, roomie," she says.

My brother steps up to the mic and a hush falls over the crowd. We all listen with rapt attention as he talks about this year's seniors and going to state again this year. Did I mention that the Montgomery Warriors are the defending state champs? My brother is in full Coach Stanton mode as he introduces his players and their stats.

"There's my man," Harley cheers when Alan announces Brad.

I smile and nod and cheer just as loud as she does. I have to show my support, not only for my brother but my team. I'm a warrior through and through.

"And now our team captain, starting quarterback, Dylan Knight!" The student body goes wild as Dylan steps forward and waves.

"Are you breathing?" Harley teases.

I know she's teasing, but I suck in a big breath anyway. He's gorgeous—dark hair, tall, lean, and muscular. He's the star of the show, one of the most popular guys in school, and in his eyes I'm untouchable. I don't take my eyes off him for the rest of the pep rally. No one notices me staring, and I take full advantage of that.

"Hey." Harley waves her hand in front of my face. "You ready? Brad just texted and said he would meet us at the gate by the parking lot."

I follow along behind Harley as we push our way through the crowd. Several of our fellow classmates stop to ask us if we're going to the bonfire. We are, of course. The plan is for everyone to go to Johnny's Pizza, which is a small local mom-and-pop joint here in town. After that we head to Brad's place. His parents have a farm, and we all pile into the field around the fire. We sit on tailgates, car hoods, wooden stumps— you name it. It's a good time.

Brad is strict on no alcohol at his parties. One, his parents would flip their shit, and two, so would my brother. He's hardcore when it comes to his players and underage drinking, swearing that, if they were caught drinking, he would bench them the entire season. Good luck getting a scholarship that way. Don't get me wrong, there will be alcohol; they'll just hide it from Brad. It's not like he's innocent, but during the season the guys keep their noses squeaky clean.

When we reach the gate, I pull out my phone and text Alan.

Me: Good speech, coach.

Alan: That's big brother to you, kid.

Me: Yeah, yeah.

Alan: Be safe tonight. Keep an eye on my team.

Me: Sure thing.

That's another thing—he always tells me to keep an eye on the team. I wonder if he's ever told them he has me watching. Maybe that's what keeps the players away from me. It's like I've been diagnosed with cooties or something. I always say I'm going to ask him, but I don't want to have the conversation that will surely lead after that one. Why do you care so much? Is there a player you have your eye on? Yeah, no, thank you. I'll endure this year until college and I can step out of his shadow.

"Hey," Brad's deep voice greets Harley. "You guys going to get pizza?"

"We are. You need a ride?" she asks.

"Nah, Dylan's driving. You're going to the bonfire too, right?"

"Yeah. We have curfew, but we'll be there for a little while anyway."

"Coach has us all on curfew so that's not an issue. Hey, Avery," he says, turning to me.

I raise my head and wave, offering him a small smile. It's then that Dylan walks up behind him. His hair is still damp from his shower, and even that's hot to me. He can make anything look good. He's that gorgeous.

"You two riding with us?" he asks Harley, his eyes slowing trailing over to me.

"No, Avery drove. We're going to be there though."

He doesn't acknowledge that. "You ready, man? We're on curfew so we need to get moving."

"Yeah." Brad leans in and kisses Harley. Just a quick peck on the lips, but the grin she's wearing is all he needs to know. She's all his. "See you there. I'll save the two of you a seat."

We watch them walk away. It's impossible not to.

"You excited?" she asks as we head toward my car.

"About?"

"Hanging out with Dylan tonight."

"Technically, I'm hanging out with you and Brad as the third wheel. I can't believe this is the first time for this. How long have the two of you been talking now?"

"Just a little over a month. They've been busy with football, and you were at the beach for two weeks without me," she fake whines.

"You were invited," I remind her.

"I know," she sighs. "Damn summer job."

We both laugh at that. She signed up to be a camp counselor this summer and it ended up taking way more of her free time than she originally thought since others kept backing out.

"Regardless, you like him. This is your chance to let him see you for who you are and not just Coach Stanton's little sister."

"Uh-huh," I agree, not really giving in to what she's saying. There is no way the team captain is going to risk it with the coach's little sister. I see a date-less, boyfriend-less senior year in my future.

Chapter
2

Dylan

I'm excited as hell for this season. It's kind of bittersweet, knowing it will be my last. I'm going to live, eat, and breathe football this year. Not that it's any different than years past, but it kind of is. Brad, my best friend, is going off to college to play ball. That's never been my plan; I'm lucky to get through high school with my grades. College is not for a guy like me, so this is it. High school is my glory years and I've accepted that, so I've made a vow to limit my distractions and focus solely on football. I want my final year of playing the sport I love to be the best yet. Last year as starting quarterback, I led our team to the state finals and we brought home the trophy. I want a repeat this year.

"You about ready?" Brad asks as he throws stuff from his locker into his gym bag.

"Yeah, I'm sure Johnny's is getting packed."

"You know it, but they always save us a booth. Star quarterback and running back!" he cheers, holding his fist out for me. I don't leave him hanging and knock mine with his.

"Harley's coming."

"What's going on with the two of you? You've been back and forth with her."

He runs his hands through his hair. "I know. It's just that she's Avery's best friend. Coach's little sister and all that."

"You like her?"

He nods.

"Then don't worry about it. Avery doesn't strike me as the type to go running to Coach. Besides, she's been to a few parties and seen things, and it never gets back to him."

"I know it's just weird as hell hanging out with Coach's sister. And those two are tight, have been for years."

"I think you're using that as an excuse. Man the fuck up," I say, slapping his shoulder and grabbing my bag out of my locker.

"What about you? You got your eye on anyone for tonight?"

"Nope. I'm steering clear of all distractions—well, as much as possible. Got to keep my head in the game until the season's over."

"You really going to stick to that, man?"

"Yep. I mean, at least for the first game of the season." I laugh.

He looks down at his phone. "Harley's meeting me at the gate. I'm going to go make sure she doesn't need a ride. Meet you at the truck?"

"All right, man," I agree and begin to pack up my bag. Once I'm finished I decide to go find him.

Maybe she'll be there. Avery Stanton. She's easily the most beautiful girl in school, and she's completely off-limits. None of us want to risk breaking Coach's little sister's heart—not that any of us has been brave enough to take the chance. He's a fair guy, but family is family. Besides, I've already sworn off all distractions until the season is over. That doesn't mean I can't look, of course. That's all I've done the last four years is look. I imagine most of my classmates, if not all of them, have done the same damn thing. Her long blonde hair, those long tan legs that she likes to cover in skirts and shorts. If her beauty isn't enough to knock you on your ass, her personality will finish the job. She's nice to everyone, always smiling. She's the full package. Avery is the kind of girl you bring home to your family. She's a forever girl. We all know it, and that's one of the reasons we stay away.

I find them at the gate and stop beside Brad. "You two riding with us?" I ask Harley, my eyes slowing trailing over to Avery.

"No, Avery drove. We're going to be there though," Harley informs me.

"You ready, man? We're on curfew, so we need to get moving," I say to Brad.

"Yeah."

At his confirmation, I turn and head toward my truck.

"She's coming back to the bonfire," Brad says, wearing a goofy-ass grin as he climbs into the truck.

"There you go. You need to nail that shit down. Stop playing games."

"I'm not playing games."

"You keep telling yourself that, buddy." I laugh.

"She's bringing Avery with her. Well, technically Avery is bringing Harley, but you know what I mean."

"And?"

"I thought maybe you could, you know, hang out with the three of us, make her feel less like a third wheel."

"What part of 'no distractions' did you not get? And besides that, Coach's little sister?"

"I didn't tell you to fuck her, just asked you to hang around, group setting and all that. Make them both more relaxed."

"We'll see how it goes," I say, not really committing. Sure, I would be crazy to not want to hang out with them. They're both nice girls and easy on the eyes. Avery has always seems so... untouchable. It might be fun to hang out with her for once.

"It's not like we haven't gone to school together all our lives."

"I know that, dumbass, but we've never really hung out with Coach's little sister before. Don't you think that's weird?"

"Just tonight," he says, not answering my question.

"Fine," I agree. It's purely selfish on my part. I want to be around her. I've admired her from afar. Sure, we've had classes together and we've interacted, passed each other in the hall, a smile or a wave here and there, but I've never actually just hung out with her outside of school. Part of me agreed so I can see if she's really the whole package that I've labeled her with in my head.

"This place is jammed," Brad says as I guide my truck into the parking lot of Johnny's Pizza.

"Looks like the entire student body."

We make our way inside and our teammates and classmates cheer for us as we enter the room.

"I saved you boys your booth in the back," Johnny himself greets us. Football players are like royalty in our small hometown. Not to mention my dad owns a very successful auto repair shop just down the street, so I'm here a lot getting food for the two of us. We're just two bachelors trying to survive.

"Thanks, man," I say, shaking his hand. A lesson learned from my father. Treat them with respect and always give a firm handshake.

We slide into the booth, one of us on each side. Brad's texting who I assume is Harley, letting her know where we're sitting. It's not until the girls appear beside our table that I realize what's about to happen. Brad scoots in, making room for Harley to sit next to him. That means Avery, the very beautiful Avery Stanton, is going to be sitting next to me. I may be on a self-imposed lockdown, warding off all distractions, but this night just got a hell of a lot better. I was reluctant before, but it's just four friends hanging out. I'm going to take what I can get.

"Hey," I say to her, sliding over in the booth.

"Hi." She waves at me and I fight back a grin. She's cute as hell.

We make small talk about what everyone is going to eat, deciding on two large pepperoni pizzas—though let's face it, Brad and I can devour one each on our own, easy. Order placed and drinks delivered, I prepare for awkward silence, but that's not what happens.

"That catch at the end of the pep rally, you had everyone in the stands holding their breaths," Avery says to Brad. Then she turns to look at me. "And you, a perfect spiral. You two really are magic on the field together."

I just stare at her, my mouth hanging open. I've never met a girl who knows about football. Hell, not even the cheerleaders seem to understand more than just the basics, and they never talk about it.

Harley laughs. "Stop showing off." She smiles at her best friend.

"Hey, not my fault my dad and brother took time to explain the game to me." She jerks her thumb at Harley. "I've tried for four years now to explain it to her and she's just not getting it."

"Maybe I can help," Brad offers, placing his hand over hers on the table. I watch as a blush coats her cheeks. He moves their hands to his lap and they're both wearing goofy grins. My boy has it bad.

"Thanks," I finally say to Avery.

"So, are you ready for tomorrow night's game?" she asks, taking a drink of her sweet tea. "After that little preview tonight, you know you all are going to kick ass."

"Yeah, first game of the season. Last first game ever."

"Still not going to play college ball?" she asks.

A flutter in my chest. I've never made it a secret that I don't plan to play college ball, but the fact that she knows that about me? It's an odd feeling.

"No." I take a huge gulp of my sweet tea. "It was always the plan for me to take over the shop one day. Don't need college for that. Dad's taught me everything he knows." I wait for her judgment but it never comes.

"That's honorable. Taking over the family business. You're very fortunate that your father is willing to pass the torch of his success."

"Well, not right away. When he's ready to retire. But in the meantime I'll be working side by side with him, learning more each day. What about you? You're heading off to college, right?"

"Yeah, Harley and I are actually going to be roommates."

"Where you headed?"

"Western University. It's a smaller university in Indiana."

I know the one. It's the same one that Brad just signed on to play ball for. He got a full ride. I find his eyes across the table and they're wide. Slowly he turns to look at Harley. "You're going to Western?"

"Yeah. Avery and I are both education majors. By some means of fate, we were able to pull off being roommates. I think it's because it's a smaller school."

"I signed with them," Brad says, his voice strange.

"Small world." Avery grins at her best friend.

For a brief moment, I'm jealous, which is an emotion I've not felt much of in my lifetime. A few times I would get jealous of Brad and the other kids who still had their moms, having lost mine when I was four. She died in childbirth with my little sister, who also didn't make it. It's just been dad and me ever since. But sitting here, knowing Brad is going off to play college ball and gets to be with these two anytime he wants, I admit I'm jealous of him.

"You sure you don't want to change your mind and join us?" Harley asks me.

If I could I would. I'm barely passing high school; no way can I manage college. It's just not in the cards for me. "Nah, I'll leave all the late-night study groups and early morning classes to you three." I play it off like it's something I've never wanted. In reality it's something I never let myself want. I knew there was no way I could hack it, not with my problem.

The rest of the night goes pretty smoothly. The girls talk about the excitement in the stands, and Brad and I eat it up.

"Y'all going to follow us to my place for the bonfire?" Brad asks.

"Yeah, we'll be right behind you."

The waitress brings the check and Brad grabs it before either of the girls can. "We got this," he says as we both reach into our pockets for our wallets.

"You don't have to do that." Avery reaches for her pocket as well.

I place my hand on her arm and can't help but notice how damn soft she is. "We got this," I assure her.

Her mouth opens, I'm sure to argue, when Harley speaks up. "Thank you for dinner."

Avery turns to face me. "Thank you, Dylan," she says softly.

I give her arm a gentle squeeze. "You're welcome." Her eyes sparkle and I force myself to stop touching her.

"Ready?" Brad asks. Harley climbs out of the booth and Brad follows, grabbing her hand and leading her out of the restaurant.

Avery stands and I scoot along the seat to follow her. Just as I'm standing from the booth, a server turns in to her, knocking her into me. I wrap my arms around her waist to keep us both from falling.

"I'm so sorry, Avery," Carrie Martin, a fellow classmate, says.

"No worries." Avery just laughs it off.

I don't know what reply I was expecting, but it's not that one. I guess I figured she'd be angry. "You good?" I ask, my lips next to her ear.

"Y-yes."

Slowly and reluctantly, I release her from my hold, then place my hand on the small of her back and lead her out to her car. I tell myself it's just to make sure she makes it out of the restaurant without further incident, but if I'm being honest, it's so I can touch her again. Trust me, you would do the same thing if you were me. This is Avery Stanton. I'm the envy of every guy at Montgomery High right now.

When we reach her car, Brad and Harley are standing at the passenger door. "I'll see you there," I say just low enough for Avery to hear.

Turning her head, she smiles at me. I feel that smile deep in my gut. Dropping my hand, I back away from her. "You ready, Harris?" I call out to Brad.

I watch him lean in and kiss Harley, then jog around the car to meet me. "Follow behind us, Av. We'll see you all there," he says.

She nods and smiles, but it's not the smile she just gave me. This one is not as... soft, if that's even possible. Fuck, I'm acting like a damn girl right now. "Let's go!" I yell, jogging to the driver side and climbing in.

"Their curfew is midnight," Brad tells me as he climbs in the truck. I look at the clock on the dash, working out the numbers. "That gives us just under four hours."

"Us?" I question him.

"I saw the way you were looking at her."

"She's fucking gorgeous, you blame me?"

"Not at all." He taps the dash to the beat of the song on the radio. "I'm stoked for tomorrow's game. We're going to crush Highland."

We spend the rest of the ten-minute drive talking plays and strategy for the first game of the season.

Chapter

3

Avery

"He kissed me," Harley says once we're in the car and following Dylan's truck.

"I noticed." I smile. She's always had a crush on Brad. I'm happy for her.

"Thank you so much, for going tonight. I'm just… gah!" She throws her head back against the headrest. "He's just… yeah, I'm excited. I mean, we've been talking for weeks and we've been on a few dates, but tonight he was different. Not as closed off, I guess."

"He's totally into you," I tell her. He is. She had his full attention the whole time we were at Johnny's.

"And what about you?"

"What about me?"

"Dylan, that's what. You two seemed to hit it off."

"If you call casual conversation hitting it off."

"Come on, Av, he paid for your dinner."

"To be nice and avoid things getting awkward."

"You keep telling yourself that, missy. This is the year. If anyone is willing to piss your brother off, it's Dylan."

"What makes you say that?" I ask.

"He's not going to college, everyone knows that. He doesn't have to worry about scholarships and all that stuff."

"Okay, but this is his last year. He's not going to risk being benched."

"So you think Alan would bench him for dating you?"

"No, but why now, after all this time? No one else has ever been brave enough."

"People change. Maybe it's because the opportunity has never really presented itself."

"All right, crazy girl. You just worry about you and your man."

"He's not mine yet. I'm working on it."

"From what I can tell, he's all yours. Maybe you should bring it up tonight."

"You think so?"

"Sure, what do you have to lose? If it scares him off, he's not in it and you need to not waste your time. This is our senior year."

"Maybe I will. I can't believe he'll be at Western with us."

"I think I remember hearing Alan say he was signing, but I didn't bother to pay attention to where." I park behind Dylan's truck and turn off the engine. I expected us to be in the field, but instead we're parked in Brad's driveway.

Brad hops out of the truck and jogs to the passenger side window. "We thought you might want to leave your car here, Avery. We'll just all pile into Dylan's truck."

"You don't have to do that. We should be fine."

"It's a little rough, don't want you tearing up your car. Pull up behind my mom's." He points to the red Ford Taurus in the driveway.

"I have an SUV," I remind him.

"This is a baby SUV." He grins at me. "Just humor me, Stanton," he says, batting his eyelashes.

"Come on, Avery." Harley's voice is almost pleading.

"Fine. I can drive, but if you insist."

He nods, moving away from the window so I can back up and park behind his mom. Before I have the car in Park, Brad is opening Harley's door, offering her his hand as she climbs from the car. I take my time turning off the ignition, gathering my keys and my phone before climbing out and locking the door.

"Come on, slow poke," Brad teases.

I roll my eyes playfully and join the two of them as they start toward Dylan's truck. I hear voices and realize they're coming from the front porch. Dylan is leaning against the white pillar, arms and legs crossed as he talks to whom I assume are Brad's parents.

"Guess you get to meet the parents," Brad says, smiling.

I see Harley tense a little. I grab her free hand and gently squeeze, getting her attention. She looks over at me wide-eyed. "You got this," I mouth to her.

"Bradley," his mom says. "Several people are already back there." She motions toward the open field just behind the tree line.

"I figured it's a big deal, first game of the season and all," Brad says.

Harley takes a step in my direction only to be pulled back toward Brad. "Mom, Dad, this is Harley," he says, not letting her get away from him. "And this"—he leans over Harley and points in my direction—"is Avery."

"Nice to officially meet you," his mom says.

"Ladies," his dad greets, and I can see where Brad gets his charm. "You boys need any help getting the fire started?"

"Nope. We got this," Brad says.

"Curfew's midnight?" his mom asks.

"Yeah. For the players, that is," Dylan answers.

"Us too," I chime in.

Dylan turns his attention to me. "We'll make sure you're back in time."

"Right, well, we're out. Avery's going to keep her car here and ride back with us," Brad tells his parents.

"You need me to leave my keys?" I ask them.

"No, you're fine. We're in for the night. You kids have fun," his dad says.

With a wave from the four of us, we head toward Dylan's truck. He goes to the driver's side and I trail behind Brad and Harley to the passenger side, assuming that's where I'll be sitting.

"Climb in," Brad says, opening the door and looking right at me. I look inside the truck and Dylan is lifting the console. *Well, I guess I'm sitting up front.* I climb in and slide over the middle, my leg pressing against

Dylan's. Brad climbs in next, then holds his hand out for Harley, who he guides to sit on his lap. Once the door is shut and we're all packed into the front seat, Dylan starts up the truck and heads toward the field. Harley giggles every time we hit a bump and she bounces on Brad's lap. He starts to tickle her and I lean in toward Dylan to give them more room, laughing at their antics.

Dylan hits the throttle, and when we hit the next bump it raises me out of the seat. I squeal and then start laughing. Dylan rests his hand on my thigh. "I got you." He grins.

When we finally reach the field, the four of us are laughing hysterically. I'm not ready for the ride to be over or for Dylan's hand to leave my leg.

As soon as we're parked, the rear end of the truck facing the fire, Dylan hops out, only he doesn't walk away. Instead he holds his hand out for me, a question in his eyes. It's like he doesn't think I'll take what he's offering. I know half the senior class is here, and when they see me slide out of his door and not Brad's the entire school is going to be talking. I study him. Does he know what he's doing?

"I got you," he says, his voice soft. Uncertain.

I smile at him and scoot over, taking his hand and allowing him to help me out of the truck. I'm disappointed when he releases me, though I try not to let it show as I follow him to the bed of his truck. Through the back glass I can see Harley and Brad still sitting on the passenger seat, her in his lap.

"Harris!" Dylan yells. This spurs them into action. Harley climbs out first, Brad soon to follow, his arm around her shoulders. My best friend is smiling so big I'm afraid her face might crack. "Time to light the fire," Dylan says.

Harley joins me at the side of the truck. I watch the guys with rapt attention as they thrown on some lighter fluid and throw a match into the pile of brush and wood. It immediately goes up into flames and the crowd cheers. I don't think there's anything those two can do that won't get cheers.

"Hop on, babe," Brad says, bending down so Harley can climb on his back.

"Where exactly are we going?" She laughs.

"Making our rounds."

That must be explanation enough for Harley, because she climbs on his back like a monkey and then they're off. Leaving me alone with Dylan. He drops the tailgate on his truck and taps it with his hand. "Have a seat," he offers.

Walking to the end of the truck, I turn my back to the tailgate, brace my hands on it, and jump. I fail miserably. "Why do you need this truck to be so damn high?" I ask him, embarrassed that I missed.

"This is a man's truck, Avery," he says like I've insulted him.

"More like a giant," I grumble. I try again and this time I almost make it.

"I can't watch this. Let me help."

Before I can accept or even decline, Dylan's hands are on my hips, gripping me tight as he lifts me off the ground and sits me on the tailgate, putting us at eye level. "Thank you," I say, looking into his brown eyes.

"Shorty." He grins.

"Look, just because you're, what, six foot doesn't mean I'm short."

"Six one," he says, taking a step closer. He's now standing practically between my legs. This is a very couple thing to do.

I'm at a loss for what to say next. Luckily I don't have to figure it out as Brad stops beside us, Harley still on his back. He turns so she can sit on the tailgate beside me. Brad doesn't move away though, staying with his back between her legs, her arms still around his neck.

"What are you two up to?" Brad asks with a grin.

"I was just asking why this truck has to be so damn tall."

"Stanton, you wound me."

I laugh. "This isn't even your truck."

"Yeah, but it's my boy's, and mine is just as tall. This is a man's truck," he explains.

"That's what I told her," Dylan says, raising his hands in the air. When he brings them down he rests them on my thighs. He's still standing close, too close for us to be just friends. Are we even friends? Classmates and acquaintances, yes, but friends?

Harley leans into my shoulder, causing me to turn and face her. She winks and offers me a view of the big cheesing grin she's been wearing since we entered Jonny's Pizza earlier tonight.

Rod Robinson, one of their teammates, yells out that we need music, and the next thing we know music is blaring from his truck, windows down and doors open. Everyone cheers and Rob starts dancing, which spurs most everyone to join in. The four of us just sit back and watch. Dylan is now turned to face them and leaning between my legs just like Brad and Harley, his arms resting on my thighs. I'm leaning back, hands braced on the bed of the truck. I'm going for nonchalant since I can't just wrap my arms around his neck like Harley is. I have a million questions running through my mind. Does he like me? Is he just being nice? Does he want a hookup? Is he not worried about Alan?

I'm not sure how we managed, but Dylan's truck is on the opposite side of the fire from everyone else. When a slow song comes on, Brad turns, lifts Harley from her spot beside me, and pulls her into his arms. I'm jealous. I want Dylan to dance with me.

Just as the thought crosses my mind, he turns around, rests his hands on my hips, and lifts me just the same. My heart beats a heavy yet steady rhythm in my chest. Once my feet hit the ground, Dylan wraps his arms around me, pulling me into his chest. We sway to the slow, steady beat of Maroon 5 crooning from the speakers of Rod's truck. My hands are around his waist too, though I'm stiff because, well, this is Dylan Knight.

"Relax, Aves," he says, bending so his lips are next to my ear. I shudder at the feel of his hot breath against my skin. And he called me Aves. I'm either Avery or just Av to all my friends; it's different and I like it. I want it to be our thing, but I know I'm getting ahead of myself with that. Dylan begins to rub his thumb back and forth over the small of my back and I relax into him. It's electric.

I'm so lost in his touch that I don't realize the song has changed. Dylan steps away, keeping one hand on the small of my back, and leads me back to the truck.

"I got you," he says, his lips next to my ear once more, when we reach the tailgate. He grabs my hips and lifts me back into my previous spot. This time his hands remain on my hips as he steps between my legs.

"Thank you for the dance," I say like an idiot. I had to break the tension.

He surprises me when he leans in and kisses my forehead tenderly. "I should be thanking you."

He's barely pulled away when Brad and Harley join us again. I don't know where they ended up, maybe on the other side of the truck in the shadows. I can't wait until we get home so I can tell Harley all about it.

"It's eleven," Brad tells Dylan, who nods, hands still on my thighs. "All right, people, curfew is in an hour. I got to get my girl home, so we're calling it a night."

Chapter 4

Dylan

Avery Stanton. She's always been untouchable to me, but now our best friends are dating and we've been thrown together, and I can't seem to stop touching her. I don't want to stop touching her. I was so close to leaning in for a kiss; I wanted to taste her lips.

Brad and I have been friends since we were five. We both started out in peewee football and we've been close ever since. So when he tells me that it's eleven, I know what he's thinking. We have an hour before the girls have to be home. That gives us roughly forty-five more minutes with them, and we don't want an audience. I never imagined that this is how tonight would end up, but I can tell you I'm fucking ecstatic that it has.

I don't move from my spot where I stand between her legs, hands resting on her thighs as Brad tells everyone it's time to pack it up and head home. There's a little grumbling, but if Coach finds out we're out past curfew it'll be sprints for the entire next week at practice. Not to mention I'm technically out with his little sister.

"Why so early?" Harley asks from her spot beside Avery on my tailgate, Brad resting between her legs, his back to her front.

"Because I have just under forty-five minutes left with you tonight and I don't want these others here," he says, not turning to look at her.

Harley wraps her arms around him and rests her head on his shoulder, a smile lighting her face.

I turn my gaze back to Avery to find she's watching me. I run my left hand up her thigh and grip her hip, gently tugging her closer, I want to be close to her. I don't know what this night is, but I want as much of her as she's willing to give. Tomorrow I could wake up and this could all be a dream.

"Where are you all staying tonight?" I ask her.

"My house. Harley is spending the night."

"You live, what, fifteen minutes from here?"

"About ten, but it's better safe than sorry."

"Finally," Brad says as Rod's truck pulls away. He was the last one to leave. "Now we need some tunes. I think I need your help," he tells Harley, lifting her off the tailgate once again. They turn the radio on in the truck and roll down the windows. But they never come back. I hear them talking near the front of the truck, but I block them out. Avery deserves all of my attention and she's going to get it.

Reaching up, I tuck a loose strand of hair behind her ear. Her blonde locks are like silk against the rough pads of my fingers. "You coming to the game tomorrow?" I ask her.

"Yeah, Harley and I go to all the games."

"Who are you going to be cheering for?"

"Well, Harley bought us face paint, so I'm guess we'll be adorned with Brad's number."

I don't like the sound of that. She should be wearing my number. I've had girls do it before. Hell, half the underclassmen do it. I've never asked a single one of them to do it for me, of course. They do it to get my attention, or hell, maybe they really are fans.

"You wound me," I say, wrapping both arms around her and holding her close where she sits on my tailgate.

"What? You know of someone else who would want me to wear his number? Is it Rod? You know, he held the door for me the other day and I thought he was just being nice, but maybe I was wrong," she says with a straight face.

"No," I reply, my voice low and firm. I take a breath, masking my emotions. What the hell is wrong with me? "I'm thinking you would look damn good with a number seventeen right here." I kiss her cheekbone. She sucks in a breath as soon as my lips make contact.

"Y-you do?" she asks shyly, quickly losing her bravado, her big blue eyes staring back at me.

"I do. You think you can do that for me?"

"I don't know—"

I cut off her reply by softly pressing my lips to hers. "Please," I whisper, only pulling away so the words can pass my lips.

"I can do that," she agrees.

"What are you doing after the game?"

"I don't know yet. We'll either end up at her house or mine. We usually stop and eat after."

"The four of us should do something."

"We won't have much time. My curfew is still midnight."

"Doesn't matter if it's ten minutes, as long as I get to see you after." She smiles up at me. "Can I see your phone?" Reaching into her back pocket, she holds it out for me. "Code?" I ask. She takes it back, types in the code, then hands it to me. I quickly add myself as a contact and then text myself before handing it back to her. "You have my number now, so call me and we'll meet up."

"Okay."

"It's a quarter till," Brad says as he and Harley join us again, their arms wrapped tightly around one another.

"Let's get you two home. Don't want you getting into trouble." I lift Avery from the tailgate and take her hand, leading her to the driver's side of my truck. I open the door for her and without hesitation she slides in. Following after, I place my hand on her leg, pulling her as close to me as I can get her. Brad and Harley climb in the passenger side and I head back toward Brad's. This trip back is different. I take it slow, wanting to keep her with me as long as possible. From the way Brad and Harley are burrowed together stealing kisses, I know they agree. I'm not sure what Avery is thinking, though I don't really care as long as she's thinking about me.

Pulling into the driveway, I turn off the ignition but make no effort to get out of the truck.

"We really need to go," Avery says, glancing at the clock on the dash.

Reluctantly, we all climb out and Brad and I walk them to her car. "Be careful, and I'll see you tomorrow," I say, holding her hand while we stand next to her open door.

"We always are, and I'm looking forward to it. Good luck tomorrow."

Her blonde hair is shining in the moonlight. It's literally hard to breathe seeing her like this. Leaning in, I kiss her softly. "Good night, Aves."

"Good night," she whispers before climbing into her car and shutting the door.

Brad and I back away at the same time, our eyes not leaving her car until they're out of sight.

"Dude? You and Avery?" he asks.

I shrug. "Not sure, really. I told her the four of us were getting together tomorrow after the game. I assumed you would be good with that."

"Hell yeah, another night with my girl."

"Is she your girl now?"

"Yeah, we cleared that up tonight. I'm officially off the market. By the looks of it you will be soon."

"Don't need the distraction."

"What the hell ever. You and I both know that if Avery Stanton is willing, you will let her distract the hell out of you."

He's right. I told myself no distractions, but Avery's different. She's worth... everything.

Brad and I head inside, him to his room and I to the guest room, which is where I always sleep. As I lie here replaying everything about tonight, I have this sudden urge to make sure she made it home okay. Grabbing my phone, I send her a text, hoping like hell I don't wake anyone in the house.

> **Me:** You all make it home okay?
>
> **Aves:** My #17, really? LOL. Yeah, we made it right at midnight.
>
> **Me:** You like that? Good, I'm glad.

Aves: Depends. Are you?

Me: If you want me to be.

Aves: Only time will tell. Good night #17.

Me: Good night, beautiful.

I'm out of my league here and we both know it, but I'm a selfish bastard. I fall asleep with thoughts of kissing her. Best damn distraction imaginable.

I wake to the smell of bacon and my stomach grumbles. Brad's mom is one hell of a cook and always makes sure we're fed well, especially on game days. Grabbing my phone, I see that it's just before nine in the morning. I pull up my text messages and read over my exchange with Avery last night just to make sure it wasn't a dream.

Me: Morning.

Aves: Morning. You ready for today?

I don't know that I've ever been with, dated—hell, even met a girl— who cared about me being ready for a game. Everyone up to this point has just wanted to hang on my arm, cash in on the popularity that comes with being the star quarterback in our small hometown.

Me: Do I still get to see you after?

Aves: Yes.

Me: Then I'm more than ready for today.

Aves: Kick ass, #17.

Climbing out of bed, I make a stop at the bathroom before heading downstairs. My nose is leading me to the bacon. "Morning, Mom," I say to Brad's mom. She's been the one and only mother figure in my life.

"Dylan, are you hungry?" she asks, setting a huge plate of bacon on the table.

"How long have you known me?" I reply, making her laugh. "Brad still sleeping?"

"How long have you known him?" she fires back. "If I had my guess, he spent most of the night on the phone with Harley."

"You're probably right."

"And what about you? No late-night talks with Avery?"

I shrug. "I texted to make sure she made it home okay, but no late-night talks. We're not dating. Last night was the first time I'd ever hung out with her."

"She's beautiful. They both are."

I just nod.

"Mom, you know bacon wakes me up," Brad says, joining us in the kitchen. He stops to kiss her cheek, then takes a seat next to me at the table. "Dad home?"

"No, he's at the hospital. Got called in for a consult this morning. He said to tell you that he would see you at the game later."

"Thank you for breakfast, Ann," I tell her when she sets a plate in front of me. She runs her finger over my head affectionately just as she does with Brad when he tells her the same.

"What are you boys doing after the game?" That's just Ann, always involved. Her husband, Jack, is too. My dad, Gary, does the same.

"I need to check in with my dad," I say, realizing that I made plans last night and didn't run them by him. He'll be fine with it, I'm sure, but his rule is check in so he always knows where I am and who I'm with.

"Taking the girls out," Brad says around a mouthful of pancake.

"Doesn't leave you much time. Those girls deserve a proper date," she scolds us.

"We know, Mom, but it's impossible on game days," Brad counters.

"We girls have to stick together." She laughs. From what I remember and from the stories Dad has told me, this is exactly how my mom would have been.

"Can we come back here? Start a fire in the pit?" Brad asks.

"Sure. Hey, I'll even pick up supplies for s'mores."

"Mom, we're seniors in high school. We're over s'mores."

"That's what you think, Mr. Know It All. Trust me, the girls will love it."

Brad looks to me for approval.

"I'm out of my element here, man. Never really cared about impressing anyone before. With Avery, I'm willing to take all the advice I can get."

He nods slowly. "Yeah, you might be right. Thanks, Mom."

"It's all about the romance, Bradley." She grins.

"Ugh, okay enough of that."

Brad might not want to hear it but I do. I need to do something to stand out from the others. This is Avery Stanton, the untouchable of Montgomery High, and she's interested in me. At least I hope she is.

Chapter
5

Avery

We won. First game of the season and the Montgomery Warriors come out on top. I proudly sported the painted-on number seventeen on my cheek. I got a few questioning looks from my fellow classmates, but those who were at Brad's last night saw us together.

The crowd is starting to thin out now that the players are headed off the field. I pull my phone out and text Dylan.

Me: Way to kick some ass, #17.

I shove it back in my pocket, not expecting to get a reply, but when I feel my pocket vibrate, I'm giddy hoping it's him.

My #17: You're my good luck charm.

I don't have a reply for that. Instead I tuck my phone back in my pocket and try like hell not to grin like a lovesick fool.

"Brad said to meet them in the parking lot," Harley says, grabbing my hand and pulling me behind her down the bleachers.

When we reach the parking lot, I see Brad's truck but not Dylan's. They must take turns driving or something.

"I would say we should let the tailgate down, but I know neither of us can get up there without the guys' help. What do you say we just climb up in the back and wait for them?"

"I still don't know why they have to have such damn big trucks."

"You have to admit it's kind of hot."

"They do just fine on their own. They don't need to drive these big monstrosities." I hike my foot up on the bumper, grip the tailgate, and begin my climb. Harley does the same as we each take a seat on the edge of the bed.

"What do you think we're going to do?" she asks.

"I have no idea. Dylan just said they wanted to see us. I didn't hear about anyone talking about coming to Brad's for another bonfire, so it's hard to tell."

She looks down at her watch. "It's a little after nine, so we'll have about three hours."

Just as I'm about to reply I see Brad walk up behind Harley. He places his finger over his lips, and before I can acknowledge him, he has his hands under her arms and is lifting her from the truck. She screams and then laughs once she realizes who it is. I want to ask him where Dylan is but I don't. Instead I watch as he cradles her bridal style and kisses her.

Strong arms rest beside me on the side of the truck and I can feel the heat radiating from his body that's aligned with mine. "Hey, Aves," he says softly. His hands come around my center in a backwards hug. "Thanks for waiting."

"Good game," I say dumbly. I'm a smart girl, but with Dylan I seem to lose my ability to hang in normal conversation.

"You ready to get out of here?"

"Where are we going?"

"Thought we would just hang out at Brad's. Did you drive or did Harley?"

"I did."

"Hey, man!" Dylan yells over to Brad. "Avery and I will meet the two of you there."

I stand and walk toward the tailgate. Dylan holds out his hand and helps me climb down. As soon as my feet hit the ground, his arms are around me in a hug. Not knowing what else to do, I wrap my arms around his center and hug him back. All too quickly he's pulling away, but we walk hand in hand to my car. Dylan opens the door for me, which

I think is super sweet. I wait for him to climb in and scoot the seat all the way back, and he catches me staring.

"What?"

"Nothing, just watching you."

His hand comes up to cup my cheek, and he tenderly runs his thumb over the paint there. "My number looks better on you than I could've imagined."

"You imagined me wearing your number?"

"I have, but it was my jersey and nothing else."

I'm blushing. I can't help it. No guy has ever talked to me this way, or even touched me really. I had my first kiss in eighth grade, and then my brother started teaching here and soon became the coach. Dating for me pretty much sucked after that.

"You're beautiful, Aves." Leaning in, he presses a soft kiss against my lips. All too quickly he's pulling away and strapping on his seat belt.

I do the same, putting the car in Drive and heading toward Brad's. Dylan reaches over and rests his hand on my thigh. It takes extreme effort to concentrate on driving and not the heat of his hand through my shorts, but we arrive at Brad's safe and sound. "They must be—" I stop midsentence as headlights of what is obviously a big-ass truck pull in behind me. Dylan and I get out of the car and greet them.

"Come on in," Brad says, leading Harley by the hand up to the front porch. Dylan grabs my hand and we follow them into the house. "My parents aren't home yet, but they will be," he laughs. "No way will they stay gone when they know the two of you are coming over tonight." He keeps walking, leading us through the kitchen and out patio doors. There's a huge deck and a fire pit below. "We thought we'd just hang out here for tonight."

"I'll get the fire started." Dylan lets go of my hand and heads toward the fire pit.

"We need tunes. I'm going to get my portable speaker. You ladies want anything to drink?" Brad asks.

"No, thanks," Harley and I say at the same time.

He nods and heads into the house, back in no time at all carrying two bottles of water and a small speaker. He sets it on the table, pulls out his phone, and taps a few times, and soon music begins to flow through the speakers, accompanied by the cracking of the fire. "Here, man." He tosses the extra bottle of water to Dylan.

Dylan catches it with ease, then takes my hand and leads me to a lawn chair around the fire pit. "Have a seat," he says, taking the one next to me.

"We're going to walk down by the pond," Brad says while they're walking away.

"Thanks again for coming tonight."

"You had a great game," I tell Dylan.

He holds out his hand and I place mine in his. "I still think you're my good luck charm."

"Great way to start out your last season as a Warrior," I say, ignoring his comment.

"It is. This is my final season period." His thumb rubs across my knuckles. "How is it that we've been in school together our entire lives and this weekend is the first time we've ever hung out?"

I shrug. "I always assumed it had something to do with the fact that I'm Mr. Stanton or Coach Stanton's little sister. I heard a rumor that he threatened to bench anyone who tried to date me."

Dylan laughs. "You can't believe everything you hear, Aves. Coach has never singled you out to any of us, not that I'm aware of. He tells us to respect all women, not just you. Although, you might be on to something about guys being intimidated because you're Coach's little sister."

"What about you? Are you worried about hanging out with Coach Stanton's little sister?" I ask, even though I'm worried as to what the answer will be. But it's better to go ahead and get it out there before I really fall for him.

"No. He's a great coach, fair. I would like to think that we could more than hang out."

"I'm not like those other girls...."

"Wait, Avery. That came out wrong. That's not what I meant at all. What I mean is that...." He runs his fingers through his hair. "I like you. I know you're not like other girls—that's a part of your charm. I would like to get to know you, more than just being friends."

"I'd like that."

"I do plan to talk to Coach, out of respect for him and for you. I want him to know that I'm interested in you and that I have good intentions."

"He's my brother, Dylan, not my father."

"I understand that, but he's my coach, and to me that's just as important as a father. Don't get me wrong, Aves, I'm not asking for his permission or his blessing. If I'm lucky enough for you to want to be with me, to get to know me, then I'm taking it. But I do respect him and you. I just think it would be good if he heard it from me, that's all."

"I guess I can see that," I begrudgingly agree.

"So, I'd like to take you out. You know, just the two of us. Are you free next weekend?"

"You have an away game on Friday. Harley and I are going."

"That's good. I'll play better knowing my good luck charm is in the stands. Saturday night? Just the two of us?"

"Okay."

"Hey, Dylan," a female voice says from the patio. "Where's Brad?"

"Not up in my room if that's what you're worried about," Brad laughs as he and Harley approach the fire pit. "You and Dad just get home?"

She shakes her head and smiles. "We did. I stopped at the store and picked up the stuff you asked for. It's in the kitchen."

"Thanks, Mom. I'll be right there." Brad turns back to us. "You ladies like s'mores?"

"Are you kidding? I'm pretty sure it's illegal to dislike s'mores, right, Av?" Harley says as she takes a seat on the opposite side of the fire from Dylan and me.

My answer is to laugh at her. My best friend has always had a slight flair for the dramatic.

After passing out the supplies, the four of us add a couple of marshmallows to the ends of our sticks that Brad and Dylan cut earlier today.

"You have to let them burn. They are sooo good burnt," Harley says, pushing her stick farther into the fire.

"Yes! Then you add the chocolate and graham cracker and it's a messy chocolaty marshmallowy goodness," I say, my mouth watering at the thought.

"Is marshmallowy even a word?" Brad chuckles.

"It is now," I say, turning my stick. We all laugh.

"Seriously, this is the best idea ever. You guys must have put some thought into this," Harley praises them.

The guys share a look and then Brad speaks up. "It was actually all my mom's idea."

"Well she's a genius," Harley tells him.

The night goes on, making s'mores and just laughing and cutting up. It's like we've all hung out like this for years. "It's eleven thirty," I say, looking at the time on my phone.

"I guess you all better head home," Brad grumbles as he taps Harley's thigh from where she's now sitting on his lap. She stands and stretches.

Dylan stands and offers me his hand. "Up and at 'em, marshmallowy girl," he teases.

"Hey." I slap his arm. Not hard, but he still acts like I about knocked him over. He's getting no sympathy from me, so he throws his arm around my shoulder and walks me to my car.

"Next Saturday, just you and me."

"Yeah. Where are we going?" I ask him.

He shrugs. "Date stuff, you know? Dinner and movie?" He says it like a question. What he doesn't realize is that I couldn't care less as long as it's him and me.

"Okay. I guess I'll see you then."

"Oh, Aves. You're going to see me before then. That's a whole seven days away." Leaning in, he kisses the corner of my mouth. "Drive safe. Text me when you all make it home."

"Okay." The words are barely a whisper. I climb into the car, Harley beside me, and we head to her house for the night.

Chapter 6

Dylan

When my alarm goes off a half hour earlier than normal, I groan. I tossed and turned all night thinking about what I'm going to do today. Hence the reason I'm up earlier than normal. I know Coach arrives early every day, so I figure now is as good a time as any to talk to him. I don't want him hearing it from one of the guys, and after the party Friday night, I'll be surprised if word hasn't already gotten back to him.

When I told Avery she would see me again, I meant it. I plan to be at her locker when she gets there today. She gave me an in, a chance to get to know her, and regardless of what anyone else says or does, I'm taking it.

After a quick shower, I grab a protein bar and rush out the door. The school parking lot is pretty empty except for a few teachers. Scanning the lot, I see Coach's truck, so I make my way to his office and tap on the door.

"Dylan, everything okay?"

"Yeah, Coach. I just wanted to talk to you if you've got a minute."

"Sure, come on in and shut the door."

I do as he says and take the seat across from his desk. "So I wanted to let you know that I hung out with Avery this weekend. And on

Saturday, she and I are going out on an official date," I blurt out. My palms are sweaty, and I'll admit a small part of me is scared that he's going to warn me away from her. Tell me that I can't date her.

"You do realize I'm her brother, not her father, right?" he asks. His eyes are intense as he stares me down.

I swallow hard. "Yes, Coach. Please don't take this as disrespect for your father, but you're my coach. We have an established relationship. It's my respect for you that has me sitting in this chair."

"I see. What does Avery say about all this?"

"She agreed to the date, and she knows that I was going to tell you."

"Are you asking for permission? Approval?"

"No, Coach. I merely just wanted you to hear it from me."

"What if I were to tell you to stay away from her? That she was off–limits?"

Shit. I wipe my palms on my jeans and take a deep breath. "With all due respect, Coach, that's not your place and I wouldn't listen. Avery is different from all the other girls. I know she deserves the best. I'm not that, but she likes me—at least I hope she does—and I'm selfish enough to see this through. I won't hurt her." I had no idea how I would answer that question until he asked it. It's true, I can't imagine ever hurting her. Avery is not a girl you let slip away. Even after just two nights of really hanging out with her, I know she deserves the pedestal I've placed her on all these years.

"That's what she deserves, Dylan. Someone who knows how great she is and shows her that every day. You're a good kid. Never say you're underserving. Treat her right."

I'm not sure what I was expecting, but it wasn't that. "Thanks, Coach. Any suggestions for our date?" I ask with a grin.

"Nice try, Romeo, but you're on your own. I'll see you at practice," he says, dismissing me.

Leaving his office, I head straight to her locker and find Brad there.

"Waiting for your girl?" I ask.

"Yeah. What are you doing here this early?"

"Had to talk to Coach."

"You good, man?"

"Yeah, I told him that Avery and I have a date Saturday. Wanted him to hear it from me."

Brad holds his fist out and we bump just as the girls approach.

"This is a good way to start off the week," Harley says as she tucks herself into Brad's arms. "Convenient that our lockers are so close." She winks at Avery.

The first warning bell rings. "You got what you need?" I ask Avery.

"I just need to put this in my locker and grab my notebook." I step out from in front of her locker so she can get what she needs. "Ready," she says, turning to face me.

I place my hand on the small of her back. "Catch you guys later." I lead Avery away. "What's your first class?"

"History."

Leaning in, I say, "So I talked to Coach today."

"About?"

"You. Us. I told him that I asked you out Saturday night." I feel her stiffen. "Was that wrong? We discussed this?"

"I know, I just don't see why it's such a big deal?"

"He's my coach, Aves. I respect him. You're his little sister. I wanted him to hear it from me."

"Let me guess, he told you to stay away?" she says, twisting away from me.

"Hey." I reach out and gently grab her arm. She stops walking. "No, and even if he did, I wouldn't. I didn't ask for his permission or his approval. I told him that I didn't want or need either. I just wanted him to know out of respect that we're going out Saturday night. Nothing more, nothing less." She's looking down at the floor, and I hate that I can't see her eyes. "Look at me, Avery." I place my finger under her chin and lift until our eyes meet. "It's just you and me, Avery. No one else matters. Just you and me."

She nods slowly "I need to get to class," she says, turning.

In one long stride I catch up with her and rest my hand on the small of her back. "I'll walk with you."

"Dylan, you're going to be late."

"Don't care. I'll walk you." Once we reach her class, I lean in close. "I'll be waiting for you when class is over."

"Dylan…"

I place my finger over her lips. "I'll see you soon, Aves." With that I turn and walk away from her, then take off running. I make it to my class just as the final bell rings.

That became our pattern for the rest of the week. I walked her to every class, barely making it to mine on time. At lunch, Avery and Harley sat with Brad and me and a few of our teammates. Talk was rampant around school, everyone always wanting to be up in everyone else's business.

Avery hasn't really mentioned it, but it would be impossible for her not to hear the whispers, see the stares. That's why for our date tonight I've decided it needs to be just the two of us. After running it past Dad, I have everything all set up.

At fifteen minutes till seven, I pull into her driveway. My punctuality is for the purpose of impressing her, but it's also just because I want to see her. Last night was a home game and we had to ride back on the bus as a team. By the time we got back to the school, it was almost eleven, so I didn't get to see her. I mean, yeah, I saw her sitting in the stands, looking cute as hell with her cheek painted. I know it's my number she's wearing because she texted me a picture right before the game started.

Grabbing the bouquet of flowers I picked up, I head to the front door. I ring the doorbell, then step back to wait. To my surprise, Coach opens the door.

"Knight," he says, holding the door open for me.

"Hey, Coach," I greet as I pass him, walking inside.

"Av!" he yells up the steps. "Dylan's here."

I try not to fidget, keeping my shoulders back and head held high. I can feel Coach's eyes on me, but I don't take mine off the stairs where I know she's going to be. When she comes into view, my breath hitches. She's a knockout. Her long blonde hair hangs in loose curls; she's wearing jeans and some kind of flowing off-the-shoulder top with knee-high boots. I want to kiss the hell out of her, but I grip the flowers tight to fight the urge.

"Hey," she says once she clears the bottom step.

"Hi. Uh, these are for you." I hand her the flowers.

"Thank you." She turns to face Coach. "Where are Mom and Dad?"

"They had plans. Mom said she told you."

"She did, but I thought they would be here to meet Dylan."

"Nope. They called me in as backup."

"You already know him," she says, rolling her eyes.

"I do. I also know what it's like to be seventeen and all alone with a beautiful girl." He smirks at me. "Not happening on my watch, Knight."

"Alan!" Avery slaps his arm before I even have the chance to reply. "We're leaving." She grabs my hand and tugs me to the door. Stopping, she turns to face Coach. "Can you put these in water for me?" She holds out the flowers.

Coach steps forward, takes the flowers with one hand, and pulls her into a hug with the other. "Be safe, Av."

"Always." She stands on her tiptoes and kisses his cheek.

"You make sure of it." He points to me.

"Always," I reply.

"Sorry about that," Avery says once we're in my truck. "You know he's just messing with us, right?"

"It's fine, Avery. He's your big brother. I would expect nothing less."

"So where are we going?"

"Well, I thought it would be nice if we got away from the whispers and stares and all that."

She throws her head back and laughs. "This is a small town, Dylan."

"I know, and I just want to spend some time with you, so I talked to Dad and got his approval for us to hang out on the rooftop of the shop."

"The rooftop?"

Reaching over, I grab her hand. "You'll see."

I can tell she's nervous, but I don't ease her mind. I want it to be a surprise—hopefully a good one.

Chapter
7

Avery

I'm nervous and trying not to show it. I have no idea what Dylan means that we'll be on the rooftop of his dad's shop. I want to spend time with him, but hanging out on a roof? My palms are starting to sweat and he's still holding my hand. The chances of hiding that are slim to none, but I don't want to pull away because then he's going to want to know why. Gah! This dating stuff is hard work.

"Here we are. Dad's still working. I told him that we would stop in so I could introduce you."

He finally releases my hand when he goes to get out of the truck, and I take the opportunity to wipe my sweaty palms on my jeans. While I'm distracted, Dylan opens my door, causing me to jump.

"Hey." He steps into the open door and cups my face in his hands. I feel the roughness from what I assume is hours on the football field and even more spent in this very shop helping his dad. "I promise, if you feel uncomfortable at any time or if you don't like what I have planned, we can leave."

I'm being ridiculous and I know it. Taking a deep breath, I nod and take his offered hand, climbing out of the truck. He leads us to an open garage door.

"Dad!" he calls out. Surveying the room, I see a head pop up from underneath the hood of a minivan. "Hey, this is Avery. Avery, this is my dad, Wayne Knight.

"It's nice to meet you," I say, holding out my hand that I pray isn't sweaty again.

"Avery." He holds up his greasy hands. "I don't want to get you all messed up. It's a pleasure to meet you. My boy here has talked a lot about you." He winks at Dylan.

"Real smooth, Dad."

His father laughs. "Just keeping it real, son. You just missed the delivery. I went ahead and took it up for you. You all have fun. No funny business, mister." He points at Dylan.

"No, sir. Just want to spend some time with her without the prying eyes of a small town. Football star and all that." He puffs out his chest.

"You need to keep an eye on this one, Avery. If his head gets any bigger, it might explode."

"Har har," Dylan says dryly.

"It's a tough job, but somebody has to do it," I say with a smile.

"Come on you. Later, Dad."

"I'll be here," he says.

Dylan grabs my hand and leads us to a door that hides stairs that I assume take us to the roof. Slowly we climb the steps that lead to another door. When Dylan pushes it open and we walk through, it's not at all what I expected. The roof is flat and decorated with patio furniture, with a flat-screen TV and a DVD player set up on a table in front of an outdoor couch and a table that holds a pizza box, which I assume is the delivery his dad was referring to. Beside the table sits a small cooler and a picnic basket.

"Dylan," I say in awe. I'm not capable of much else.

"This spot, this is special to my dad. He and Mom used to do this. It doesn't get used much anymore, but I wanted to be alone with you without hanging out in my truck. I ordered pizza, and we also have pop and water. I even have dessert. We have the satellite box hooked up so we can order pay-per-view or on demand, or we can find something on one of the regular channels, whatever you want to do." He leads me closer to the setup and farther onto the roof. "Over here we have a radio so we can listen to music, or just sit and talk and just… be."

"I can't believe you did all of this."

"I'm going for complete honesty here, Avery. I've admired—no, that sounds creepy. I've always thought you were beautiful and different, you know? You're never mean or vindictive, at least not that I've ever seen. To me you were untouchable, but something happened the other night. I just... hanging out with you, I want to do more of that. As much and as often as you'll let me."

Is this real? I pinch my leg. "Ouch."

"What are you doing?"

I feel my face heat. "I had to make sure this was real. That it wasn't a dream."

Slowly he walks toward me. Lifting his hand, he tucks a strand of hair behind my ear. "Not a dream, Aves."

"I wanted it to," I whisper the confession.

"Wanted what?"

"Last weekend. When I found out that you were going to be with Brad, I wanted what happened to happen."

His smile is blinding. "You did, huh?" he asks, stepping closer.

I nod.

Dylan leans in and I brace myself. He's going to kiss me, I just know it. As he nears, I close my eyes and wait for his lips to press to mine. That never comes. Instead his lips land on my forehead. "Let's eat," he says, backing away and leading me to the couch. "I just got pepperoni. I wasn't sure what you liked."

"Pepperoni is perfect." I watch as he reaches into the picnic basket and pulls out paper plates and napkins. "You thought of everything."

"Not really. My dad had a lot to do with it."

"So this is the Knight version of 'date stuff'? Dinner and a movie on a rooftop?"

"Maybe," he says, adding two pieces of pizza to a plate and handing it to me, then making one for himself. "Just thought it might be nice to hang out up here."

"It's great, really. I've not done the date thing that much, so that makes this the most interesting to date."

"Why is that?"

"What?"

"Why do you not date much?"

"Really? I don't exactly have guys knocking down my door. Being Mr. Stanton's little sister, or Coach's little sister to the football team, tends to keep suitors at bay."

"Suitors?" He grins.

"You know what I mean." I laugh. "I'm actually really surprised that you asked me out tonight."

"You've seen you, right?" He's completely serious, his face void of any humor.

"My brother is your coach," I remind him, deciding to ignore his question. How in the hell am I supposed to answer that anyway?

"He is. That doesn't mean he's your father. I respect him, but my coach has no say in whom I date. What about you? Does he influence your decisions?"

"No. I mean, he's my older brother and I trust him, but he doesn't make decisions on whom I date either."

"Hence the reason you're here."

"What? You think he would try to talk me out of it? You're his team captain, Dylan. He likes you, trust me."

"As a football player, yes. For you? Only time will tell."

"What movie are we watching?"

"I have Netflix, so we can watch whatever you want. And like I said the satellite box is hooked up to. We can search on both."

"Netflix and chill, huh?" I ask, a stern look on my face.

"No, I mean, yes, but no. Damn it. I want to hang out with you eat this pizza and watch a movie, nothing else. Well, I mean not nothing, but... fuck!"

I can't stop the laughter from falling from my lips. "Dylan," I say reaching over and resting my hand on his arm. "I get it. I'm just messing with you."

Slowly he lifts his head and looks at me. I watch as the grin pulls at the corner of his lips. "What am I going to do with you?" he asks.

I shrug. "Eat pizza with me and, I don't know, watch a movie?"

"Har har." He picks up the remote and starts surfing through the channels.

"Wait, that one," I say when he passes over *The Hunger Games*.

"You sure?"

"Definitely. Have you ever seen it?"

"No. If I'm not on the football field, I'm here with Dad. Don't really do the dating thing."

"Yeah, I think I've heard that about you."

"Don't believe everything you hear, Aves."

"Trust me, I know that too." I smile at him, which seems to help him relax.

Side by side we sit on the outdoor couch, eating our pizza and watching the movie. The sun has set and it's almost completely dark outside. It's romantic, but I don't think that was his intention. That's just me, finding the romance in every situation. Dad says I'm just like Mom; we're always searching for the happy ending. Every minute that passes I feel more and more comfortable with him, up here on this roof.

Plates empty and pizza forgotten, I kick off my shoes and curl my feet up under me. Dylan lightly grabs my ankles and sets my feet on his lap, never taking his eyes off the screen.

I suck in a deep breath, trying to calm my racing heart. I have the hottest guy in school sitting next to me, lightly trailing his fingers up and down my legs.

"You're cold," he says before reaching beside him and grabbing a blanket.

I can't tell him that it's his touch causing the goose bumps to break out on my skin. The night air is thankfully a little chilly, so I just let him believe it's the weather. Dylan drapes the blanket over my lap, covering me, then stretches it over my legs. His hands remain under the covers and he continues caressing… if that's even the right word for what he's doing to my legs. It's a new experience for me. I've been on a handful of dates one-on-one, as well as a few group dates, but none of them compared to this.

This is one of those movie moments that Mom and I will talk about for days after the movie is over.

This is romance at its finest and he has no idea.

Chapter 8

Dylan

When I mentioned to Dad that I had a date with Avery, he immediately suggested the rooftop. As soon as he said it, I knew it was a great idea. I wanted to impress her, show her I put thought into our date, not just the normal dinner and a movie. She deserves more than just normal. I was a little worried that it would be too intimate for a first date, but Dad assured me that for girls who are worth the effort it can never be too soon. I'm out of my element with wanting to impress a girl, so I took his advice and ran with it. Before I went to pick her up, Dad helped me set up the TV and carry everything upstairs, then ordered the pizza when I left so it would be here when we got back. Everything to this point has been great.

When I felt the goose bumps against her skin, I was glad he suggested a blanket. It might be odd that he set his teenage son up with a girl on a private rooftop with a blanket and a couch, but he knows me better than that. He raised me to respect women, and no way is anything more than a kiss going down on this rooftop tonight, no matter how much my hormones scream otherwise.

As we sit here, I try like hell to focus on the movie and not the feel of her soft skin under the rough pads of my fingertips. She's so damn soft. *Focus, Knight.* I turn my attention back to the television.

"What the hell?" I ask when the movie ends. I turn to look at Avery. "They can't just leave us hanging like that."

She laughs. "They can and they did."

"Have you already seen this?"

"I have. It came out earlier this year."

"Why didn't you tell me? Is the next one out yet?"

Again, she laughs. I like making her laugh. "Nope. Not until next year sometime."

"Shit. Well, pencil me in. We've got to watch it."

She tilts her head to the side and studies me.

"What?"

"You think this"—she points between us—"will still be… a thing next year?"

Well hell. "I don't know, Aves. I like you. I mean, I know you're going to college and stuff, but maybe when you come home to visit, we can watch it then."

"That's right, no college for you?"

I hate talking about this with her. I know she deserves someone better than me, but I won't lie to her either. "Nah, not my thing. I'm struggling with high school. I'm not good with taking tests and things. College just isn't for me."

"Dylan." She pulls her hand over mine that's resting on her thigh under the cover. "You can do anything you want. Don't let the fact that testing is not your best thing keep you from it."

"I'm not," I say, probably a little more defensively than I should. "Look, I've always known what I was going to do after high school. I want to work here with Dad. Take this place over some day. That's always been the plan." I've never been good in school. Even if my football skills are good enough for a scholarship, I would never be able to keep my grades where they need to be to keep it. Not with the vigorous football schedule and sleeping. I have to study twice as hard, twice as long, and it's just not something I want.

"Sorry, I don't mean to preach. You have your dad for that. I just… see more in you."

Leaning in to her, I cup her face in my hands. "You're beautiful." She seems shocked and so am I. It's not like me to wax poetic to a girl. I've never cared enough to tell someone I think she's beautiful. I've never dated anyone like Avery either.

"You already got me here, Dylan. You don't have to try and woo me."

"Woo you?" I laugh. "Aves, you're beautiful. No wooing needed. I just call it like I see it."

She looks up at me from under her lashes. "Thank you," she whispers.

I can't take it anymore. Leaning in, I press my lips to hers. It's slow and I can tell she's hesitant, so I just leave my lips there, feeling the softness of hers. I can feel her jaw relax in the palm of my hand. That's my cue to press for more, just a taste. I trace her lips with my tongue and she gasps. Taking advantage, I slip my tongue past her lips. She doesn't kiss me back at first, but I start to explore her mouth and that seems to spur her into action, her tongue mimicking mine.

I don't want to push her too far, but I'm not ready to stop kissing her. Slowly I lean back against the couch and bring her with me. I have one hand behind her neck, the other across her lower back. Once my back hits the arm of the patio couch, I relax and bring her into my arms.

"Dylan," she whispers between kisses.

"Aves."

"What are we doing?" I can hear the hesitation in her voice.

Pulling away, I hold her face mere inches from mine. "I'm kissing you, Avery Stanton. I'm memorizing the taste of your lips. I don't know if you're ever going to give me another date after tonight, and I don't ever want to forget this, forget you. So for as long as you let me, or until I have to get you home for curfew, I'm going to kiss you."

She licks her lips. "I-I want that. All of it."

My heart literally skips a beat in my chest. I'm not shitting you. I feel like I'm living out some sappy chick flick. Only this one I want to watch to the end. Hell, I don't ever want it to end. I bring her lips to mine and get lost in her. Lost in her taste. Lost in the feel of her in my arms. Lost in the idea that this doesn't end tonight.

I don't know how long we've been lying on this couch in what feels like our alternate universe, but reality comes crashing back when I hear the beeping of her cell phone.

"That's my alarm. I have to be home in a half hour."

"You set an alarm?" I ask her.

She blushes. "Yeah, I just… didn't want to get caught up in whatever it was we were going to do and be late."

I kiss her nose. "I better get you home before you turn into a pumpkin."

Her musical laughter echoes into the night. "No pumpkin turning, I promise." She sits up and I follow her. "I'll help you clean up first."

"No, I got it." I stand to stop her. "This will take me no time. I'll have Dad come up later and help me move the TV back downstairs. Let's get you home." I hold out my hand and she takes it. I want to scream into the night that this girl, this beautiful, amazing girl, is mine, but she's not. Not yet. Time to step up my game. Now that I've had a taste of her, I never want to let her go.

When we make it to the bottom of the steps, I see the light on in the office. "Let me tell Dad I'm taking you home." I don't let go of her hand; instead, I lead her down the hall and stop in the doorway of his office. "Hey, Dad, I'm taking Avery home. I'll be back."

"You kids have a good night?" he asks.

"We did. It was a great idea, thank you," Avery says.

"Son, you weren't supposed to tell her it was me," he says, smiling and shaking his head.

"Can't keep it from this one." I squeeze her hand.

"You kids be safe. Straight home, Dylan. I'll meet you there," he says, closing his laptop.

"You got it." With a final wave from both of us, we head out to my truck. I hold her hand all the way there, not ready to end this night or this newfound connection we have.

I kill the headlights when I pull into her drive and see lights on in the house. "Can I see you again?" I ask, turning to face her.

"I'd like that. Thank you for a great night, number seventeen."

"Me too, Aves." I bring our joined hands to my lips and kiss her knuckles. "Can I kiss you for real? Should I worry about your dad coming outside after me?"

She chuckles softly. "Yes, please, and no."

It takes me a minute to process her answer before I lean in and kiss her softly. "Thank you for coming out with me tonight."

"Thank you," she says, kissing me one more time.

Reluctantly I release her and climb out of the truck. With my hand on the small of her back, I walk her to the front door. "Sweet dreams, Aves," I say, my lips next to her ear.

"Night, Dylan. Please drive safe."

I nod and watch her disappear behind the door. When I know she's safely inside, I head back to my truck and drive away. It's dark in the cab, but if I could see my face in the mirror I know what I would see. I can't erase the grin the whole way home.

I'm going to make Avery Stanton my girl.

Chapter

9

Avery

Tonight's game was a home game, and of course our Warriors kicked ass. Dylan had a great game, as did Brad. Actually the entire team was on point. Harley and I are standing outside the locker room waiting for the guys. There are a few other girlfriends doing the same.

"So what are we doing tonight? I asked Brad about a bonfire and he said no. Has Dylan said anything?"

"He wouldn't tell me, just that you and I were not to make plans. He gave me strict instructions that we wait for him here after the game. Oh, and he wanted me to ask you to drive."

"Yeah, Brad pretty much told me the same thing. He even asked me to drive. Those two are definitely up to something."

I try to hold back my smile. Things have been going really well with Dylan and me. He walks me to all of my classes, and we hang out after practice. I've been helping him with his homework, much to his dismay. I do want to be a teacher, after all. We eat lunch together; Brad and Harley sit with us, as well as a few other players from the team. The rumor around school is that we're an official item. I'd like to think that too, but technically we've never talked about it. I don't bring it up and neither does he. He tells me that he can't get enough of me, that spending time with me is all he wants. He even went as far as contemplating skipping football practice one day. I convinced him that Coach Stanton, aka my brother, would kick both our asses. He went, but he made sure I knew it was because I asked him to. He said he would much rather spend time with me, just the two of us. That sounds to me like we're official, but I'm still waiting for that conversation.

"Hey, pretty lady," Brad says loudly enough for anyone within walking distance of the field to hear. Harley jumps into his arms, laughing.

"My girl," Dylan says low enough for only me to hear while wrapping his arms around me from behind.

"You think so?" I ask. His front is pressed to my back and his chin rests on the top of my head.

He squeezes me tight. "Hope so." I like that these moments are between us. I don't need a loud verbal declaration; I just need Dylan.

"You got plans to make that happen?" I ask. My tone is teasing, but it's hard as hell to keep the quiver out of my voice. I *really* want to know the answer.

"I thought I already was." Leaning down, he kisses my cheek. "You ready to get out of here?"

"Where are we going?"

"Brad's."

He says it so nonchalantly that I assume it's just to hang out by the fire like we did after the first home game for the season.

"Brad, you all ready to head out?" Dylan calls out to him.

"Yeah, we're right behind you."

With that, Dylan grabs my hand and leads me out to his truck. Before I can open the door, he pushes my back against it and lowers his lips to mine. I'm hesitant because we've really not done this in front of anyone at school. Sure, we've held hands, and he's had his hand on the small of my back or his arm around my shoulders as he walks me to class. There have even been a few pecks on the cheek and forehead kisses, but this... this is new for us.

"Dylan," I mumble against his lips.

He chuckles. "What? Am I not allowed to kiss my girl?"

That's the second time tonight he's referred to me as his girl, and it's hard for me to not get my hopes up about it. I want to be his. I mean, I'm already his, but is he mine? Maybe one day I'll get up the nerve to ask him. I don't want to be one of those clingy girlfriends or… whatever I am.

Dylan steps away, pulling me with him so he can open the door for me. "Why did you need me to have Harley drive?" I ask as I climb into the cab.

He holds up a finger with a grin. Stepping away, he closes the door and runs around to the driver side.

"Come here." He pats the seat next to him.

I raise my eyebrows in question, but do as he asks and slide to the center of the bench seat.

"This," he says, laying his hand on my thigh and pulling me closer. "I can't seem to get you close enough." Leaning over me, he fastens my seat belt and kisses my temple before latching his own belt. He keeps his hand on my thigh for the duration of the drive to Brad's house, surprising me when he bypasses the house and heads toward the field behind the tree line.

"Field party?" I ask.

"Not exactly." He doesn't elaborate so I don't ask.

When we reach the field, it's empty. Not another car anywhere. "Are you sure you told everyone?"

"Yep." He smiles over at me. We drive to the corner of the field before he puts the truck in Park and kills the ignition.

"Dylan?"

He turns sideways in the seat to face me. "Can you do me a favor, Aves?"

"O-okay."

"Can you close your eyes for me?"

"What are we doing, Dylan?" I can hear the panic in my voice.

"Babe, I promise you'll love it. If you don't, we can leave. I just need you to give me a few minutes. Can you do that?" he asks, cupping my cheek.

I nod.

"Close your eyes," he whispers.

Taking a deep breath, I do as he asks. I feel his lips kiss each eyelid tenderly. It's not until I hear his door open that I start to panic again. "Dylan?"

"I'm right here. I have to get something in the back of the truck. I'll be right back."

Taking a deep breath, I try to calm my nerves. I can hear my mom now telling me how incredibly stupid I am to willingly go to a dark field with a boy. I know Dylan would never hurt me, but my mind is running wild with what he could possibly be doing right now. I hear another truck and I cheat just a little, opening my eyes slightly to see Brad's truck driving to the opposite end of the field from us. Quickly I squeeze my eyes closed. "Come on, Dylan," I say under my breath. That must be all it takes because suddenly he's there.

"Keep them closed, babe. Take my hand." I feel his hand wrap around mine. "Slide toward me." I do as I'm told. "I'm going to lift you in my arms. I'm just taking you to the back of the truck. I need you to keep your eyes closed, but hold on tight around my neck, okay?"

"Okay." What else can I do but trust him? He's never done anything to hurt me, and his voice is soft, almost tender, when he speaks to me. I just wish I knew what we were doing. I've never been good at surprises.

Chapter
10

Dylan

When Brad told me that his parents were going out after the game tonight, we immediately started planning something we could do with the girls. Not brave enough to be alone with them in the house, we came up with blankets in the back of our trucks. Actually, it's an idea I got from Dad. He's told me story after story about how he and Mom used to do this when they were dating. Aves liked the rooftop date, so I figured Dad was on to something. I could've told her what we were doing, but I like to surprise her. It's the smile she gives me. That night on the rooftop, her smile was blinding and all for me. It's something I've come to crave from her.

Sliding my arms under her legs, I lift her from the truck. She giggles. "Hold on, babe."

"Can I open my eyes now?"

"Almost." I manage to kick the door closed without dropping her and carry her to the bed of my truck. I have the tailgate down, and the makeshift bed and pillows are calling our names. Carefully, I sit her on the tailgate. "Okay, open."

She blinks her eyes open and I wait for her vision to adjust. "What are we doing?" she asks.

Time to see if the old man's idea is a good one. "It's just us. Well, Brad and Harley are over on the other side. We just… I just wanted to spend time with you. We thought it would be cool to lie out here and watch the stars for a few hours. Just until curfew. Brad's parents won't be home until late, so we thought tonight was as good as any."

She looks across the field at Brad's truck and then back to me.

"Turn around, Aves." I point to the bed of my truck.

Slowly she turns her head. "Dylan," she whispers.

I step as close to her as I can, resting my hands on her hips. "You up for watching the stars, Avery?"

She turns back to face me, placing her hands on my shoulders. "Dylan Knight, you're a romantic." She smiles. It's the one that lights up her entire face, the one I was hoping for.

Pulling her into a hug, I whisper in her ear, "Just for you, beautiful. Just for you." We stay in this spot, in this moment, under the stars with her in my arms for what seems like hours even though I know it's mere minutes.

"What are we waiting for?" I step away from her and she swings her feet up on the tailgate of the truck. I watch as she slips off her tennis shoes and crawls into the bed before lying back on one of the pillows.

"I'm not sure how comfortable it'll be. I used like five blankets," I say, hopping up on the tailgate and sliding off my shoes. I crawl into the bed of the truck and lie beside her. "Come here." I open my arms and she settles her head on my chest as I wrap my arm around her.

"It's perfect."

I run my hands through her silky blonde hair. It's so damn soft. I close my eyes and just feel—her soft hair, her soft body pressed into mine. The boys and I brought home a win and here I am with my girl under the stars. This is the perfect ending to the night.

"Your eyes are closed," she says, lifting her head.

"Yeah, just taking it all in."

"How can you take the stars in with your eyes closed?" she asks, resting her head back on my chest.

"Not the stars, Aves. You."

"Me?"

I rest the hand I was running through her hair on her hip and give it a gentle squeeze. "Yes, you, Avery Stanton. Can a guy not just sit and enjoy holding his girl?"

"You mentioned that earlier."

I know what she's asking, and I've been waiting to have this conversation with her for weeks now. "I did."

We're both quiet. I'm trying to decide how to bring it up when she finally breaks the silence. "Am I your girl, Dylan?"

Slowly I shift to lie on my side and she does the same. I need to be looking at her for this part of the conversation. "I guess we haven't really established titles. I think we should change that tonight." I tuck a stray strand of hair behind her ear. She doesn't say anything, her eyes watching me. "Avery, you're all I think about. You've quickly become the most important person in my life. Will you do me the honor of being my girlfriend? When I call you my girl, I want to know that you know what that means. That you're it for me."

I watch as a lone tear trails down her cheek. Leaning in, I kiss it away.

"Yes," she whispers as her lips find mine.

As gently as I can without breaking the kiss, I lay her back on the bed of blankets. My hands roam her body, over her breasts, down her stomach. I slide my hand under her shirt and slip my index finger under the waistband of her jeans. Her breath hitches. I trail kisses down her neck, tasting her. Avery buries her hands in my hair, holding me in place as I devour her. "Dylan," she breathes.

I trail my fingers up her belly until I reach her bra-covered breasts. My mouth waters at the thought of tasting her there, my vision blurring at the idea of seeing her creamy white mounds. My cock grows stiff at the thought of the sounds she'll make as I slip her sweet nipple into my mouth. I cup her breast, bra and all, and she moans.

I need more.

Pulling away, I look into her eyes as I trace the swell of her breast under her shirt. I want more, but I don't want to push her. I would never push her. I'm just about to ask her how far she's willing to let me go when she sits up and pulls her shirt over her head. I look over at Brad's truck; no way am I taking the chance of anyone seeing her like this. Avery takes it a step further and efficiently renders me speechless when she reaches behind her back and unclasps her bra, her eyes never leaving mine as she slides the straps from her shoulders. She holds it in place, almost as if she's asking for permission.

I swallow hard. "I've never seen you more beautiful." My voice is gruff. "The moonlight is shining on this blonde silk." I reach out and push her hair over her shoulder, exposing her even further. "This creamy flawless skin. You're glowing." I trace the swells of her breasts as she holds the cups of her bra in place.

"I've never done this, Dylan."

I pause. "You don't have to now," I tell her, and I mean it. I would never force her.

"I want to." She looks to her lap. "I don't know what to do. I mean, I know it's going to hurt, but…"

"Hey." I place my index finger under her chin and lift until her eyes meet mine. "We'll only go as far as you want, but I'm not making love to you tonight. Not here in the bed of my truck. Not with our friends just across the field. You deserve better. When you tell me you're ready for that, we'll be in a bed where I can worship you."

That must relax her, because the next thing I know she's pulling her bra all the way off and tossing it beside us on top of her T-shirt. Reaching behind my neck, I grab my shirt and pull it off. It's not something I've ever done before with a girl.

I've had sex with one person, and it was quick in the back of her car this past summer. My jeans were around my ankles while she slipped out of her shorts and straddled me. Brad and I went to Bracken University for a college visit, and a few of the guys on the football team invited us back to a party at their house. Two BU cheerleaders latched on to us, promising the guys to show us a good time. It was over just as fast as it started, which was a good thing since Brad's parents were waiting for us at their hotel room. We quickly called a cab and headed back having both lost our virginity that night.

There's something about Avery that makes me want to do it all with her. Experience everything life has to offer. I want to brand her skin with mine. I want to do whatever it takes to remind her that she's mine.

With a shaking hand, I run my fingers over her side and under the swell of her breast. I watch as she closes her eyes and takes a deep breath. Unable to resist, I run the pad of my thumb over her nipple. It hardens at my touch. "Can I kiss you here?"

She nods, not opening her eyes.

Leaning down, I run my tongue over her nipple, much like I did with my thumb. She sucks in a breath. My hand finds her other nipple while my lips latch on and suck deep. She arches her back, which spurs me on. I nip, lick, and suck as I take my time, not willing to rush this. Her hands are buried in my hair, holding me to her. When I come up for air, I knead the nipple that was just in my mouth with my fingers and latch on to the other. I know in this moment that I will never have enough of her.

"Dylan."

"Yeah, baby?" I say, releasing her nipple. I lie down beside her and pull her chest against mine. The sensation of skin on skin is like nothing I've ever felt. I close my eyes and try to brand this moment into memory. I never want to forget what this feels like, what she feels like, her bare breasts pressed against my chest. My cock is screaming for release, but I'm content to just hold her. I'm not the most experienced, but this is all new to her; she needs to know that this, just holding her, is good too.

A ringing from her pocket echoes into the night. "My alarm," she sighs.

"Hey, this isn't a one-time thing with us. You're my girl now. We made that official, so there's gonna be more of this, more of us in our future." I kiss her quickly and pull us both into a sitting position. "Let's get dressed so we can get you home."

"I want to stay here with you."

I cup her face. "I can't have you getting in trouble, because I need to be able to see you every day. I need my Avery fix." I hand over her bra and shirt while I pull my shirt back on as well. Just as she's pulling hers over her head, I see Brad's headlights starting toward us.

I push my feet into my shoes and hand Avery hers, then grab the blankets and pillows and toss them in the back seat.

"You two about ready? They have just under thirty to get home," Brad says, stopping his truck next to mine.

"Yeah, we're right behind you." I lift Avery off the tailgate and set her on the ground. She's already in the truck, sitting right in the center when I join her. When we reach Brad's, the house is still dark; I breathe easier knowing we're in the clear. I turn off my truck and face her. "Thank you for tonight, Aves."

"I had fun. I mean, I didn't know it could be like that, you know?"

I do an internal fist bump that she liked it just as much as I did. "It's because it's us, Aves." I kiss her one more time before sliding out of the truck and walking her to Harley's car.

Once the girls are on the road, Brad and I stand there like lovestruck fools until we can no longer see Harley's car. "This is becoming routine for us," he laughs.

"What's that?"

"Standing here watching them leave."

"Yeah."

"She like it?" he asks.

"She did. What about Harley?"

He grins. "Your old man knows his shit. You got any other good ideas?"

"I'm sure he does." We head into the house and off to bed. I stare at the ceiling waiting for Avery to text me that they made it home okay.

> **Aves:** We made it to Harley's.
>
> **Me:** Good. Night, beautiful.
>
> **Aves:** Night, Dylan.

I toss my phone on the nightstand and drift off to sleep thinking about my girl.

Chapter 11

Avery

"Dylan, we have to focus. My parents are in the other room," I hiss. He kisses my neck one more time before pulling away. We're sitting at the dining room table working on our history homework. "I'm over history," he grumbles.

"Fine, but playoffs are coming up. It would suck for you to be sitting on the sidelines."

"Fuck," he hisses under his breath.

We've been dating for a few months now. This isn't the first time I've had to play hardball to get him interested in keeping his grades up.

"I have you. I don't need the playoffs."

I know he means it, but I also know he loves football and this is his last season. It's my job to be the hardass girlfriend and keep him on track.

"I'll tell you what. Let's go over the study sheet two more times, and then we can quit and do whatever you want. It's only two o'clock now. If we hurry to get this done, we'll have a couple of hours before I have to be home." It's Sunday afternoon and my curfew is ten on a school night.

"Deal." He pushes the study guide toward me and shuts the book. We spend the next hour going over it and by the second round, Dylan gets all the answers right. I know that doesn't mean he'll ace the test since he's not much of a test taker, but he says our study sessions seem to help him. We get to spend time together, so it's a win-win situation in my eyes.

"You kids finished?" Dad asks, taking a seat across from us.

"Yeah, we just finished. Where's Mom?"

"She ran to the store. She has to make brownies for work tomorrow."

"Do you care if I go to Dylan's for a couple of hours?"

"Your dad going to be there?" he asks.

"Yes, sir," Dylan answers.

"You kids have fun. Av, you be home at ten," he reminds me.

"I will, Dad," I say, fighting the urge to roll my eyes. I quickly clean up my books and run them up to my room. When I come back downstairs, I find my dad, Dylan, and my brother sitting around the table talking about the playoff games that start next week.

"Av, you can't be keeping him out all night. He needs to rest up for practice this week."

I give Alan a hug. "You excited?" I ask, ignoring the jab.

"Hell yes, I am. My boys are going to go all the way."

I chance a look at Dylan and he's grinning at my brother.

"You ready?" I ask. He stands and says goodbye to my family, and then we load up in his truck. He always wants to drive me, says we get to spend more time together this way. I admit he's right, but I'm not naive enough to think our parents aren't on to us.

Dylan's dad is sitting on the couch when we walk in. "Hey, kids," he greets.

"We're going to go to my room and watch a movie," Dylan tells him.

He stares at us for a long time. "Door open. Above the covers. Don't think I won't be checking," he warns us.

"Got it." Dylan grins, grabs my hand, and leads me back to his room. "It's nothing great, but it's mine," he says, guiding me to the bed.

I take in the surroundings: black and gray comforter on the queen-size bed, matching gray walls, dresser covered with trophies and a helmet. "Was that yours?"

"Yeah." He reaches over and picks it up. "This was my very first helmet. I was five. They got new uniforms the next year and Dad bought everything from the school. Pants, jersey, helmet—all of it."

"Aw, he's such a softie."

Dylan just shakes his head. "Don't encourage him."

"So, what are we watching?"

"Anything you want," he says, pulling me into his arms.

"Hmmm, how about... *The Notebook?*"

"Whatever you want, baby, you know that." He kisses my forehead, then steps away to grab the remote from his dresser. I watch as he kicks off his shoes and grabs a blanket out of a laundry basket.

"He said no blankets."

"I know that, but I know you like to snuggle with a blanket when you watch a movie. You can be under and I can be over. Don't worry about Dad."

"Always thinking about what I want." I stand on tiptoes to press a soft kiss against his lips.

"Just you, Aves. All I think about is you." He pulls away from me and climbs into his bed. I wait for him to adjust the pillows and get situated, and then he opens his arms for me. "Come here."

I waste no time climbing in beside him. He throws the cover over me, making sure I'm all covered up before he wraps his arm around me, pulling me to his chest before starting the movie.

This is one of my all-time favorites, but I can't help but fight sleep. I'm all bundled up and warm, with Dylan caressing my back, his scent surrounding me. It's not long before I'm drifting off to sleep.

"I thought I said no covers," I hear Dylan's dad whisper.

"You did," Dylan whispers back. "But Aves likes to snuggle with a blanket when she watches movies. I wanted her to be comfortable. I stayed on top."

"I see that. Looks like you're holding on pretty tight, son."

I keep my eyes closed, trying not to let them see I'm awake.

"Damn right," Dylan says.

His dad chuckles softly. "She's good for you."

"I know."

"You're going to miss her when she's gone."

"Like a limb, but she's worked hard to get that scholarship. Her dream is to be a teacher. I'll be here waiting for her when she finishes college. I'll even drive up to visit. It's just a five-hour drive."

"You know how hard that's going to be?" I can hear the sorrow in his voice. "To be without her that long."

"I can imagine," Dylan says. "You know what though? I can't imagine my life without her in it at all. She's my reason, Dad."

"Don't ever forget that, how you feel right now with her here. It's going to be a long four years."

"Don't care. The end game is me and my girl and whatever the future holds. I'll make sure she knows I'm not going anywhere."

"Don't let her forget it. Even when there are miles between you, never let her forget how much she means to you, or how much you miss her. Remember to always be honest with her. It'll all work out like it's supposed to." I hear footsteps and his voice sounds farther away. "You probably ought to wake her soon to get her home before curfew."

"I know. The movie just ended. I wasn't going to wake her until I had to."

"You be safe driving her home. Love you, son."

"Love you too, Dad."

The bed shifts and Dylan's runs his finger down the side of my cheek. "Babe, it's time to wake up." I don't do anything at first, keeping up with the ruse that I'm still sleeping. "Aves, baby, it's time to wake up." This time he presses his lips to mine. I roll over and stretch, blinking like I'm just waking up.

"What time is it?" Luckily my voice is groggy from my nap and I don't have to fake it.

"Just after nine. I need to get you home."

I burrow under the covers and curl into him. "I missed it, all of it. The movie, our snuggle time. I'm sorry."

"I'm not. I got to hold you, watch you sleep. No regrets on my end. Come on, sleepyhead. Up you go."

I let him pull me from the bed. I grab the blanket to fold it but he reaches out and stops me. "You don't have to do that. I'll be sleeping with that tonight."

"What? Why would you do that? You've already got a blanket on your bed."

He smiles down at me and my heart melts. "It smells like you, Aves. You'll be here with me all night."

"I'm jealous," I say, not realizing what I've said until the words are out of my mouth.

Dylan studies me, then looks around his room. He grabs a Montgomery Warriors hoodie that he wore yesterday and hands it to me. "I only had this on for a few hours yesterday, so it's not really dirty."

I bring the shirt to my face and breathe him in. "Thank you." I wrap my arms around his waist for a hug.

"Let's get you home."

In normal Dylan fashion, he walks me to the door. I get a soft kiss to my forehead with a promise to text when he gets home. I don't bother watching him leave; I know he won't until I'm safely inside.

I find my parents in the living room, Dad sitting on the end of the couch with Mom's head in his lap. "Hey, kiddo," he says.

"Hey, what are you guys watching?"

"Dad's watching *How It's Made* again. I'm reading." She holds up her Kindle.

"I'm going to head up to bed. Good night." I wave and head upstairs. After quickly changing clothes, I wash my face and brush my teeth. My phone pings just as I climb into bed.

My #17: Just got home. Sweet dreams.

Me: Good night, Dylan.

I plug my phone in and leave it to charge on the nightstand. Holding Dylan's sweatshirt close to my chest, I think about the conversation he had with his dad. I love how honest he is, even with his father. It's one of the reasons why I love him.

And I do. I'm madly in love with him. I want to tell him, wanted to tonight, but I don't want to ruin it. What if he doesn't say it back? I know he cares about me, but love? That's huge. So huge that my heart is spilling over with it.

I'm in love with Dylan Knight.

Chapter 12

Dylan

We won. We fucking won state! The bus back home is rowdy and loud, everyone still pumped up from our win. I can't wait until we make it back to town—I need to hug my girl. Avery and Harley as well as Avery's parents drove up for the game. They offered to let me head back with them, Brad too, but Coach insisted we all ride back as a team. I had maybe two minutes with her, and we were surrounded by her family, my teammates. I didn't get to hug her. That's what I need.

> **Me:** I need a hug, Aves.
>
> **Aves:** You won the game, you should be celebrating.
>
> **Me:** I will be when I have you in my arms. You're who I want to celebrate with.
>
> **Aves:** I'm proud of you, Dylan.
>
> **Me:** I need a hug.
>
> **Aves:** LOL. I'll see you in an hour.
>
> **Me:** Are we there yet?

Aves: Stop texting me and celebrate with the team. I'll
see you soon.

God, I love her. I type out those three little words and erase them. I can't be that guy, the one who tells his girl he loves for the first time over text message. No, I have bigger plans for that. I just hope it all works out.

"That your girl?" Brad asks, falling into the seat beside me.

"Yeah, they're on their way back. She and Harley are going to meet us at the school."

"Did she say anything?"

I look at him like he's crazy and he laughs. "What the hell are you talking about?"

"Nothing." He grins. "Just pumped up about this win. My head's all over the place."

I know the feeling so I don't think too much of it. We replay the entire game for the next hour. Coach sits up front and just grins at our antics as we announce play for play. He's a great guy, and we've managed to keep my relationship with Avery separate from our relationship on the field. I'm kicking myself in the ass for not asking her out sooner. Look at all the time I wasted that I could've been with her. Dad says everything happens for a reason, and maybe he's right. I was really struggling this year with grades, and if it weren't for Avery I'm not sure I would've been on that field tonight with the rest of my team. She's my lifeline.

As soon as the bus turns into the lot, Brad and I are on our feet at the front of the bus, anxious to see our girls.

"Where are you two off to?" Coach asks.

I look at him and grin. "Gotta hug my girl," I say, patting him on the shoulder as I walk off the bus.

Brad scoffs. "Dude, that's his little sister."

"Dude, that's the love of my life. Season's over."

Brad doesn't have time to reply before the girls are running our direction. We both drop our bags and brace for impact as they throw themselves into our arms.

"I'm so proud of you, Dylan," Avery says, wrapping her arms and legs around me and burying her face in my neck.

I don't say anything. Not because I don't have anything to say; I'm just afraid I'll blurt it out here in the school parking lot. That's not how I want her to remember it. Instead I hold her as tight as I can and soak up her warmth.

"Best behavior tonight," Coach says as he walks past us.

"What's he talking about?" I ask Avery.

Pulling back, she grins at me. "Brad didn't tell you?"

"Tell me what?"

"We're all staying at Brad's tonight. Brad's dad talked to mine and Harley's. He promised no funny business and they said yes. I mean, technically we're all eighteen and adults, but we are still in school for a few more months and living under their roofs," she rambles on.

"Aves!" I say to get her attention. "What are you saying?" *Did I hear her right?*

She giggles. "Harley and I are spending the night at Brad's, and so are you. She and I are going to camp out in the basement with his mom while you guys are upstairs like you normally are."

"I don't understand," I say, looking over at Brad.

"My parents knew we would be pumped about the win. This is our last high school game, and for you, the last game ever. They grabbed some snacks and talked our girls' parents into letting us all stay at my place. We're going to hang out, watch movies, and then when we finally crash, Mom will stay downstairs with the girls while you and I are up in our rooms."

I look back at Avery. "All night?"

She nods.

"Can we find a way to cheat the system so I can hold you? I just want to hold you."

Her face softens. "We'll see what we can do, big guy. Right now I'm freezing my buns off, so we need to get going."

I give her a quick kiss before releasing her. "We're riding back with Brad's parents. We'll see you two there." She waves over her shoulder.

"Dude!" I say, getting Brad's attention once they pull away. "Why in the hell did you keep this from me?"

"Didn't want to distract you from the game."

"What about you?"

He laughs. "I didn't find out until the game was over. You were with Avery's family when Dad pulled me aside and told me the plan."

"Your parents are cool as hell."

"Right? Although Avery's right. Technically we are all eighteen now. And if we really want to get technical, all of our parents are cool as hell for agreeing to this."

"Holy shit! We gotta go." I tug on his hand as we walk to our trucks.

"Don't be speeding, Romeo. The girls will be there when we get there."

I get what he's saying, but I don't understand how he's not more stoked about this. I know he cares about Harley, but maybe he doesn't love her the way I do Avery. I'll have to ask him—another time though. Right now all that matters is getting to her.

Just when I think life can't get any better…

Chapter
13

Avery

Brad's parents drive us to their place, making small talk about the game and our plans after graduation. I'm still surprised my parents agreed to this. Dad simply said I'm technically an adult and that he trusts me. He also said this will be a good trial run for when I leave for college in a few months.

My gut twists at the thought. I hate even thinking about it, about leaving Dylan. We've not talked about it much, I've been holding off, not wanting to add anything to his stress level until the game was over. Now that it is, we're going to have to talk about it. I don't want to leave him. I've even been looking at colleges close to home that have education programs. It's a little late to apply for scholarships, but I can try. I'm willing to do whatever it takes to stay with him. He's my heart.

"Thank you again for doing this," Harley tells Brad's mom. The three of us are in the kitchen getting some snacks together.

She smiles at us. "You're welcome. This is a big deal, their last game of their high school career. I asked Brad how he wanted to celebrate and he said he wanted to take you out. I knew there was no way these boys would want to wait until next weekend to celebrate and that your curfew would come way too soon." She glances over at the clock. "You would have to leave here in fifteen minutes to be home on time."

"Thank you for including me," I say, pouring some salsa into a bowl.

"Dylan is my second son. That boy owns a piece of my heart. No way could we not include the two of you in our little mini celebration."

"Not many parents would do this," Harley says.

"You all are good kids. As a parent I would rather know you're here under my roof than trying to sneak around to see each other. It's a big night, a big win, and a celebration is in order."

"Hey," Brad says, coming to stand behind Harley. I watch as he places his hands on her hips and kisses her cheek. Harley says she's not sure how he feels, but from my view he loves her. Anyone can see that.

Arms wrap around my waist, a kiss pressed to my temple. "Missed you," Dylan whispers just for me.

"Okay, Brad and Dylan, carry down the pizza boxes. Avery and Harley, do each of you mind grabbing a tray? We'll set all of this up downstairs." We do as asked and carry all the food down to the basement. "You kids go ahead and dig in. I'm going to go upstairs and change." Brad's mom looks over at him. "Your dad and I will be down in a little bit."

Brad walks to where she's standing and scoops her up in a big hug, lifting her feet off the floor. "Thank you for this. I love you," he says.

"Love you too," she replies as he sets her back on the floor.

Then Dylan picks her up, only he swings her around. "Thank you, love you," he says. It's low, not a proclamation like Brad's. My heart aches for him, losing his mother at such a young age. I'm glad that he's had Brad's mom to semi-fill those shoes for him.

We fill our plates with junk food and settle onto the couches. There are three of them set up kind of like a sectional to make a U shape. The other wall holds a huge TV, and there's not a bad seat in the house.

"You all kicked ass tonight," I say before taking a big bite of my pizza. They both grin at my praise.

"Your parents are seriously the best for doing this. Av and I were plotting ways to sneak out to see you," Harley tells them.

Dylan looks at me. "That true?"

I shrug. "Tonight was a big deal for you, both of you. We just wanted to be there to help you celebrate. Who knows if we would've actually pulled it off? Thanks to Brad's parents, we didn't have to."

He leans over and kisses me. "That right there, that made my night." He must see the question in my eyes because he continues on to say, "To know you were willing to risk getting caught to see me." He opens his mouth like he's going to say more but quickly closes it.

"I ate too much," Harley complains, standing to throw her paper plate away.

"Me too." I grab Dylan's plate and toss both in the trash. Harley and I close the pizza boxes and place the lids back over the dips. "Should we put this in the fridge?" I ask Brad.

"Nah, leave it for now. I'm sure my parents will come down and eat eventually. Hurry up, you two, it's movie time." Harley and I are wearing matching grins as we join them on the couches.

Brad jumps up to dim the lights over where we're sitting. It's a pretty cool setup down here. Dylan stands and walks toward the small area off the kitchen, back in no time with two blankets in his hands. He hands one to Brad and sets the other on the back of the couch we've been sitting on. He lies down and pats the couch in front of him.

I look over at Brad. "It's fine, they won't freak out," he answers my silent question. His parents have been great; I don't want to push my luck.

"We've done this before with his parents, Av. It's cool," Harley reassures me.

I sit on the couch in front of Dylan and stretch out, resting my head in the crook of his arm as he wraps the other around my waist. "I need you closer," he whispers, and I wiggle back to where my body is aligned with his. I feel his breath against my cheek as he exhales. Reaching up, he grabs the blanket and places it over me. I bunch a portion of it up in my arms and snuggle it close. "That's my girl," Dylan says, his lips next to my ear.

My body breaks out in goose bumps from the heat of his breath against my skin. It makes me think of that night in his truck. There hasn't been another one like it. Yeah, there's been some groping in his room, or in his truck or my car, but nothing like that night under the stars. We haven't even been able to make it up to the rooftop again. It's only been stolen touches here and there, and it's done nothing to quench this craving I have for him.

Chapter 14

Dylan

The movie Brad picked plays in the background, but I can't tell you what it is. My sole focus is Avery. She's snuggled up in my arms and nothing else matters. Not today's win, not the fact that in a few short months she'll be leaving me; right now, all that matters is that she's in my arms where she belongs.

"Hey, hey, there're my champions," Brad's dad says, coming down the stairs.

"Shh!" Brad shushes him. "The girls fell asleep."

"Party poopers," his dad teases. "I thought this whole setup was so you all could celebrate together."

"Dad, what am I doing right now?" Brad whispers.

"Lying on the couch watching a movie?"

"And who is lying here with me?"

"Harley."

"So let's recap, shall we? Tonight my best friend and I took home the state championship. Now just a few hours later, I'm lying on the couch, holding my girlfriend, asleep or not. This tops whatever it is you and Mom had planned."

His dad looks over at me.

"No complaints." I grin.

He shakes his head and grins. "We raised you boys right." He walks over to the table of food and starts making a plate.

"Aw, they fell asleep," Brad's mom says softly as she makes a plate and joins her husband on the other couch. We sit in silence and watch the movie. Well, I pretend to watch it. I don't care what's on; I just care about Aves. Brad was right when he said they didn't tell us because we would've been distracted. I wonder what the chance of them letting us sleep like this is.

I must've fallen asleep because when I open my eyes, the TV is off and Brad's parents are standing over him, trying to wake him but not Harley. "Brad," his mom whispers. He opens his eyes. "Time for bed."

"Night," he says, burying his face in Harley's neck. I fight to hold back my laughter.

"I promised their parents," his mom says.

"I know, but this is all we're going to do, sleep. You can come down and check on us anytime. You can sleep on the other couch."

She looks over her shoulder at me and finds me watching them. "I don't want to move," I tell her. Of course, if I have to I will, but I'm hoping not.

"I know you all are eighteen, but these girls, their parents trusted me to keep them safe from the two of you." She gives us both a pointing look. "Do not make me regret this decision. Your dad and I are going to sleep in the bedroom down here. No funny business."

"None," I say with conviction. I want there to be funny business, but if that's the trade I have to make to hold her like this all night, there's no contest.

"Thanks Mom, Dad," Brad whispers.

His mom nods and walks to the downstairs bedroom. His dad holds his fist out for Brad and then me. "You boys be good to them. Never take for granted what you have. You've found good ones. Hold on tight."

"I'm trying," Brad says. I repeat that exact phrase in my head.

I'm trying.

Sliding my hands under the covers, I hold her close, waiting for sleep to claim me. It never comes.

I don't know how much time has passed when Avery wakes up. "Hey," I whisper in her ear.

"Dylan, we're going to get in trouble." I hear the panic in her voice.

"We're fine. His parents know we're sleeping like this. They're just down the hall in the downstairs bedroom. They made us promise no funny business."

"Will you show me where the restroom is?"

I nod and tap her leg for her to stand. We tiptoe down the hall and I wait outside the door for her. The bedroom door opens and Brad's mom steps out.

"Everything okay?"

"Yeah, Aves just had to use the restroom."

"What about you?" she asks.

"I'm waiting for her."

The corners of her lips tip up in a smile. "Dylan, I think she can find her way back to the couch."

"Probably, but I'll wait anyway."

"No funny business, mister." She points at me.

"You have nothing to worry about. Thank you for doing this, for trusting us and giving me this night with her."

She steps closer and pulls me into a hug. "Dylan, your mom would be so proud of the man you're becoming. I know I can never fill her shoes, but I love you just as I do Brad. You're a part of this family."

I hug her back. "Thank you. I love you all too."

"Everything okay?" Aves asks, catching us in our hug.

"Fine. Just giving this one a hard time about waiting outside the door for you. Then I went and got all sentimental on him."

"I don't mind," Aves says.

"Oh, Avery, of course you don't. He's one of the good ones. Make sure he always treats you this way. If not, you come to me and I'll knock some sense into him."

"Deal." Avery smiles.

"Let's go back to sleep," I say, holding my hand out for her. I wasn't sleeping, but I'm anxious to get her back in my arms. Where she belongs.

Stretching out on the couch once more, I hold my arms open for her. She doesn't hesitate to lie down next to me. "Turn over," I whisper.

She rolls on her side so she's facing me, and I pull the blanket over us and hold her close. She rests her head on my chest and I lay my cheek against the top of her head. "I've thought about this," she says, her voice soft, low. "Thought about falling asleep like this, with you."

"You're all I think about," I admit, keeping my voice soft as well. It's on the tip of my tongue to tell her that I love her. This isn't how I had planned it would happen though. She snuggles closer and places a kiss over my heart. It's through my shirt, but I swear I can feel her lips on my skin. "I love you, Avery." The words tumble out and I don't regret it. I can't keep how I feel about her to myself.

She raises her head and her tear-filled eyes look up at me. "I love you too."

Leaning down, I press a chaste kiss to her lips; anything more than that and I might be breaking my promise to Brad's parents. Avery places her head back on my chest and I tighten my hold on her. Now that I've said the words, not a day will go by that I don't tell her how I feel. We only have a few months before she leaves for college. It's going to suck, and it's going to be hard as hell to be away from her for long periods of time, but she's it for me. We'll make it work no matter how hard it is.

Avery Stanton owns me.

Chapter 15

Avery

I wake to the sunlight streaming into my room. I know it sounds cliché, but I feel different this morning. Yesterday was graduation day and it was bittersweet. I'll miss high school, but I'm ready for the next chapter in my life—college and my future with Dylan. It's been nine months now, and I know that may not seem like a long enough time to know that he's my forever, but to me it's more than enough time. There is not one aspect of my future that I don't see him as a part of.

My phone pings from its spot on my nightstand. I see Dylan's contact name and realize I should probably change it since football's been over for months now.

> **My #17:** Morning, beautiful.
>
> **Me:** Morning. You all packed?
>
> **My #17:** I was packed the day we booked the cabins.
>
> **Me:** I'll see you soon.
>
> **My #17:** I love you, Aves.
>
> **Me:** Love you too.

Dylan, Brad, Harley, and I rented cabins at Lake Grant. Our parents protested at first, but we reminded them that we're eighteen and high school graduates, so really they didn't have much of a leg to stand on. It also helps that my parents really like Dylan, and Harley's like Brad. We're leaving at noon today and spending four days there.

Brad's parents and Dylan's dad paid for the cabins as part of their graduation presents. Harley and I both offered to pay our share but they shut us down. I can still remember Dylan's exact words. "I love you, Aves. This is the best gift he could've given me. Four days with you, no interruptions. Just us. No way are you paying." How could I argue with that?

I hop out of bed and head to the shower, taking my time, shaving every inch. Dylan and I haven't had sex yet. We've come close a few times but he keeps stopping us. But I'm ready and he's ready, so I don't know what the holdup is. I hope that changes this weekend.

After the night we spent at Brad's together, even though nothing happened, my mom took me to get on birth control. I fought it, saying we didn't need it. She said that was fine but she was taking me anyway so when we did decide to have sex, I was covered. It was a little uncomfortable talking to her about it, but I'm glad I have her, that she's there for me for stuff like this. It's kind of a relief, really; I won't have to stress over the possibility of getting pregnant if and when it happens.

Harley says I need to take control. She and Brad slept together for the first time a few months ago. I don't know why, but Dylan insists on waiting. I know he's faithful; that doesn't concern me. I'm going to be patient until he decides he's ready.

I also hope to talk to him about college while it's just the two of us. He's been good at putting off this conversation, but we have to have it. I've been accepted to the local university. I was too late to apply for scholarships, but I can get loans and work. Whatever it takes not to leave him.

I've just finished zipping up my duffel bag when Mom yells up the stairs. "Av, they're here."

I make one last mental check: phone, charger, bag, money. I think I've got it. I head downstairs to find Dylan, Brad, and Harley talking to my parents. To my surprise, Alan is here too. "Hey," I say, clearing the final step.

"You ready?" Harley asks. I can hear the excitement in her voice.

"No speeding," my dad says to Brad. We're taking his mom's Tahoe.

"No, sir, we've got nothing but time," he replies.

Alan puts his arm around my shoulders. "You know you can call me to come and get you. No questions asked. I won't even tell Mom and Dad. You need me, you call," he says just for me.

I hug him tight. "Love you, big brother."

"Okay, so you have all of our cell numbers. Brad's mom said when they were there a few summers ago, service wasn't an issue."

Mom pulls me into a hug and Dad hugs us both. "You all be safe. We love you. Call us if you need us, no questions asked."

I understand I'm the baby of the family, but we're going to be fine. It's only two hours away. "We will. Love you guys." I give them all one more hug.

Dylan takes my bag from my shoulder. "I'll put this in the car." He turns and walks outside, Brad and Harley following close behind.

"You sure we can trust him with Av?" Dad asks Alan.

He laughs. "He's a good kid. You all know that. They'll be fine." He winks at me.

I make a mental note to get him a little something extra for Christmas this year. "I'll see you all in a few days," I say.

After another round of hugs, they walk out to the front porch with me. Brad and Harley are already in the front seat and Dylan's standing at the bottom of the steps, waiting for me.

"I promise I'll take good care of her." His voice is the most serious I've ever heard him.

"We know you will, Dylan. You kids have a good time," Mom tells us.

Dylan takes my hand and leads me to the Tahoe, opening the door and climbing in behind me. I don't bother scooting over; there's nowhere else I want to be than close to him.

We stop at a small grocery store before heading to the cabins. We decided that we'll all eat together for each meal to save on groceries. "There's a restaurant there too and they have good food. We can eat there as well."

After loading up on camping essentials—burgers, corn on the cob, s'mores ingredients, and lunchmeat—we head to the cabins.

"We can just keep the food in our cabin," Harley suggests. "It'll be easier to keep it all in one spot."

"Definitely," I agree.

Our cabins are side by side so it makes it easier for Dylan and me to help carry in the groceries. It will also make it convenient when it comes time to eat.

I thought I would be nervous for this weekend, but I'm not. Excited and hopeful is more like it. He already owns my heart and soul; now I'm ready to give all of myself to him.

Chapter 16

Dylan

We're sitting around the fire behind Brad and Harley's cabin. I look at Brad and he nods. It's time for us to get our girls alone. I won't lie, I'm nervous. I've waited to be with her; I know it's her first time and I want it to be perfect.

I know she's been frustrated with me. I haven't been able to explain it to her so she understands. She's my world; I want nothing but great things for her, and that includes her first time. I know it's going to hurt her, and that kills me. I refuse to rush, and this is really the first true opportunity I've had to take my time. Although I'm not a virgin, there are still experiences I have yet to have with a girl. I want those with her, and I want to take my time to enjoy them, to enjoy her.

"You ready to go?" I ask Aves from where she's sitting on my lap.

"Yeah."

"We're going to head out. See you all in the morning."

Avery stands and I follow, grabbing her hand. "You need help with the fire?" I ask Brad. It's not much of one as we've been letting it die down, but I still offer.

"Nah, I'm going to throw some dirt on it and call it good."

With that, I lead my girl through the backyard to our cabin. Once inside, I make sure both the front and back doors are locked. "You ready for bed?" I ask her.

"I'm ready to snuggle with you," she says, wrapping her arms around my waist. I rest my chin on top of her head.

"I'm always down for some Aves snuggles," I say, causing her to laugh.

"I think I'm going to take a shower before bed."

My mind immediately goes to the gutter, wet soap sliding down her body. I close my eyes and try to block the image. "Okay, babe." I kiss the top of her head and release her.

Not three minutes later, I hear her call out, "Dylan!"

I make my way to the bedroom, pushing open the door, "You…" My voice trails off at the sight before me. Avery, my beautiful Avery, is standing before me completely naked. Her legs are crossed and her hands are covering her breasts, a slight blush coating her cheeks.

"I thought that maybe you might want to take a shower with me… you know, save water and all that." Her final words are so soft I barely hear her over the thunderous beat of my heart.

"You sure you want that?" I ask, taking one step toward her.

"I want you." She exhales, uncrosses her legs, and drops her hands from her breasts.

I don't move. I stand there, staring at my girl naked. It's my first look at all of her and I'm trying my hardest to memorize every curve, every inch of her gorgeous body.

"Dylan." There's a quiver in her voice.

"You take my breath," I say honestly.

She holds her hand out to me, asking again for me to join her. This time I don't hesitate to place my hand in hers. She walks us to the bathroom, then turns to face me. Neither of us speaks as she grabs the hem of my shirt. I lift my arms above my head and allow her to pull my shirt off. She places her hands on the waistband of my shorts, but I'm painfully hard and I don't want to scare her. "I can do that." I unsnap my shorts and pull them and my boxer briefs off at the same time, kicking them to the side.

Her gaze never leaves mine. "The water should be ready," she says.

I nod, place my hand on the small of her back, and follow her into the shower. She keeps her head down, looking at her feet.

"Aves, we don't have to do this," I tell her.

Her head pops up. "I want to, I just... I don't know what to do. Will you show me?"

"Baby, I've never been in this situation before." I place my arm around her back and pull her naked body to mine. I hold her like I have a thousand times before, but this time it's different. We're skin to skin. I rest my chin on the top of her head as she wraps her arms around my waist, her head on my chest. My erection is pressed against her belly.

"You're trembling," she says.

"I've thought about this moment a million times. Now that we're here, I don't know what to do. I want to devour you, taste every inch of you. This is new to me too, Aves."

Lifting her head, the corners of her lips tilt in a slow smile. "So we learn together?"

"Yeah, we can learn together."

"I've never seen one," she says, her head still resting on my chest. "I can feel you, but I've never actually seen one."

I'm sure she can feel the thunderous beat of my heart in my chest. I swallow hard. "You can look. I'm yours." No truer statement has ever been said.

"Can I touch you?"

My cock twitches against her belly. "Only you."

Slowly she steps back and looks down. Again my cock twitches. She doesn't move, and to be honest I'm not sure either of us is breathing. Tentatively, she reaches out and traces the tip with her index finger. "It's so soft," she whispers. "I don't know what I expected, but not... soft."

My knees weak, I turn my back to the wall and lean against it. Avery continues her exploration, taking my cock in the palm of her hand. "Aves," I moan.

"Am I hurting you?"

"No, babe, you're not hurting me. You are, however, driving me mad. Having your hands on my... that's different, you know. It's different than through our clothes. Your hands are soft and warm."

"You're hard and soft at the same time." She runs her hand up and down my shaft, slowly pumping.

I grit my teeth, fighting like hell not to lose control. Two seconds with her hand on me and I'm ready to blow. "Aves." I place my hand over hers. "That feels better than I could ever explain, but if you keep doing that…"

Her eyes widen. "This makes you feel good?" she asks, pumping me again, this time a little faster.

"Yeah," I breathe, resting my head back against the shower wall. She doesn't stop, her hand sliding up and down my shaft in a steady rhythm. "Aves," I moan, fighting my release. "Babe, I'm close."

She doesn't stop, and within seconds I'm releasing into her hand. My eyes are closed, my head still against the wall of the shower while I try to catch my breath. That's why I didn't see what was coming next. When I feel her lips press against the head of my cock, my eyes shoot open and I look down. It's an image I will carry with me until my dying day. Avery is kneeling before me, licking her lips as she tastes me for the first time. Her nose is scrunched up.

"Aves."

"It's not what I expected," she says, climbing to her feet.

"What did you expect?"

"I don't know, but it was warm and salty. It's not terrible."

"Come here." I can't keep from smiling as I pull her wet, naked body to mine. "I love you, Avery."

"I love you too."

I grab the body wash and pour some into my hands, rubbing them together before placing them on her shoulders. Slowly I run my soapy hands down her arms, her breasts, over her stomach; I don't leave one single inch of her creamy skin untouched. Once I've completed my task, I guide her under the spray and watch as the suds roll off her. It's the most erotic moment of my life.

"My turn," she says as she gives me a shy smile.

I nod, standing stock-still while she runs her soapy hands all over my body. After we're rinsed off, I turn off the water and step out of the shower, grabbing a towel and wrapping it around her before handing her another for her hair. I make quick work of drying myself off, then step out to give her a few minutes.

I don't bother with clothes, not because I expect her to have sex with me but because I have plans to hold her all night long. Sure, I think about what it's going to be like when I slide into her for the first time, but I can wait for that. I want her to be sure. Losing your virginity is a big deal.

I wish I would've waited.

For her.

Chapter 17

Avery

I rush through drying my hair, in a hurry to get back to Dylan. Tonight's the night; I can feel it. I don't know what he's been waiting for, but he can't keep putting me off. We have this cabin to ourselves for four nights and I plan to utilize them. I want to give him the one piece of me that he doesn't already own.

I find Dylan lying in bed with nothing but a thin white sheet draped over him. He's completely naked, and I fight the urge to celebrate. *This is really happening.* Shutting off the bathroom light, I walk slowly to the bed with only the guidance of the moonlight. Dylan holds the sheet up for me to crawl under. I move over next to him and he immediately wraps his arms around me.

"Make love to me, Dylan."

"Aves, I don't expect—"

I place my finger over his lips. "I know you don't expect it. I do. I want to give you the last piece of me."

"Avery." He leans down and kisses my forehead.

"Just hear me out." I wait for his confirmation; it comes with a simple nod of his head. "I love you, Dylan. Not just high school 'he's my boyfriend' love, but a soul-deep, 'feel it in my bones' kind of love. My heart and soul have your name on them. There's only one thing left and

I want you to have it. No matter where we end up, where our futures lead, I want to know that you have that piece of me. The one piece that I will never be able to give another."

"You're my future, Aves. I love you."

"I love you too." Deciding I need to be bold, prove to him this is what I want, I reach over into the nightstand and pull out the new box of condoms I stored there earlier. I straddle his hips. "Make love to me, Dylan."

He hooks his hand behind my neck and pulls me down into a kiss. His tongue strokes my lips, my tongue as he kisses me senseless. He rolls us over so he's now on top, his hips resting between my thighs. I prepare myself for more of his kisses, but instead he sucks a nipple into his mouth. It sends a rush of heat and what I can only assume is desire running through my body. He takes his time, giving each of my breasts equal attention. When he lifts his head once more, his eyes are dark, intense.

Resting his weight on one elbow, he slides his other hand between us, through my folds. "I want to kiss you here. Can I do that, Aves? It will be a first for me. Something I can give you."

I know he wishes he had waited for me. He's told me that before, that he feels guilty, but he shouldn't. One of us needs to have a better understanding of what's going on here. "Only you."

Bending down, he trails kisses down my neck and over each breast. He moves down my belly and I can't help but quiver with anticipation. "You okay?" he asks.

"Yeah, don't stop." I know if he thinks I even remotely have reservations he won't keep going. I really, *really* need him to keep going.

He continues to move lower until his head is now between my thighs. Lifting onto my elbows, I look down at him. He never breaks eye contact until after the first swipe of his tongue; I watch in fascination as he squeezes them shut and lets out a slow breath. "I love you, Avery," he breathes against my heated skin before going back for more.

The sensation of his tongue down there, it's... everything. I don't know how to explain it. I do know he's driving me crazy with need for him. I lock my fingers into his hair and hold on for the ride, which seems to spur him on as he pushes my legs further apart and unleashes on me.

"Dylan," I moan, because that's all I'm capable of. I feel as if I'm about to lose control. He doesn't stop, just keeps stroking his tongue against me, and the wave hits me before I know it's coming. I hold on tight to his hair and ride the current as it races through my veins.

When I finally come to, Dylan is lying beside me, tracing small circles on my belly. "That was… I don't have the words, Aves."

"Make love to me."

"You're sure?"

"No questions, no hesitations, no regrets. I want it to be you, Dylan."

He grabs the box of condoms. I refuse to take my eyes off him as he tears the little foil packet with his teeth and slowly rolls it down his length. He settles himself between my legs and rests his weight on his elbows on either side of my head. "Promise me if you need me to stop you'll tell me."

"I promise," I say, running my hands up and down his back. "I want this, Dylan."

He doesn't reply, just leans down and kisses me. It's slow and sensual, his tongue teasing my lips. I grab his arms, bracing for the impact, and I can feel him trembling. I kiss him with everything I have in me, losing myself in him, until I feel his hard length at my entrance. I don't stop kissing him as he inches his way inside me for the first time. His pace is painfully slow, so I wrap my legs around his waist and squeeze. "I'm okay," I whisper.

"That's good, babe, but I'm not. It's so hot, so tight, I don't know that I can hold on."

"Don't. I just want to feel you, all of you. It doesn't matter how long. I know this time is going to be fast, but I want it. We have the next four days to practice our longevity."

He chuckles softly and rests his forehead against mine. "Avery, I don't know that I'll ever be able to last with you. This is…you feel incredible. It wasn't… I've never felt this."

"This is us, Dylan." I raise my head to kiss him and he slides the rest of the way in. I freeze, not from the pain, really, but from the sudden impact of having him fully inside of me.

"You good, Aves?" he asks. His eyes are closed tight and he's breathing heavy.

"I'm good, just full. Move, Dylan. Take what you need. I'm right here with you."

He kisses me one more time before he gently rocks his hips into mine. I have no concept of time—it could have been thirty seconds or thirty minutes—but I do know when he reaches his climax. I'm fully aware of how he calls my name as he pulses inside of me. It's a feeling I will never forget.

"I'll be right back." Dylan kisses my forehead, then pulls out of me. I immediately feel the loss of connection, of his body pressed to mine. I lie there in bed, watching the shadows play off the ceiling.

"Hey, open your legs," he says softly.

I do as he asks, willing to give him anything, do anything for him. He places a warm cloth between my legs and cleans me up.

"Come here, Aves." He climbs into bed and opens his arms for me. "Thank you for that. I'll never forget this night. You're a part of me, Avery Stanton. Nothing will ever change that."

I mumble something even I don't quite understand as I let the warmth of his skin and the safety of his arms help me drift off to sleep.

Chapter 18

Dylan

Four nights and I'm never going to be the same. It doesn't matter how much time or distance is between us—Avery will always own me. My skin is branded from her touch.

We're on our way back to drop her off at her place, but I'm fighting a losing battle as I try to keep the grin off my face. That's all I need to do is drop her off with the "I just made love to your daughter more times than I can count and I'm planning the next time I can be inside of her" face on. Not a good plan.

Grabbing her bag in one hand, I lace her fingers through mine with the other. No way can I not touch her. I need the connection for a few more minutes.

"Thank you for—"

I drop her hand and place my finger over her lips. "I love you, Aves. Never thank me for spending time with you, or for… anything else, for that matter."

She smiles up at me. "I'm not ready to say goodbye."

"I know, but I'm sure your parents miss you. Dad has texted me twice wanting to know when we're going to be home."

"Tonight?"

"Yeah." I push her long locks behind her shoulder. "You just text me and I'll come and pick you up."

"I really want to kiss you," she whispers.

I'm tempted, I am so damn tempted. It's not like they assume we've never kissed, but I just spent four days inside of her; not sure I'm willing to push my luck at this point. I know they're watching. "Tonight."

"Tonight." She stands on tiptoes, kissing my cheek. She's grinning when she pulls back.

I wait for her to be safely inside before I head back to the Tahoe. Our next stop is Harley's house, where she and Brad pretty much have the same goodbye as Avery and me. When he climbs back in the Tahoe, he rests his head back against the headrest and exhales.

"That was harder than I thought," he says.

"What's that?"

"Dropping her off."

"The sooner we get home to our parents, the sooner we can get back to them," I remind him. At least that's my plan. I'm not sure what he and Harley are doing, but I know I'll be seeing my girl in a few hours.

"Yeah, we're going to hang out at my place tonight."

"I'm picking Avery up later but we didn't make definite plans. Just hanging out."

"You all can stop by if you want."

"Thanks, I'll let you know."

The rest of the ride back to my place is in silence. We're a couple of lovesick fools and neither of us wants to talk about it to the other. We know where we are with our feelings and that's all that matters.

Lugging my bag inside, I find Dad sitting on the couch. "Hey, I thought you would be at the shop."

"Can't a guy just be home to see his only son?" he asks, placing a hand over his heart as if he's offended.

"I hear ya, old man." I laugh.

"How was your trip?"

"Good."

"Just good?"

"Amazing." I can't stop my grin from showing.

"Avery have a good time?"

"She did."

"Dylan," he says.

"Yeah?"

"Were you safe? I mean, I know we discussed this before you left, but please tell me you took my advice to heart."

"We were safe, Dad."

He studies me for a minute and I fight the urge to squirm under his gaze. "You love her."

It's a simple statement but means so much more. Not only to Avery and me but to Dad and me. Over the years, he's told me story after story about Mom and how much he loved her. How she was the light of his life. He's always told me to never settle, and when I find the light to follow it. "I do."

"She's going away to college soon."

I nod. "Yeah, it's a couple of hours' drive. I figure I can drive up a couple weekends a month to see her."

"Long distance is hard."

"It is, but she's worth it."

"She okay with this plan?"

"We've not really talked about it too much. I mean, she knows I love her and that I want her for as long as she'll have me. Forever."

"Seems like something you two should be discussing. When does she leave?"

"Two months from tomorrow." I know he's right, but I've been dreading the conversation and the date. It's going to suck ass to not see her every day, but this is her dream and she has a full scholarship. That's huge for her and her family. It'll also be nice for us when we start our lives after she graduates. We won't have any loans hanging over our heads.

"That's not a lot of time, Dylan. You need to talk to her. Work it out. Remember, being open and honest is the only way to make a relationship succeed. Without honesty, your love means nothing."

"I will." I take a seat next to him on the couch. "So fill me in on what's been going on at the shop. Did you get the Shelby fixed?"

We spend the next hour or so talking about the shop and my transition in. Dad wants me to work part-time this summer and then full-time once Aves goes off to college. He said I should enjoy my summer being a kid before all the responsibility hits.

My friends get their college years, not me. I'm okay with that though. I plan to save it all while living at home with Dad. I'll help out with the bills, but I want a nest egg built for us for when she graduates. I should have a really good down payment on a house in four years.

I'm just getting ready to grab a shower when my phone vibrates in my pocket.

> **Aves:** I'm riding to Alan's with him to help with paint colors. You want to just pick me up there?
>
> **Me:** Sounds exciting. Yeah, just tell me when to be there.
>
> **Aves:** Give us an hour or so.
>
> **Me:** Got it. Love you.
>
> **Aves:** Love you too.

"I'm going to hop in the shower, then go pick Avery up at her brother's."

"You just spent four days with her." Dad chuckles.

"And if I had it my way, I never would've dropped her off." I rush upstairs with the sound of his laughter following me.

I rush through a shower; it's not near as fun without Avery here to help me. I'm ready thirty minutes earlier than I need to be, so I head out early. I'm sure Coach won't mind. No man wants to discuss paint colors for an hour.

I pull up behind his truck and I hear voices in the backyard. I've been here a few times for team meetings. Couch has a huge back deck, and if they're sitting out there, I know the paint conversation is done. Walking around the side of the house, I stop when I hear my name.

"How does Dylan feel about you leaving for college?" he asks her.

"I don't know. We haven't really talked about it." She's quiet for a minute and I'm just about to walks around the corner when she starts again. It's wrong to listen, but I can't stop.

"What if I told you I was thinking about staying local... you know, for college."

"That depends. What's your reasoning?"

"I don't want to leave him. I know we care about each other, but long distance is hard and I can't ask him to do that."

"Don't you think that's his choice to make?"

"Not really. I mean, it's my education. I should have the final say on where I go."

"What about your scholarship?"

I'm now leaning against the house, trying to process what I'm hearing.

"It's too late to apply for a closer school. I can get a loan. I won't be the only college kid doing that, Alan."

"I know that, Av. I just know a full ride is a big deal. When you graduate you won't have any debt hanging over your head."

"We'll figure it out."

"Are you sure he's worth it? Don't get me wrong, Dylan is a great kid and one hell of a ball player, but how are you sure that he's it, the one? Look at me, Avery. I'm twenty-eight and still living the single life. You really think you've found your happily ever after at eighteen?"

"I know."

My girl is steady in her answer, and that makes me want to kiss the hell out of her, but I can't let her do this. I can't let her give up her scholarship, her dream to go to college with her best friend, just because I'm not smart enough to go too. I won't let her do this. I'm going to have to convince her that long distance is the best option. But from the conviction in her voice, I've got my work cut out for me.

Taking a deep breath, I school my features and walk around the side of the house and up the deck steps.

"Hey! You're early." Avery stands and gives me a hug.

"I was ready early. How's the paint colors coming?"

Coach laughs. "She thinks this place is too much of a bachelor pad. How I let her talk me into changing the living room, I'll never know."

"It's because I offered to do all the work." Avery laughs with him.

"I can help," I offer automatically. Anything she needs. Always.

"What are you two getting into tonight? Didn't you just spend four entire days together?"

"We did, and we're going to spend a few hours tonight too." She turns to look at me. "Harley said they're hanging out at Brad's if we want to come over."

"If that's what you want." I should really tell her that we need to talk. Maybe I can convince her to hang out on the roof of the shop with me tonight. Stargazing sounds like a good idea; get her nice and relaxed before we start our talk. I know she's going to fight me on this.

"Sure." She shrugs. "You." She points to Coach. "We're going this week to pick up the paint and supplies. You need a little color in your life."

"Uh-huh. You two have fun tonight."

"How about the rooftop?" she asks as soon as we're in my truck. "I didn't want Alan to think we were trying to be alone after four days, but I think we have some things to talk about."

"I was going to suggest that. We need to get our plan together for when you leave for college. Visits and things like that." I say it even though I know that's not what she's thinking.

"We can talk about it," she says. I'm not convinced, but that's because I know better. If I hadn't heard their conversation, it might've been too late. She might've given up her scholarship before I figured it out and she would grow to resent falling in love with the guy who's not smart enough for college.

Chapter 19

Avery

The ride to the shop is quiet. I guess it's going to be Dylan's shop one day. He's got his future planned out as do I, but I just need to make a few alterations to keep him in it. I know he's going to disagree with me switching colleges, but once I explain it to him, he'll understand. No way can I spend four years only seeing him a few days a month. Plans change.

Once I tell Dylan and we get our game plan, I have to break the news to my parents. I should've made sure I told Alan not to tell them. That's a part of the big brother code or something, right? Don't tell the secrets of the little sister as long as she's not in danger or hurt.

"Does your dad know we're coming?" I ask Dylan when he pulls behind the shop.

"No, but he's not going to care." He grabs my hand and leads me into the building, making sure to lock the door behind us.

When we reach the rooftop, Dylan adjusts the cushions on the outdoor couch and sits, pulling me into his lap. "So I was thinking I can drive up to see you every other weekend."

"Dylan," I try to interrupt but he stops me.

"No, it's only a couple of hours to get there. I can stay in a hotel. I'm going to be working full-time and living at home until you graduate, so the cost isn't an issue."

"Dylan!" I say louder this time. "I'm not going away."

He doesn't look as surprised as I thought he would be. "What do you mean?"

"I'm staying here, locally. I've checked out the education program and it's as good as any. I don't want to go the next four years only seeing you a few days a month."

"You have to go, Aves."

"No, I don't. I don't want to leave you."

"Your scholarship."

"So I'll get a couple of loans. I'm not the first and won't be the last."

"Think about this, Avery. You have a full ride. That's zero debt after graduation. What about all the plans you and Harley have made? Being best friends and roommates? You can't give all that up." He runs his fingers through his hair.

"I can and I will."

He stands and sits me on the couch, then kneels in front of me as he gently cups my face in his hands. "Avery Stanton, I love you. I want you, all of you, for as long as you'll have me. I refuse to let you give up your dream. We can do this, Aves. It's you and me. This"—he motions between us—"can't be broken. We're solid, and we'll stay that way even with you being away at school. I'm going to work and save up and when you graduate, I'm going to build us or buy us a house, whatever you want. We've got this, baby. You have to go."

"Why are you pushing this?" I ask him.

"Because, Avery, you busted your ass to get those scholarships. I'm so fucking proud of you. Do I want to be away from you? No. Do I want to see your dreams come true? Hell yes, I do. I'll be here, babe."

"Dylan, I appreciate what you're saying, but I've made up my mind. I'm going to tell my parents soon. I'm staying here with you."

He hangs his head before eventually laying it in my lap. I run my fingers through his dark hair.

How can I possibly go weeks without this? Without him?

I can't.

I won't.

"I'm doing this, Dylan. Everything is going to work out, you'll see."

He doesn't say anything, doesn't move from his position. He's stock-still while I run my fingers through his hair. We sit there for so long his legs have to be numb.

"Dylan." He doesn't look up. "Dylan, will you look at me?" He raises his head and his face is somber. I don't want that. I hate arguing with him; this is really our first and I don't like it. "Will you lay with me?"

His response is to stand. I do the same and wait for him to lie down on the couch. He opens his arms for me and I don't hesitate to stretch out next to him. His arms wrap around me and he's holding me tight. I feel him kiss the top of my head.

"It's going to be fine, Dylan. You'll see." Again no reply—he just holds me. We spend the rest of the night just lying there in each other's arms. Neither of us says anything. I don't know what to say. I knew he would argue with me, but I didn't expect him to take it like this.

He's just going to have to learn to deal. I'm sure he will in time. I'm not leaving him.

Chapter
20

Dylan

Yesterday I was high on life. I had just spent four days with my girl and our best friends, and in my mind our future was mapped out. That all changed within hours.

Last night, she rocked my world. I've known from the beginning that Avery was too good for me, but I pursued her anyway. Never in my wildest dreams would I have thought that she would give up her dreams for me. Sure, she can still go to college and become a teacher, but not the way she had always planned. Falling in love with me shouldn't change those plans. I'm not worth that. She deserves nothing but the best, right down to her education and living out her dream of rooming at college with her best friend.

Last night, we didn't talk much. She wasn't budging and I know her well enough to know she won't. That leaves it up to me to make it happen. I'll do whatever I have to do to make her dreams come true. She can't change the path just because she added a stop. That stop being me.

I talked to her a few hours ago, and she's still convinced this is the best option. She's going to talk to her parents this weekend, which doesn't give me much time. I have to fix this.

When I called Coach and asked him if we could talk, I could tell he was confused and curious at the same time. I need his help.

Walking to the front door, I knock.

"Dylan, come on in." He steps away from the door.

"Thanks, Coach."

"Alan, I am your girlfriend's brother." He laughs.

"Right."

He can tell something's up. "What's going on? Is Avery okay?"

"She is, or she will be. I heard the two of you yesterday. Last night we talked about it. About her giving up her scholarship."

"I see."

"She can't do it. I won't let her. Not for me. She's busted her ass to get where she is, and I can't let her stay behind because I'm not smart enough to join her and our friends at college. I won't let her," I say again.

"Tell me, Dylan, how do you plan to change her mind?"

I shake my head. "I can't. I've tried. She's convinced this is the best way. Sure, she can still get an education close to home, and regardless of where her degree is from she's going to be an amazing teacher, but she needs to go where she's always dreamed of." I walk to the window and stare out into the street. "Last night, after I dropped her off, I went home and looked at our freshman yearbook. We had to do interviews of where we thought we would be as seniors and what we wanted to be, go to college, all that stuff. Avery and Harley both said college roommates at Western and teachers."

He nods. "They've had that plan for a while."

"I know." I swallow hard. "I can't let her give that up for me. She's everything, the light in the darkness, the sunshine on a rainy day, the best part of my day, the best part of me. I love her, Alan. With all that I am, I love her. I know what you're thinking, that we're young and we'll move on, but I know it will always be her for me. That's what makes this so hard."

"What are you talking about?"

I don't answer him at first. It takes everything in me to say the words I never in my lifetime thought I would say. "I'm going to break up with her."

"What?" he asks. His voice is low and I can tell he's shocked.

"I have to, man. She can't give up her dream to stay here and I've tried convincing her, last night and then again this morning. She's planning on talking to your parents this weekend so I don't have much time."

"Why are you telling me all this?"

"Because it's going to break her. My heart is bleeding from the mere thought of letting her go. I need you and your family to know that I love her and I always will, but I need her to not give up this opportunity. This is the only way I can think of to make her go."

"Just like that?"

"Fuck! No, not 'just like that.' How else am I supposed to do this? I can't make her go unless I'm no longer in the picture."

"So you break her heart?"

"I don't want to. God, I never want to be the one to cause her pain, but she's stubborn. I love her enough to set her free."

"What if this little plan of yours backfires? What if she still gives it all up?"

"You can't let her. You have to help me convince her to go. That's the other reason I'm here. I wanted you to hear my side and ask you for your help. Help me guide her to the future she's always wanted."

Chapter 21

Avery

Dylan and I argued again this morning and I hate it. I wish he could see how this is all going to work out. We're going to be together all the time. All the things he talked about last night can still happen. I can even work part-time and help save for that house he was talking about or to put toward my loans. We can make it happen.

He just called me again and wanted to know if we could go somewhere and talk. I hope he's seen this is the best option. I pull in behind the shop and park next to his truck. He's sitting inside with his head resting on the steering wheel. He doesn't move to greet me, which is not like him. Slowly I climb out of the car and walk to his door, knocking softly. He still doesn't make a move and now I'm worried. What happened to make him act this way?

"Dylan," I say through the window. Slowly he lifts his head and looks over at me. He doesn't smile or give me any indication that he's okay—he's just staring. Finally, after what seems like hours but in reality is mere seconds, he reaches for the handle. I back away, giving him room to climb out of the truck.

"Hey," I say hesitantly as I wrap my arms around his waist.

Leaning down, he buries his face in my neck. "Hey." His voice is barely a whisper. Breaking away, he grabs my hands and leads me inside.

Just like always, he locks the door behind us. Silently, we climb the stairs to the rooftop.

"You ready to tell me what's wrong?" I ask, keeping my voice calm. I'm trying not to freak out on him, but he's really starting to scare me.

"Avery, you can't give up your scholarship."

Seriously? This is what has him looking like someone kicked his puppy? "Dylan, there is no discussion here. This is my choice. I choose to attend the local university. I choose to be close to you. It's not your decision or anyone else's."

"Avery, try and see this from my side. I've watched you work so hard this year to maintain your grades for this scholarship. Going away and being roommates with Harley has been your plan long before me."

"Plans change." I shrug. I really don't see the issue.

"I came across our freshman yearbook. Even then you wanted this plan. You've worked your ass off to make it happen. This is your dream."

"Dylan, it's college. I'm still going to be a teacher—that's not going to change."

"It is. Can't you see that? You're giving up something you planned for years, just to be closer to me. You're giving up a full ride, Avery. A full fucking ride. Do you know how many students in our graduating class alone would give anything to be in your shoes right now? Full-ride academic scholarships are almost unheard of and you did that. All you, Aves."

"I'll give you that, but they didn't put in the work I did."

"Exactly!" he screams. "Avery, I want that for you. I want you to have every experience you've ever dreamed of. Please, you can't give up this opportunity for me."

He's really pushing for this but I can't give in. I won't. This is my decision and I want to stay here. Like I said, plans change. "My mind is made up. I already told Mom and Dad that I needed to talk to them this weekend. I sent back the acceptance letter. It's done."

"Have you told Western that you won't be there?"

"Not yet. All I have to do is make a phone call. There's plenty of time for them to replace me."

"What about Harley? What does she think about all of this?"

"She gets it. She's going to miss me, and the plans we made, but she gets it. Brad is going to be at the same college. They don't have the same obstacle to face that we do."

He drops his elbows to his knees and buries his face in his hands. I give him time to work through this. I hate that he's so upset, but it's not his decision to make. I refuse to be in a relationship where what I want doesn't count. I still don't even really understand why this is such a big concern for him.

"I love you, Avery." He lifts his head and his eyes are watery. "You are the air I breathe. I would give you anything, but I can't give you this. I can't let you give up your plan for the future because of me. I'm a small-town guy who isn't smart enough for college."

I try to protest but he holds his hand up to stop me.

"I knew that first night… hell, I've always known that I'm not good enough for you. I would never forgive myself if I let you give up this opportunity for me. Five, maybe ten years down the road, you might grow to resent me for everything you missed out on. I don't want that for you. I don't want that for us." Reaching over, he grabs my hands and pulls them to his lips. "There is never going to be another you, Avery. For as long as I live I will never love anyone the way I love you." He takes a deep breath. "Do you hear me? You are it for me. There will never be anyone who even comes close to my heart. Just you."

"Dylan." I've never seen him like this.

"Baby, we can't do this anymore. We can't stay together. If staying together means you give up your dream for me, then we're over." He chokes on the words.

I stand still, frozen in time as I try to process what's happening. "W-what?"

"Don't make me say it again," he says, his voice low. He's barely hanging on.

"Why are you doing this? You don't get to choose." I hit his chest and he stands to move away from me. I follow him and hit him a little harder this time. "You just told me you loved me." I'm sobbing now that the words have sunk in. This can't be happening.

"I do, Aves. I do, more than you will ever know. That's why I can't let you do this." He tries to pull me into his arms but I take a step back.

"No! No! No! You don't get to rip my heart open and then attempt to soothe the pain. This is what you want?"

He stares down at his feet. "Honestly, no. There is nothing I want less, but this is how it has to be. I can't let you do this for me. I'm here. I only have eyes for you. We can do long distance."

"No. That's not what I want. I won't make it without you."

"How do you know, Avery? We've never tried. Just try it for me."

I shake my head. "No. You've made your decision. It's done." I'm crying so hard I can barely see as I turn to leave. I don't hear footsteps behind me; he's not coming after me. I literally feel like my heart is cracked wide open in my chest. How can he say he loves me but end us? I fumble with the lock and finally make it outside. Falling to my knees, I let the sobs break free from my chest. I feel two strong arms wrap around me and my heart flutters with hope. *He came after me.*

"I got you, Av," Alan's says.

My brother. "W-w-what are you doing here?"

"Dylan."

One word and my heart breaks all over again. He knew this was going to happen. He planned to break my heart and end what we have. Did he ever really love me? Yeah, he says he does, but if he did how can he let me go like this?

"Let's get you home."

"No. I don't want to go home."

"Okay." He pulls me to my feet and wraps his arms around me. "We can go to my place."

I don't say anything as I let him lead me to his truck.

Chapter 22

Dylan

The last eight weeks have been harder than I ever could've imagined. I've avoided life, not wanting to run into her. I spend just as much time at the shop as Dad, and when I'm not, I'm at home in my room. Hiding.

Brad has been over a few times. He keeps me updated on how she is. After that night when I broke it off, she called me several times a day for a week. She stopped by the house and the shop, but then all of a sudden she stopped. I should be glad; that means she knows I'm serious and she's moving on.

I've been keeping in contact with Coach too. He and his dad actually surprised me with a visit about five or six weeks ago. Their dad thanked me for doing what was right for his daughter. I spilled it all out, how much I love her and how I'm not good enough. I even went as far as to ask him to take care of her. To say I was a mess is an understatement. I still am.

Today they're leaving for Western. My plan worked. Brad, Harley, and of course her family convinced her to take the scholarship. Brad did say she mentioned something about being out of this town where everything reminded her of me. I know she's mad, and to her that's a blessing, but to me, this town is what keeps me going. To sit on the rooftop and think about all the times we spent up there, every single place where we made a memory engraved in my mind. I want to be here, to feel closer to her. I still feel like this is what's best, but I miss her.

I knew it would be hard as hell, but I never thought it would be like this. I can't eat, haven't slept a full night in eight weeks. I grab my phone to text her a thousand times a day. I'll hear a song on the radio that reminds me of her or something we did while the song was playing. Our time together plays out like a movie reel.

I fucking miss her.

I'm sitting on the couch holding my phone like a lifeline. Alan, as I now refer to him, promised he would let me know when they get on the road. I check my phone yet again, and this time a text comes through as I tap the screen.

Alan: They're headed out.

Attached is a picture of the back of her Kia Sportage with "Western Bound" written on the back window in shoe polish. I have to rub the spot over my chest as the familiar pain lets me know it's still there. I have no doubt that it will always be. I will love her until the day I take my last breath.

Me: Thanks.

I shove my phone back in my pocket and close my eyes. She's gone, and she's taking my heart with her.

Chapter
23

Four years later

Avery

Leave it to Harley to plan a wedding three weeks after graduation. I've been with her every step of the way. I've pushed the fact that I'll be walking down the aisle with Dylan to the back of my mind. I know he and Brad remained close. He even came to Western to visit several times. Harley warned me every time, and I always took the opportunity to drive home. I knew on those trips that I was safe, that I wouldn't be running into him.

Now here I am, car packed full as I move back home. With my parents. This is going to be a huge adjustment for me. Not only will I be back under their roof, but I can also no longer hide from him. I have no desire to see him. To make awkward small talk about things I couldn't care less about. He made his choice; we both have to live with it.

My phone vibrates from where it sits in the cup holder. Glancing quickly, I see Harley's face smiling back at me.

"Hello."

"Hey, Av. Where are you?"

"I'm about two miles outside of town. Where are you?"

"We just got to Brad's parents' place."

"I bet you're wishing you would've listened to him and signed that lease on the apartment last month," I tease her.

"Nope. You know his parents are great. Besides, I can't see paying rent when we wouldn't be living there. Not to mention that neither of us has started our new jobs yet."

"Fair point. So what's up?"

"Just checking in on you. I was thinking tomorrow we could go through the RSVPs and work on the seating chart."

"Sounds like a plan. I'm all yours until the school year starts."

"Gah! I'm so excited that we're going to be working together. What are the odds that we'd both get picked up by our old high school?"

I laugh. "We just got lucky that Mr. and Mrs. Garret both decided to finally retire this year."

"Truth! Okay, well I'm going to run to Mom and Dad's for a bit. You want to meet here tomorrow?"

"That sounds good. See you then."

I drop my phone back in the cup holder. I fought the urge to ask her if Dylan was going to be anywhere around. I hate that part of me wants to run into him. It's been four years and my heart still calls for him. Maybe seeing him is what I need to get over him. I haven't laid eyes on him since the day he told me we were over. Harley and Brad—hell, even my family—have tried to get me to forgive him. They all claim that what he did was out of love and that he was just looking out for me. I call bullshit. I mean, I can see their point, but end us? He said he loved me and then just ended it. No calls, no texts, no more visits. Just like that, he was done. That's not love. You can't just let it go like that. I was a fool and still am to this day because I've never stopped loving him.

Pulling into my parents' drive, I barely have the car turned off before Mom is opening my door.

"I'm so glad to have you home," she says, yanking me into a hug as soon as I'm out of the car.

I laugh. "I missed you too, Mom. Don't get used to it though. Once school starts and I start getting a steady paycheck, I want to look for my own place."

"Honey, you know you're welcome here as long as you need. This will always be your home."

I do know that. I also know that after four years, moving back home seems daunting. Only time will tell how it'll be living with my parents again.

"Come on in. Dad and Alan are manning the grill out back."

"Mo-om," I whine. Yes, I am very well aware that I am an almost twenty-three-year-old woman and I just whined to my mother. "I thought I said I didn't want any kind of coming home shindig."

She grins. "It's just us—me, you, your dad, Alan, and Kara."

Kara is Alan's girlfriend. They've been dating a little over a year now. I keep waiting for my big brother to pop the question. Everyone can see that the perpetual bachelor is now whipped. He's crazy about her.

"That's not so bad," I say hesitantly. "As long as you didn't invite anyone else."

"I wanted to, but your brother warned me not to."

I make a mental note to do something really nice for my big brother. I don't bother unloading my car as I plan to get Dad and Alan to help with that. Instead, I just grab my phone and follow Mom into the house. She stops off at the fridge and gets us both a bottle of water before we head out onto the back deck. "Look who's here," she announces like I'm the freaking Queen of England or something.

Dad rushes me first. "Glad to have my baby girl back home." I don't comment on his use of baby, because I know to him I will always be his little girl. Instead I hug him tight.

"Hey, Dad," I say, my face buried in his chest.

"My turn." Alan pulls on my hand to get me out of Dad's embrace. He wraps his big hulking arms around me. "Missed you, Av." He kisses the top of my head. Even though he's ten years older than me, Alan and I are close. He was there for me when everything happened with Dylan. Now that I think about it, I never did ask him how that conversation went down. How he knew to be there that day outside the shop. I remember him saying Dylan's name but I was so upset it didn't even register until now. Not that it matters at this point.

"Missed you too," I say before whispering, "When are you going to make an honest woman out of her?" He knows who I'm taking about. He just smirks and winks. Just as I suspected, big brother has a plan.

"Good to see you, Avery," Kara says from beside us.

I chance a quick glance at Alan. He's smiling, so either she didn't hear us or he couldn't care less if she did.

"Kara!" I give her a big hug. She's only five years older than me, making her five years younger than Alan. I really like her and hope she becomes my sister one day. "How have you been? I didn't get to see you the last time I was home."

"Good, just working and trying to keep this one in line." She points at Alan who is now standing behind her with his hands wrapped around her waist.

"How's work going?" Kara is a social worker and based on some of the things she has to see, I don't know if I could do her job. Then again, as a teacher, I'm going to be subjected to some of those things as well. It's sad but true.

"Good days and bad." She smiles. "Both are still rewarding."

"You kids ready to eat?" Dad calls over.

He doesn't have to tell us twice. We load up our plates and gather around the patio table. After we finish eating, we spend a couple of hours just sitting around and catching up.

"Well, this has been fun, but I'm exhausted from the move. I'm meeting Harley tomorrow to go over the seating chart, so I'm going to head to bed."

"We'll get your stuff." Dad stands from the table.

I wave him off. "No need. I have clothes to sleep in, so we can do the rest tomorrow." I make my way around the table, giving each of them a hug. Not sure how living back home is going to be, but I will admit I missed my family.

I'm jolted awake by my ringing cell phone. Without opening my eyes, I pat around on the nightstand until I find it. Peeking open one eye just enough to swipe Answer, I place the phone next to my ear. "Lo."

Harley laughs. "Good morning, Sunshine. How about we meet for breakfast before we start working on wedding stuff?"

"What time is it?"

"A little before eight."

"We've been college graduates for maybe a minute. Did you already forget how to sleep in?" I say a little more awake.

Again, she laughs. "We have a wedding to plan. Now drag your tired ass out of bed. I'll be there in thirty minutes to pick you up."

"You're buying," I grumble before ending the call. *The things I do for my best friend.*

I take a quick shower and throw on some shorts and a T-shirt, then blow-dry my hair and pull it up in a knot on top of my head. Foregoing makeup, I grab my phone and purse and head downstairs.

"Where are you off to?" Mom asks.

I fight the urge to roll my eyes. *Gotta love living at home.* "Harley will be here any minute to pick me up. We're going for breakfast, and then we're going to go over the seating chart for the wedding." I hear a car outside; looking out the window confirms it's Harley. *Speak of the devil.* "She's here, see you later." I wave and rush to the door, stopping only to slide my feet into my flip-flops.

"I expected to have to pull your ass out of bed," she teases once I'm in the car.

"Where are we eating?" I ask, ignoring her comment. She knows if I need to be up and moving that I am. She's the one in college who I had to constantly wake up or she would've missed the majority of her morning classes.

"The diner. Where else is there to get a decent breakfast in this town?"

"My mouth's watering just thinking about it. It's been years since I've eaten there. The last time was…" My voice trails off when my mind pulls up the memory of the last time I was at the diner.

"Av?" Harley questions.

"I was with him, with Dylan, that last time I was there."

"We can go somewhere else. McDonald's?" she offers.

I sit a little taller in my seat and take a deep breath. This is my new reality. No more hiding from him, from the memories. I can't stay locked in my parents' house. Not to mention I'm going to be teaching in the school we attended senior year.

"No, I'm good. Just not something I've thought about in a really long time." I remember the night he and I were there. Dylan made the comment that he couldn't wait until he could wake up with me, and then we could go to breakfast because he would be afraid to feed me his cooking. So we took a nap on his couch; he said his dad wouldn't freak out if he came home and we were asleep on the couch. When we woke up, Dylan took me to the diner and we had breakfast—which they thankfully serve all day—for dinner.

"You sure?"

"Yeah." I give her a weak smile at best. "They do have the best breakfast in town."

"Food in town," she reminds me.

"So where are we going to work on the seating chart?"

"I have it all set up in the basement at Brad's."

"You getting excited?"

"Yes!" she squeals. "Who would've thought I would be marrying my high school sweetheart."

"People do it all the time. You're a lucky girl. Brad's great."

"He has his moments," she laughs.

"So what all is left to do?" I ask once we've placed our orders.

"Seating chart, finalize head count for the caterer, final dress fitting, final meeting with the photographer."

"So not much." I laugh. "Are you sure you won't let me throw you a bachelorette party?"

"Nope, Brad and I both decided against it. We don't need it. The shower is more than enough. Oh, I forgot to tell you, Brad has an interview on Monday with the local bank in town for an open mortgage broker position."

"That's great. It's still hard for me to wrap my head around the fact that Brad is that fond of numbers."

"Right? Crazy man."

"Listen to you, Miss History Teacher."

"And you, Miss English Teacher."

"What can I say, I've always done well in English. It's a gift," I say, blowing on my nails and brushing them on my shoulder as if it's no big deal.

"It's all those books you read."

"Hey now, don't be hating on my books."

She holds her hands in front of her in surrender. We talk all things wedding while we eat, then head to Brad's parents,' which is Harley's place too for now.

"I have it all set up downstairs," she says, leading me inside the house. "And here you have it, wedding central."

The small dining table is covered with all things wedding, and there are boxes of decorations stacked against the wall. "That everything?" I ask her, pointing to the boxes.

"Uh, no. Mom has several more at her house too." She grins.

"Okay, so who all's invited?"

"Yes." We sit at the table and she opens a box. "On my laptop." She points to where it sits next to me on the table. "There's a list of who all was invited. This"—she points to the box—"has the RSVPs we've received so far."

"When's the cutoff?"

"It was two weeks ago, but they're still rolling in. And Mom suggested that some forget to send them, so I either need to reach out, which I think is kind of tacky, or I need to plan for a few extras just in case."

"I'm sure there will be a few who say they're coming and end up not showing."

"More than likely, so if we pad the list and the tables, we should be fine."

"Agreed, so where do we start?"

"How about I pull up the spreadsheet of the invites and you call off the names." She holds up the box. "Then I'll know who hasn't replied. Some of them we know just won't show up. We all have a few of those in our families."

"True story. Okay, let's do this." We get to work and before I realize it almost three hours have gone by. "That didn't take long." I laugh.

Harley rests her elbows on the table. "Yeah, and now the seating chart."

As soon as the words leave her mouth, I hear Brad yell down the steps, "Babe, you down there?"

"Yeah," she calls back.

I hear heavy footsteps as they tromp down the stairs. "A-very. Hi, didn't realize you were here," Brad says cautiously.

"I told you we were working on the seating chart," Harley reminds him.

"That was hours ago."

"This takes time, Bradley," she says.

I look up to give him a hard time and my breath catches in my chest. Dylan is standing beside him. His eyes find mine and we hold each other's gaze. It's been four years since I've laid eyes on him. Now that I have, I can't look away.

How am I going to do this?

Chapter
24

Dylan

Avery. I blink hard to make sure I'm not seeing things. When I open my eyes she's still there, and she's so fucking beautiful.

I stand still beside Brad, not moving a muscle; hell, I'm not sure I'm breathing at this point. I'm waiting for her to realize I'm here. I'm not sure how she'll react. She's made it clear to our friends and family that she didn't want to see me over the years. I honored that and never tried to reach out, but I watched her. Sounds like I'm a damn stalker, but I did what I had to do. I had to see with my own two eyes that she was okay. Brad or Harley, even her parents or Alan, would tell me where she was going to be and I would show up in the shadows, just to get a glimpse of her. Not a single day over the past four years have I not thought about her, loved her.

Now she's back. I told myself that if she was with someone once she graduated, if she was happy, I would back off and let her be just that— happy. But she's not with someone. Brad, Harley, Alan, her parents, all of them have made sure to tell me that. It gives me hope that they're rooting for me, for us.

Her eyes find mine and she stills. I don't look away. I can't. Instead I ball my hands at my sides, fighting the urge to pull her into my arms.

"Dylan," she whispers.

That's when I break eye contact. As soon as I hear my name roll off her lips, I close my eyes and remember a time when that alone put a smile on my face. I'm fighting that same smile now, but I know I need to keep that shit locked down.

"Aves," I use the nickname that only I ever used. I hope that's still the case. By the way her eyes are now closed and her chest is rapidly rising, I would say so.

"Look," Harley says. "This was bound to happen, considering the two of you are walking down the aisle together in the wedding that is just three weeks away. You both said this would not be an issue." She stands with her hands on her hips, a worried expression on her face.

"It's good to see you," I say, ignoring Harley.

Slowly she opens her eyes and I can see the hint of tears. I take a step toward her, but Brad reaches out and puts his hand on my arm, stopping me.

"Is it?" she chokes out.

Fuck me! "Avery—"

"Don't bother, Dylan. I promised Harley and Brad this wouldn't be an issue and it won't be. Unless it's wedding-related, I don't want to see you. We're going to have to find a way to live in this small town together. You did fine with it that summer, so I'm sure we can do it for the next fifty years."

The only thing I want to do for the next fifty years is love her. That's all I've ever wanted, to love her and for her to follow her dreams and be happy.

"Dylan?" Harley says.

"It won't be an issue." The words are sour rolling off my lips. I don't like this plan, not one fucking bit. I need to convince her that I did it for her, show her that I still love her. Remind her what we're like together.

"We needed a break anyway. You ready to head home?" Harley asks Avery.

"Yeah, thanks."

I watch as she stands and places her phone in her back pocket. I'm in the path of the basement steps, which means she has to walk right past me. I should move, but I don't. Instead I wait patiently as she rolls her eyes and walks past me.

Reaching out, I grab her hand. She whips around, surprise all over her face. "I missed you," I tell her.

"I'm not buying your bullshit, Dylan. It's been four years. If you missed me, you would've contacted me. Where were you, huh?"

I bite my tongue, not wanting to out our friends.

"That's what I thought." Jerking her arm out of my hand, she stomps up the stairs.

"Well, that went well," Brad says.

"Dylan," Harley sighs. "Why didn't you tell her?"

I shrug. "It's not the right time. She's still pissed and she's not ready to hear it. Besides, I don't need her pissed off at the two of you before the wedding. Let's get through the big day and see what happens." I know my Avery; she's not one to let go easily. Once she finds out that our friends and even her family helped me see her over the years, she's going to be pissed. I don't want anything ruining the wedding, so I'm just going to sit back and plan.

Harley surprises me when she wraps her arms around me in a hug. "You're a great guy, Dylan Knight. She loves you even if she's not willing to admit it."

"For now, I love her enough for both of us." Over the years, I've embarrassed myself in front of our friends and family with my outbursts of missing her. I took tears and beers to a whole new level.

"I'll be back later. I don't want to leave her right now" Harley says to Brad.

"Do what you need to, babe. We were just going to play some pool. Be careful, I love you." He leans down and kisses her.

"That was not what I expected," Brad says once Harley's upstairs.

"What did you expect? Tears of joy and we live happily ever after?"

"No, dick." He punches me in the arm. "I expected tears and more… yelling."

"There were tears." He looks at me like I've lost my mind. "She was close to exposing them. Did you hear her voice crack?"

"Then why did you stop her when she was trying to leave?"

"Because I needed her to know that I missed her. I meant what I said, I won't mess up the wedding, but after that it's no holds barred. I'm going to fight for her."

"Great plan, but what happens when you lose the fight?"

Losing isn't an option. "At least she and I both will know that I tried."

"So you'll move on, just like that?"

"Not even close. She's it for me."

"So, single for life if she shoots you down?"

"It wouldn't be fair to anyone else to only get half of me."

"Random hookups?"

I shrug. I'm not capable of more than that with anyone other than Avery.

"That's some deep shit, D."

"Rack 'em," I say, pointing to the pool table. Talking about it gets me nowhere; I need to decide how I'm going to go about this. I'm heading into the fight of my life, and I'll be damned if I go down easy.

A few hours later, I find myself driving past her parents' place on my way home just to see if I can get a glimpse of her. I still drive the same old pickup truck, and yes, I still live at home with my dad. I did what I told her I would do. I worked and saved every penny, and now I have a pretty nice nest egg for us to start our life together.

My phone vibrates as soon as I pull into the drive.

> **Alan:** I hear you got to see her today.
>
> **Me:** Yeah.
>
> **Alan:** I figured you would tell her everything the first chance you got.
>
> **Me:** Nah, I don't want to ruin the wedding. She's going to be pissed at all of us.
>
> **Alan:** She will, but she'll get over it.
>
> **Me:** I hope so. Not going to be an easy fight.
>
> **Alan:** You fighting?
>
> **Me:** For her, always.

I don't wait for a reply; I know I won't get one. In the house, I find Dad making a sandwich.

"You want one?" he asks.

"No, thanks. How was the shop today?"

"Same old." He adds some chips to his plate, then takes a seat at the table. "I hear Avery's back from college."

"She is."

"For good?"

"Yeah, she graduated."

"I know that. Is she staying around?"

I nod. "She's going to be teaching at the high school."

"You talk to her?"

"I said hello in passing at Brad's."

"You got a plan?" Dad's always a man of few words, but when he does speak, you listen.

"Working on it."

"Good."

"I'm going out," I say, turning to head back out the door.

"You just got home."

"Need some time."

"Be safe, Dylan."

Waving goodbye, I head out the door, drive to the shop, and park around back. Unlocking the door, I make my way up the steps to the roof. I've spent a lot of time up here over the past four years. This is where I brought her for our first date and many more after that. This is also the place where I broke us. Being up here makes me feel closer to her.

I lie down on the old patio couch and close my eyes. If I try really hard, I can feel her here with me. I remember every minute, every touch, every kiss, and every breath of our time together.

Now I need to remind her.

Chapter 25

Avery

How is it that I spent four years at college and came home often without running into Dylan? Yeah, I know I would come home when he was visiting Brad, but that's not the only time. There were holidays, birthdays, "just because" visits, and not once did I run into him.

I've been home for a week. One week and I've already managed to run into him five times. That first day at Brad's, then the next day coming out of the library of all places. That same day I passed him at the bank, he was leaving as I was going in. Last night, he was at the grocery store; I was already too far down the ice cream aisle to back up without being obvious.

That brings us to today. I'm meeting Kara for lunch and, lo and behold, there he sits at a booth right across from ours.

"Aves," he greets me, then goes right back to eating. Like I'm just another acquaintance in this small town of ours. I know that's what I wanted, but he's so nonchalant about it, as if it's easy as hell for him to forget what we had.

"So much for him missing me," I say under my breath.

"Oh, honey, he misses you," Kara says, sliding into the booth.

Shit. That must have been louder than I thought. "You heard that, huh?"

She nods. From the corner of my eye, I glance over at Dylan and his jaw is tight. *Damn it. He heard me too. Well good. He needs to know I'm not falling for his games.* "How's your day?" I ask Kara to move the subject away from Dylan.

"Uneventful, which in my line of work means it's a good day. How about you?" She raises her eyebrows.

"Good, though I'm going stir-crazy, so thanks for meeting me."

She laughs. "I would've thought Harley would have you busy with the wedding."

"Oh she does, but it's just… different living at home again. They want to know where I'm going and with whom. I know they're parents and it's ingrained in them, but come on."

We both laugh at that.

"How's the wedding planning coming?"

"Good, but it's a lot of work. If I take anything out of this experience it's that I don't want a big elaborate wedding. Not that I'll be getting married any time soon, if ever," I add at the last minute.

"Come on now," she says.

Before I can reply, I feel a shadow looming over me. I don't have to look up to know it's him. Dylan leans down and places his lips next to my ear. I shiver when I feel his hot breath against my skin. "I missed you, baby." I feel a featherlight kiss against my cheek before he says, "You'll have the wedding of your dreams, big or small. I'll see to it."

And then he's gone, his long-ass legs carrying him away from me where I sit across from Kara. My mouth hanging open and my mind racing with his words. I'm trying to get my traitorous body under control from being close to him again.

"Avery." I hear Kara say my name, but I can't seem to focus on her. "Avery," she says again, this time reaching over and resting her hand on top of mine. Her touch pulls me out of this fog I'm in.

"I…" I have no words right now.

"Yes, that really happened." She laughs. "You okay?"

I nod.

"That was pretty intense."

Again, I nod.

"Did he rob your ability to speak?" She giggles.

Another nod.

"Snap out of it, here comes our food."

The waitress brings our food while I reach for my glass of water and down it. "I'll be right back with a refill," she says.

"I can't believe him," I finally blurt.

"What? He's never gotten over you. Ask anyone in this town. I'm surprised he's waited this long to tell you."

"He didn't tell me anything. He said he missed me last week too, but that doesn't mean anything. He's messing with me."

"What about the wedding comment?" she asks.

"You heard that, did you?"

"I did. I'm telling you, he's not going to just go away now that you're back in town."

"I don't expect him to. We both have to live and work here. It's going to be an adjustment for both of us."

"Keep telling yourself that."

"Eat, your lunch is almost over." I give her a mock glare and she throws her head back in laughter.

I know she means well, but she doesn't know the history with Dylan and me. It wasn't just a high school crush. Well, I guess it was when you think about how he crushed my heart, but the love I had for him, it was real. I would still like to think that he loved me too, even though he ended us. He told me he did that day, but...

I shake my head to clear my thoughts. No more thinking about Dylan Knight.

Kara and I say our goodbyes after lunch; then she heads back to work and I go back to my parents.' Harley is coming over later to work on the seating chart again. I didn't want to risk another run-in with Dylan, so I convinced her to lug it all here.

"Hey, Av," Mom greets me.

"Hey. Where's Dad?"

"He and Alan went fishing today."

"What? Alan's not whipping the next round of Montgomery High state champs into shape?" I tease.

She laughs. "Not today. What do you have going on the rest of the day?"

"Harley's coming over so I can help her work on the seating chart for the wedding."

"Two more weeks. You ready for this?"

"It's not my wedding."

"I know that, Miss Smarty Pants. I meant walking with Dylan."

I shrug. "It's four quick walks down the aisle between the rehearsal and the real thing, and then it's over. I can do that for Harley and Brad."

"What about the dance?" she asks.

"What dance?"

"Avery, the new couple dances and then normally the wedding party joins them. You're going to have to dance with him too."

"Harley didn't mention that. She must not be holding to that tradition."

Mom gives me an "Are you crazy?" look. "This is Harley, Avery."

Shit, she's right. "Well, Little Miss Bride and I are going to have a chat when she gets here." I stalk up to my room, cussing myself and Harley the entire time. I should've thought about that; this isn't the first wedding I've been to, after all. I was so wrapped up in the walking down the aisle thing that anything else involved with the wedding slipped past me. I mean, I know I have to walk down and back at the rehearsal and the wedding, but the dance? Damn! I even thought about the wedding party table, but guys are on one side and girls on the other, so that's distance between us.

"Is it safe?" Harley asks from just outside my bedroom door. She has a big bag on her shoulder.

"You forget to tell me something?"

"Avery, listen. I knew you would stress over it."

"Harley!"

"I'm sorry. I just knew you would do it and not make a scene at the wedding, and no way can I get married without my best friend as my maid of honor. What was I supposed to do? You refuse to talk about him or even be civil."

"Because he broke my heart!" I yell. "He didn't want me, and no matter how hard I try, I can't stop loving him." My voice is barely a whisper now.

"Av, he loves you too. We all see it. Maybe the two of you should talk."

"Oh, we talked today."

"Really?" she asks, surprised.

"Yep. He was at the diner when I met Kara for lunch." I go on to tell her what happened, and her reaction is to grin like a fool. "What in the hell are you grinning at?"

"I'm right. He loves you and you love him. Let's make this happen."

"Come on, Harley. He broke me."

"If I recall correctly, he did it because he loved you. Isn't that what he said?"

"That was his excuse," I correct her.

"All right. This is the last time I'm going to say this, and then we're going to stop talking about Dylan and work on the seating chart. I'm your best friend, so I'm going to give it to you straight. I think you're hiding behind the pain. You're using it as a shield. You didn't get your way. You wanted to make the decision for both of you and it was one Dylan couldn't live with. He wanted to stay together, long distance. He wanted you, but you refused to try things his way. We all stood behind you, but maybe, just maybe, you're being selfish."

I open my mouth to fire back at her and she places her hand over my lips. "No. I said my piece. I love you, Avery Stanton. You are my best friend, my sister from another mister. Just think about it. Watch him in the next couple weeks and at the wedding. Just clear your mind and let go of the pain. Try and see things from his point of view. You were young, we all were, but you're older now. Open your mind and your heart. You might be surprised at what you find."

"Seating chart," I croak out past the emotion in my throat. My mind is racing. What if she's right? What if Dylan really does still love me? My heart stutters at the thought.

"You want to do it up here?"

"No, let's go down to the kitchen." I follow her downstairs and push thoughts of Dylan out of my mind. I need to get our best friends married, and then maybe I'll think more about what she said.

Chapter
26

Dylan

My plan to wait until after the wedding has sucked ass. I've run into her several times, some because I knew that's where she would be and others just by coincidence. It's so damn hard to not spill my guts, tell her everything. Tell her I love her just as much today as I did the day I destroyed us.

Today is finally the rehearsal dinner. Three long weeks of watching, waiting, and wondering if I'll ever be able to make her mine again.

"Dylan, Avery, your turn," Harley's mom calls to us. I step in line as instructed and so does Avery. I can smell the coconut lotion that she's always worn. I've not been this close to her since that day in the diner. I was afraid that my little confession would start an argument, that she would seek me out. Part of me hoped it would. Instead, I heard nothing from her. I'm glad she knows, but the question is does she believe me?

"Okay, everyone, link arms," Brad's mom instructs.

I hold my arm out for Avery without looking at her. Staring straight ahead, she does as asked and slips her arm through mine. I close my eyes at the feel of her skin. That's always been my thing with her.

We stand here side by side, arms linked, both staring straight ahead. No longer able to fight the pull, I lean down and whisper in her ear, "You look beautiful, Aves."

She doesn't acknowledge me. She doesn't need to; I can see the rapid rise and fall of her chest. I'm watching her as she bites her bottom lip. She wants me to think she's not affected, but I know better. This is my Avery, after all.

Deciding not to push my luck, I turn back to the front of the venue. I keep my gaze straight ahead and wait for our turn to walk down the aisle. Before the day I broke her heart, I always thought this would be us. To be honest, that's my end game. I want all of her. Forever.

"You're up, you two," Harley's mom whispers to us.

I take a hesitant step forward and Avery follows my lead. I stand up tall while trying not to take "giant steps," as she used to call them. I'm all about taking my time considering the beautiful woman on my arm. Once we reach the altar, I have to let her go. She releases my arm and takes her spot. I take mine as well, right behind a grinning Brad.

"Careful, man, or your face might crack," I goad him.

"Fuck off," he says under his breath.

I chuckle. When the wedding march plays, we all turn our attention to the back of the room. Harley appears with her dad, wearing the same damn smile as Brad. I'm happy as hell for the two of them even though I am a little jealous. I've gone over that night more times than I can count. Was I being selfish? Should I have let her make the decision? Everyone has assured me that I did the right thing, but right now, with this pain in my chest, the one laced with heartbreak, love, and envy that this could be our wedding, I'm not so sure.

Glancing at Avery, I see a soft smile on her lips as she watches our best friends. Her eyes mist with tears, and even though I know they're happy ones, I still fight the urge to pull her into my arms and hold her. I don't take my eyes off her during the entire trial run. I want to tell her that I'll give her this, all of it. She just has to let me.

The run-through is quick and before I know it, I'm stepping next to her and offering her my arm yet again. She takes it, still keeping her gaze straight ahead. When we reach the end of the aisle, we're directed to stand in line beside the bride and groom to greet the guests as they move into the formal dining room. I make a mental note to give Harley a big-ass hug when this is all over. Without knowing it, she's putting me with

Avery more than I thought I would be. Then again, maybe she did know. She's been one of my biggest supporters, pushing me to come clean to Avery that I kept tabs on her.

Avery unlinks her arm from mine and lets it fall to her side. When the rest of the wedding party joins us, she has to scoot closer to me. Instinctively I place my hand on the small of her back, standing a little behind her, giving her the space she needs to not feel crowded—well, by anyone except me.

The guests tonight consist of the parents and the venue staff, but tomorrow we'll be standing here a lot longer. I don't hate the idea. Tonight she pulled away from me, but she won't make it obvious at the wedding.

"All right, wedding party, make your entrance into the formal dining room first, and then the bride and groom will be announced. Link arms," the lady who's been directing the night informs us.

I hold my arm out for Avery and she takes it, still not looking my way. I wait our turn and then lead her, at her pace, into the formal dining room. There's a long table set up in front of the room, a banner stating "bride's crew" on one side and "groom's crew" on the other. I take notice that all the other guys are leading their partner to their seat and pulling out their chair for them. I do the same with Aves and she whispers a soft "Thank you," which in my eyes is progress.

Taking our seats, we wait for the happy couple to enter. "Okay, once the bride and groom are seated, dinner will be served. After dinner, they will have their first dance. The second song will be just the wedding party before the floor is opened up to everyone. The next step will be speeches and then cutting the cake. The bride and groom will dance with their parents and new in-laws, and then it's party time," the planner explains.

Much to my disappointment, we're then released from further duties for the night.

"Just one more thing," Harley says, getting our attention. "Thank you all so much for being here for us." She leans in to Brad and he kisses her on the top of her head. "We have a little something for each of you. Bride's crew come with me. Groom's, follow my future husband." She grins.

I and the other guys follow Brad up to his room. "Hey, guys," he says. "Thanks for being here." He hands each of us a small black box. "Go ahead." He gestures for us to open them.

Inside are leather money clips engraved with our initials. "Thanks, brother." I lean in and give him a quick hug and tap on the shoulder. The rest of the guys follow my lead.

"Now, you all have your own rooms as you know. All I ask is that you stay sober until all the important parts are over. I want this to be everything Harley imagined it would be. After that's all over, there's an open bar."

"Shots!" Anthony, a fellow groomsman Brad met at college, calls out.

We all agree with him, and as best man I figure it's my job to toast. I wait until Anthony has the glasses passed out. "To Brad and Harley." I raise my glass and the others follow my lead before we throw back our shots.

"Well, since I can't see my girl tonight, it's up to you jokers to entertain me," Brad says.

"I'm thinking the bar for some pool," I suggest.

"Sounds good. Harls and the girls are in for the night, so no chance of running into them."

Although I'm disappointed, I'm also relieved. I don't think I could handle seeing any of the guys at the bar hitting on my Avery.

Chapter 27

Avery

Instead of going back to my own room last night, I stayed with Harley. We stayed up way later than we should've, just talking about well everything. I was waiting for her to bring Dylan up again, but she never did. Of course, I didn't either, even though I've done nothing but think about what she said the other day, and about Dylan and our time together. Then I remember that day it all ended and the years we lost and I get angry. I'm just not sure who I'm angry at anymore.

"Today's the day," Harley says from her spot next to me in this king-sized bed.

"It is. Are you nervous?"

"Nope. I'm so ready to do this. What time is it? We have hair appointments at ten."

"It's a few minutes before nine."

"Okay, well, breakfast is being delivered here at nine thirty in this suite, with hair and makeup immediately after."

"No chance in seeing the guys?"

"Not a single one." She laughs. "Before I forget, I have something for you."

"You already gave me my gift last night." She gave each of us a long-sleeve button-up shirt with our initials embroidered on the pocket.

They'll come in handy today so we don't mess up our hair or makeup when we're getting dressed.

"Here." She hands me a small black box.

Opening the lid, I find a heart-shaped locket. Opening it, I feel tears prick my eyes. Instead of pictures, there is a small piece of paper on each side. On the left it reads "maid of honor today" and "best friend forever" on the right. "I love you, Harls. I'm so happy for you," I say, wiping tears.

"I love you too." She hugs me tight. "Okay, enough of that. Let me call the girls before breakfast gets here."

The rest of the morning passes in a blur of breakfast, hair, makeup, and dresses. The suite is a whirlwind of activity, and then there's a knock at the door telling us it's time to make our way downstairs.

"Make sure Brad is already down there. I'm not risking him seeing me," Harley tells June, the wedding coordinator.

"I've already double-checked. He's in his place, and the groomsmen are waiting on these lovely ladies."

I take a deep breath, trying not to panic at all the time I'll have to spend with Dylan tonight. Last night's rehearsal wasn't so bad, but it brought back memories and feelings. I just need to stay focused on Harley and get through this night; then we can go back to status quo like the last three weeks.

With one final check for each of us and an extra for the bride at her insistence, we make our way downstairs.

"Places," June says, causing a flurry of activity while we all pair up.

Dylan joins me at the back of the line and offers me his arm. I take it, pretending like this isn't my Dylan, that he's just another groomsman. That plan is short-lived when he leans down and whispers, "You take my breath away, Aves."

I don't have time to reply before the line starts to move. I stare straight ahead, and as soon as the two in front of us start down the aisle, I plaster on a big-ass fake smile and follow Dylan's lead.

When we reach the front, we're supposed to just part ways, but Dylan has other plans. He pulls my hand to his lips and places a kiss on my knuckles. It happens so fast that he's already let me go and is walking toward his spot beside Brad before I can comprehend what just happened. Thankfully, I'm on autopilot and find my place at the front of the line without making a spectacle of myself.

The wedding is flawless—well, unless you count my smeared makeup. Dylan kept his gaze on me the entire time. I tried to ignore it, but I couldn't help but think that this could've been us. He took that away. I know he loved me—you can't fake what we shared—but he was so quick to end us.

But was Harley right? Am I being selfish hiding behind the pain and not willing to see the forest for the trees?

Before I know it, the ceremony is over; now it's time to link up with Dylan again. I take the arm he offers and let him lead me to the big hallway just outside of the formal dining room. Just like last night, he steps a little behind me and places his hand on the small of my back. I want to tell him to move it, but I miss the warmth of his touch and I don't want to ruin the night for the newlyweds. Instead I'm going to pretend. I know it's wrong, but for the next however many minutes I have to stand here to greet guests, I'm going to pretend that Dylan is still mine and that we're next.

It's not a new dream for me, not even close.

After the final group of guests are through the line, June appears. "Wedding party, enter just as you walked down the aisle. Please take your seats at the front table."

Dylan offers me his arm, but this time he rests his hand over mine in the crook of his elbow. I can't pull away, nor do I really want to. He walks me to my seat and pulls my chair out for me. I slide into it and scoot a little closer to the table. I thought Dylan was gone until I feel a kiss on the top of my head. My face heats from his attention, in front of everyone we know. Looking out to the crowd, I see Mom and Dad both smiling at me, which is not what I would've expected after what just happened.

"You're glowing," I say to Harley once she and Brad are seated.

"We did it." She has the biggest, brightest smile I've ever seen gracing her face.

"Being married looks good on you," I tell her.

"Your damn right it does." Brad leans in and kisses her, the crowd clapping and cheering for them.

Dinner is served and I pick at it, my stomach in knots for the next step of the night. *One dance and then I'm off the hook. I can do this. He's just Dylan. We have a past, that's it. I can do this.*

"Can I have Mr. and Mrs. Harris on the dance floor?" Jane announces over the PA.

I watch the two of them, so in love. Back then, Dylan was all I wanted; I know Harley felt the same for Brad, and they did it. They made it work. I'm so happy for the both of them.

Just as the song comes to an end, the guests start chanting "kiss," which drowns out the music. The happy couple don't disappoint as Brad tips her back and kisses her.

"Can we have the rest of the wedding party out on the dance floor?" Jane calls through the PA.

Before I can scoot my chair back, Dylan is there, helping me and then offering me his hand. Knowing that all eyes not on the bride and groom are on us, I take his hand and allow him to lead me to the dance floor as Brett Young's "In Case You Didn't Know" begins to play. I'm tempted to run from the room, but instead I keep the smile on my face and allow Dylan to take me in his arms.

"It's me, baby," he says next to my ear.

I want to yell at him, scream that he can't keep calling me that. He lost the right when he dumped me. But I hold my tongue. Not even a minute being in his arms and I'm fighting the pull to rest against his chest like I always used to.

"I got you," he says and pulls me tighter.

I give in and rest my head on his chest as Brett sings to us. He could be singing for me. I wonder if Dylan feels the same. Will I ever know? Probably not if I keep freezing him out. I'm beginning to think Harley might be right. She's going to love hearing that.

When the song comes to an end, I know I have to pull away from him. As of right now, my commitments that involve Dylan are complete; I have no reason to stay out here with him. Lifting my head, I try to step away, but Dylan holds on strong.

"One more, Aves. Please, baby, let me hold you just one more?" His voice is pleading. Which confuses the hell out of me.

"Dylan." His name on my lips is also a plea. "We can't do this," I finally say.

Surprisingly, he leaves one hand on the small of my back and leads me back to the table.

I made it through the dance, but my heart is aching for him, for what we could have had, for what it seems like he might be offering.

A waiter places a new glass of champagne in front of me and I drain it quickly, motioning for another. I need to forget, just for a little while.

Chapter

28

Dylan

After our dance, I watched her down an entire glass of champagne. Now that we've each made our toasts to the happy couple, she's had two more. I hate that she's drinking to forget. I'll give her tonight, where I'm here to keep a close eye on her.

Tomorrow is a brand-new day. The wedding will be over and the gloves are coming off. I'm not going to give up, not without a fight.

"I don't think you've taken your eyes off her all night," a deep voice says from behind me.

I don't have to turn to know who it is. "Mr. Stanton," I greet Avery's father.

"Good to see you, Dylan. Thanks for keeping an eye on my girl."

I don't acknowledge his comment.

"Listen, Dylan. I think I might've played into this thing more than I should have. When Alan told me what happened, all I wanted to do was thank you for putting her first. Not many young men your age would've done that."

"I love her."

"I know you do. That's why I feel as though maybe I've played a part in the two of you staying apart all these years. I knew how both of you were feeling, yet I still encouraged her to stay at Western."

"That's what was best for her."

"A year ago—hell, six weeks ago, I would've agreed with you. Seeing the two of you together again, you both wear it on your sleeves. She's hurting, Dylan, because she still loves you. I just want to see my little girl happy. That's what she deserves."

"Me too. That's what I've always wanted."

"Fight for her, Dylan."

"I plan on it, sir." He gives my shoulder a tight squeeze and disappears into the crowd.

Over the years, her parents have been good to me. Her mom would stop by the shop and drop off cookies or brownies for Dad and me. Her father, Alan, my dad, and I have been fishing a few times too. They've kept me close, just as they would have if Avery and I were still together. Her mom even told me that she was confident that we would end up together one day. I can only pray that she's right.

"There's my best man. What are you doing over here all alone?" Brad asks as he stops to stand next to me.

"Just taking it all in." I nod toward the dance floor.

"Ah, I see. You ready to make your move?"

"I was being considerate of you and your wife. I didn't want to ruin the wedding."

He grins. "My wife and I are behind you one hundred and ten percent."

"Good to know." I watch closely as the girls head toward the bar and order a round of shots. They toast and then toss them back. My eyes zone in on Avery, her long slender neck as she drinks. I always did like kissing her there. If my memory serves me correctly, she liked it too. Just one more thing I need to remind her of.

I spend the next hour standing around with Brad and the rest of the groomsmen. Avery is never out of my sight, as I continue to keep an eye on her.

It's not until "Slow Hands" by Niall Horan starts playing that I start to get worried. Avery and the girls are dancing in ways that would bring any man to his knees. Brad and another groomsman excuse themselves to go dance with their wives. Avery is wasted, and I don't want some other asshole grinding up on her. I can't stand by and watch that, not again. I did it a few times over the years, hidden in the shadows watching over her. Tonight, I'm here and she knows I am. No chance she's leaving here with anyone but me.

I make my way to the dance floor just as some guy I've never met before heads toward Aves. Reaching her before he does, I place my hands on her swaying hips and give him a look that says "Fuck off, she's mine." He gets the message and backs away. Avery continues to sway her hips and push her ass into me. At this point, I have no idea if she even knows it's me behind her, but I keep my hands on her hips, moving in time with her.

I tense up when she turns in my arms. She looks up at me and I see sadness in her eyes. She stops moving and wraps her arms around my waist, burying her face in my chest. There is no hesitation on my part as I wrap my arms around her and hold her tight. We're the only couple standing still in the mass of bodies bumping and grinding, but I couldn't care less. Avery is in my arms. I hold her a little tighter, knowing her walls are down from all the alcohol. I don't know how long it'll be before I get to hold her like this again. Nothing and no one can pull me away from her—well, except for her.

When the song ends, she doesn't let go and neither do I. I'm not going to, not until she does. I can stand here all night. I *will* stand here all night, if she lets me hold her. For two more songs we stand here in the middle of the dance floor, not really moving, arms locked tight around each other.

She pulls away slowly. "I think it's time for me to call it a night." She sways a little on her feet.

"Let me help you to your room."

"I've been doing just fine the last four years, Dylan. I can manage," she slurs. There is no hate in her voice, no anger; she's just matter-of-fact.

"I know you can, but it would make me feel better if you let me make sure you get in okay."

"Whatever." She turns and wobbles on her heels.

Reaching out, I place my arm around her waist to steady her. I don't say anything as I lead her to the elevator. I catch Brad's eye as we leave and he nods, knowing I'll take care of her and Harley doesn't have to worry. I keep my arm around her on the elevator, and to my surprise she lets me.

"What room?" I ask her.

She pulls a keycard out of her garter and I fight the urge to groan. We stop outside her door and she manages to get the key in and unlock it. Walking inside, she holds the door open for me. I assumed she'd kick me to the curb at this point, but I'm taking any chance I can to be with her.

"I need your help. I can't do it on my own."

I nod, afraid to speak and have her change her mind. She turns to me and raises her blonde locks, revealing her neck and ultimately the zipper to the dress. With shaking hands, I grab the zipper and slowly, painfully so, I lower it. Her back is exposed, and of course she's not wearing a bra. Unable to resist, I run my index finger down her spine. She takes a step away from me and the dress falls to the floor. I don't speak, just bite down on my bottom lip. I don't take my eyes off her in nothing but a white lace thong as she pulls a tank top out of the dresser and slips it over her head. It's one of those that hangs around her neck, leaving most of her back exposed. Finally she turns to face me, and I can see her nipples through the thin white fabric. She doesn't say anything as she climbs onto the bed and lies on her stomach, one arm under her head as she looks in my direction.

"That should've been us tonight, Dylan."

"It still can be," I tell her honestly. If she were sober, I'd take her to the nearest airport and we'd be in Vegas or whatever tropical destination she has in mind. I would take her anywhere. I would marry her in a heartbeat.

"You don't want me," she says softly, her eyes closed.

"You're wrong," I tell her. I kneel beside the bed and move her hair away from her face so I can see her. "I've never stopped wanting you."

"Why does this seem so familiar?"

I can't tell her it's because it is. Two years ago, Brad and Harley were visiting home and Avery decided not to come with them. They called me and I followed her, to make sure she was okay. She and some friends ended up getting shit-faced, much more so than she is now, so bad she could hardly stand. She recognized me, so I was able to get her to come with me, even though she talked to me as if I was a dream to her. I got her back to their apartment and tucked into bed, then stuck around for a few hours, making sure she was going to be okay before slipping away. Brad and Harley know, but they never told her. She even went as far as to tell Harley how real the dream was. Just one of the things I need to come clean to her about, but not tonight. She won't remember tonight.

"Sweet dreams, Aves." I lean in and kiss her temple. Standing to leave her like this is hard as hell.

"Dylan," she calls out.

Looking down, I see her eyes are still closed. "Yeah, baby?"

"Will you stay, maybe until I fall asleep? My heart hurts when you're not here."

I swallow back the emotion. "Anything for you, Aves." I drop back to my knees beside the bed and gently rub her back.

"Lie with me?" she whispers.

Standing, I kick off my shoes, take off my shirt and undershirt, and throw them over the chair. Climbing on the bed, I kiss her shoulder before resting my face against her cheek. Her hand grips the sheets. I lace mine with hers and we hold on tight to one another. I know her barriers are down from the alcohol, but this moment, this right here, gives me hope for us.

"I love you, Aves," I whisper next to her ear.

"My Dylan," she whispers before falling to sleep. Rolling onto my side, I pull her in to me and hold her tight while she sleeps. I don't close my eyes—I can't. I never want to forget this time with her. I don't know what the future holds for us, but I do know I'm going to fight like hell to hold her like this every night for the rest of our lives.

Chapter
29

Avery

I wake up hot. I blink a few times and realize there are two strong arms wrapped around me. I stiffen until I smell him and hear his voice at the same time.

"It's me, Aves."

Dylan.

I take a few deep breaths to calm my racing heart. He never breaks his hold on me—of course, he never did. Slowly I turn in his arms to face him. His face is scruffier than yesterday. This is a good look for him. I rest my palm against his cheek. "You're not a dream."

"No." His voice is soft and low. "I'm not a dream."

"I asked you to stay." I remember last night. The details are a little foggy, but I remember him holding me on the dance floor for what seemed like forever and then me needing to get out of there. Dylan came with me. He told me he loved me and I asked him to stay.

"I couldn't make myself leave. I had plans to hold you for a few hours and then slip out, but I couldn't seem to let you go." He closes his eyes as I run my fingers over his facial hair.

"You haven't slept," I say, seeing the exhaustion in his eyes.

"How can I sleep with you in my arms? I don't know if I'll ever have this chance again, Avery. I refused to miss a single second of my time with you."

"You did this, Dylan."

"It wasn't just me. You weren't willing to compromise. To just try it to see if we could make it."

"We were young."

"We were, but that didn't mean that I didn't love you."

"That was years ago."

"Doesn't matter, Aves." He places his hand on my face. "I've never for one second stopped loving you."

"I can't take losing you again, Dylan. I won't live through it."

"I'm here, Avery."

I close my eyes and relish the feeling of being back in his arms. I'm sober this time, yet I continue to lie here next to him.

"We can take it slow," he offers. "We can date again, see if the memories are still our reality."

"What happens when you figure out that I'm not what you want? I can't do it again, Dylan. I can't."

"I won't. You're all I've ever wanted. There are some things I need to tell you about the last four years." I tense up. "Nothing bad, baby. Just what's been going on, you know?"

"Dylan, I care about you."

He leans in, his face close to mine. "You love me. You want to know how I know?"

I nod. "Because your heart races any time I'm near. Your eyes still light up like they used to when you would see me. It only happens when you're looking at me." He pulls my hand from his face and places it over his heart. "You live here, Aves. Not one day has gone by that you haven't been here with me. No matter what you decide, that's something that'll never change. Let me show you. Give me one more chance to love you like you deserve to be loved. We have no obstacles in our way now. Just… let me love you."

I think about what he's asking. He's right, I love him just as much now as I did then, but I don't know if trying again is the right answer. What if our time is over?

"Aves, we'll go slow, at your pace, baby. Just let me show you."

"Slow. We have to take it slow, and I can't—"

He places his finger over my lips. "Slow I can do. Be ready to be reminded."

"Reminded?"

"Of how good we are together." He kisses my forehead and pulls me in to his chest.

We're already here, and since I insisted on slow, it's going to be a while before I have this opportunity again. I relax into his hold and just live in the moment, with him.

My phone rings. Dylan reaches over me and grabs it from the nightstand for me. "Hello."

"Av, hey. We're checking out and I wanted to check on you before we left. You okay?" Harley asks.

"Yeah, Dylan, he, uh, got me back to my room and stayed to make sure I was okay." My eyes never leave his, and I see them soften when he hears my confession. I'm sure he thought I would hide this from her. I told him I was willing to go slow and I am; I need to see if these old feelings are lingering because of how we ended or if my heart still really is his like I think it is.

"He stayed?"

"He did. He's here now."

Dylan grins.

"Well, okay then. You're in good hands."

"You think so?"

"I know so, Avery. He loves you. You two have fun. I'll see you in a few days."

"Enjoy your honeymoon, Mrs. Harris."

She giggles. "Bye. As soon as I'm back, we have some catching up to do."

"You got it. Love you, Harls. Give Brad a hug from me."

I end the call and Dylan kisses my forehead. "Can I take you to breakfast? I know you said slow, but we both have to eat, right?"

My stomach growls loudly. I didn't each much last night. "Yeah, we can do breakfast. I need a shower."

"I'll run to my suite and shower, pack up. I'll be back to get you. Did you drive here?"

"No, I rode with Harley. I was going to call my parents to pick me up today."

"I'll take you."

"Thank you, Dylan."

He stands from the bed and slips back into his shirt and shoes. Leaning down, he kisses my forehead. "I'll be back, Aves." And then he's gone.

I stare at the door. I never would've dreamed that this is how things would turn out last night. One day at a time, I remind myself. We'll take it slow and see where it leads us.

Realizing that Dylan's going to be back soon, I hop out of bed, grab some clothes, and rush to the shower. I've just finished throwing everything back in my suitcase when there's a knock at my door.

"Hey." Dylan smiles when I open it. "I'm really glad to see you," he says.

"Were you expecting someone else?"

"No." He shakes his head. "I just wasn't sure this was real, that last night happened and that I'm really taking you to breakfast."

"It happened and I'm starving. You ready to go?"

"More than ready. Let me get your bag." He grabs mine and his, then leads us to the elevator.

Chapter 30

Dylan

When I pull into the diner, I look over at Avery and she smiles. "Bucket list," I say, and she laughs.

"Technicality. We've had breakfast here before."

"You're right, we have. What we haven't done is wake up in the same bed together and have breakfast for breakfast. Bucket list," I say again.

Avery shakes her head before climbing out of the truck. I catch up with her just before she reaches the door and I open it for her. One hand on the small of her back, we enter the diner. It's not busy yet, since most people are still at church.

I lead us to a booth in the back.

"I'm starving. It smells so good," she says, picking up a menu.

"Order one of everything," I tell her.

"Right. I'm hungry but no way can I eat all of that."

"That's what I'm here for."

She studies her menu. "I'm thinking the farmer's breakfast. Although the French toast looks good too."

"I'll get that so you can have some of both." I don't bother looking at the menu.

"Dylan, get what you want."

"I'm trying to do just that."

Her head lifts and she studies me. "We said slow."

"We did. However, that doesn't change how I want things to go. You're what I want, Avery."

"Welcome, can I start you off with coffee or orange juice?" the waitress asks.

"Just water for me, and I think we're ready to order." She looks over at me for confirmation and I nod. "I would like the farmer's breakfast. Eggs scrambled, with wheat toast."

"I'll have a large order of French toast with strawberries on the side and water to drink."

The waitress rushes off to put our order in.

"You don't eat strawberries on your French toast."

"I know, but you do."

She shakes her head as if she can't believe that I would still know something like that about her. I've never forgotten a minute of my time with her.

"So, you're working at the shop with your dad?"

"Yeah, we pretty much run the place together these days. I've learned a lot about running the business. Of course, college helped."

"College?" she asks, surprised.

"Yeah, I went to community. Took me three and a half years to get my associate's in business, but I wanted to…"

"Wanted to what, Dylan?"

I guess I need to start filling her in slowly. "I never thought I was good enough for you, Avery. I'm a small-town mechanic, not smart enough for college. I wanted to do it to have an education, to help Dad run the business. It's going to be mine someday, and I wanted to make sure I knew what the hell I was doing. I can fix cars all day, but the other stuff, payroll and taxes, I had no clue. I wanted to make sure I could provide for you, for our family, if one day I was ever lucky enough for you to be mine again. I wanted to be ready."

She's quiet. I don't know what she's thinking because she's looking at her hands that are folded in front of her on the table.

"Hey," I say, reaching out to lift her chin. What I find takes my breath. There are tears in her eyes. "I'm sorry, Aves. I'm not trying to hurt you. Shit!" I start to climb out of the booth so I can comfort her.

"Dylan." I stop and look at her. "I'm fine. I'm just processing. You have to give me a minute." She grabs a napkin and wipes her eyes while I scoot back in the booth. "I never saw you like that, Dylan. Not once did I not see a guy who was loving and attentive. You made me happy, Dylan. That's all that matters. It's not your job to support me. It's our job to support each other. I want someone I can lean on through life, so when I fall I know without a doubt that person is there to catch me. That's what I always saw in you, in us."

"I thought maybe you felt like you had to give up your scholarship because I didn't get one." I hang my head at my admission. It's not one I've spoken until now.

"Dylan, I loved you so much that the thought of not seeing you every day killed me inside. You were my heart. It had nothing to do with your education and everything to do with the fact that I loved you too much to move away from you."

"Yeah, but look at you. You're graduated with a job already lined up. You're kicking ass and taking names."

"I could've done that staying local too. Only difference is that I would've had you by my side every step of the way. Instead I mourned what we had. I dated, but I compared them all to you. No one ever lived up to the way you were with me, to me."

"I feel like I should apologize for that, but I'd be lying."

She smiles. "I'm proud of you, Dylan."

"Here you go," the waitress interrupts as she delivers our food.

I add syrup to only half of the plate; I know she likes the flavor from the strawberries better without it. I spoon a little of the strawberries onto the corner of one piece and cut off the French toast. "Taste," I say, holding my hand under the fork and offering it to her for a bite. She hesitates for only seconds before she leans in and wraps those soft lips around my fork. I could watch her eat all day.

"Yum." She smiles. "Try mine." She scoops up some eggs and hash brown and offers it to me." I take my time letting the fork slide past my lips, watching as she swallows hard. Good to know she's just as affected as I am.

"How's your dad?"

"He's Dad, you know. Staying busy at the shop. I've learned a lot from him. We're actually restructuring a few things. He's taking my input to heart, which is a good thing."

"That's great. He knows you're his ace." I raise my eyebrows in question and she continues. "He knows what he has with you. Sure, you're his son, but you're smart and you care about the business. I'm sure with your degree you're now a double threat, and he's taking full advantage of that."

"I've missed you, Avery."

She takes a sip of water. "Me too."

We spend the rest of our meal dealing in small talk. I pay the bill even though she tries to argue. "Let's get you home." I walk her to the truck and open the door for her. The ride to her parents' place is filled with more small talk, but I'm okay with that. She's nervous and, to be honest, so am I. This is my one shot to win her back, after all.

"I always loved that house." She points at a two-story with a wraparound porch.

"I know." I smile over at her.

"Mom said it was only on the market for a day before it sold. I wonder who's going to be living there."

I wasn't going to tell her yet, but I refuse to lose her from keeping something as small as this from her. Hell, I have a laundry list of things to confess; I don't need to add another. "I am," I finally say.

She turns to look at me. "You? You bought the old Hampton place?"

"I did," I say cautiously. I can't tell if she's mad or not.

"Why?"

"You love that house."

"Dylan," she breathes.

"That was last July, almost a year ago."

I can hear the wheels turning in her head while she tries to work this out.

"You said you still lived with your dad."

"I do."

"So it's a rental?"

"No."

"Why are you not living there?" she asks.

I pull into her driveway and turn to face her. "I know you love that house, Avery. You used to talk about it all the time. I bought it for the chance that one day you and I might be able to live there together, as a family."

"What happens if this"—she points between us—"doesn't work? Then what, Dylan? You can't just buy a house for the off chance that we might get back together."

"I did. We're going to work out, Aves."

"Dylan! You don't know that. I'm being serious."

"Then we can sell it, burn it, you can live there, I don't care. I'm not going to live there without you."

"You know that sounds crazy, right? I mean, you pay a mortgage and don't even live there."

"I put a lot of money down, so the mortgage payment isn't even enough to call it that. More like a car payment."

"But you don't live there," she says again.

"Not without you."

"That was almost a year ago."

"It was."

"What if I was with someone?"

"It was a chance I was willing to take."

She's quiet for several minutes. "I don't know what to say, Dylan."

"Don't say anything. You know why I bought it, you know what I want. You take your time getting there with me."

"Dylan—"

I hold my hand up to cut her off. "I'll fight for you, Aves. Until you can look me in the eye and tell me you don't want me, that you don't love me anymore, I will fight for you. I don't care if it takes six days, six months, or six years."

She nods, then reaches for the door handle.

"Aves, do you have the same cell number?"

"No. I changed it when I left for Western."

"Can I have your number?"

She holds her hand out for my phone. I hand it over. "I need your passcode." She tries to hand it back.

"It's your birthday."

She stops, closes her eyes, and takes a deep breath. When she opens them again, her hands shake as she types in the digits to her birthday. When the phone unlocks, she looks up and shakes her head. Looking back at the screen, she freezes. I know what she sees. It's a picture of us at the cabin—my favorite. She's smiling so wide her whole face lights up. I'm staring at her, a look of wonder on my face.

She taps on my contacts and enters her contact information.

"Send yourself a text," I tell her.

"I don't want to get into your messages."

"I have nothing to hide from you, Avery. There are a few more things I need to tell you, but none of them are bad." Her fingers fly across the screen and I hear her phone beep in her pocket. "I'll help with your bag," I say once she hands me back my phone. I quickly hop out of the truck and grab her bag from the back seat, then follow her up the sidewalk and onto the front porch. "Thank you."

"For? You're the one who bought breakfast. I should be thanking you. Thank you," she says with a hint of a smile.

"For last night, for letting me stay and hold you. For today, letting me take you to breakfast. For agreeing to give me a shot, no matter how slow we have to go."

"There have been a lot of revelations in the last twenty-four hours."

I chuckle. "That there has. I'll be in touch. I'd like to take you out."

"We agreed to go slow, Dylan."

"I know, but we have to date, right? In the meantime, you need me, you call, text, carrier pigeon—whatever you have to do. I'm there."

"Goodbye, Dylan."

"Bye, Aves." I wait until she's in the house, just like I always used to, before turning to leave.

I drive home in a daze. It almost feels like I've been living a dream. I can only hope that dreams really do come true.

Chapter 31

Avery

"That you, Av?" Mom calls from the living room.

I'm still a little dazed and confused from information overload. "Yeah," I say, joining her and Dad and taking a seat on the recliner.

"I've been waiting for you to call for a ride," she says.

"Sorry, it's been a crazy morning. Dylan and I actually had breakfast and he dropped me off."

"Dylan?" Mom's face lights up.

"Yeah."

"Everything okay, sweetheart?" Dad asks.

"Just have a lot of my mind. Did you guys know that Dylan bought the old Hampton house?"

"We did," Dad says.

"Why didn't you say anything?"

"It wasn't our place."

"Do you know why he bought it?"

"We do," Mom answers.

"So, what? You want us together now? You agreed that I should go to Western."

"We did, Avery," Dad agrees. "As your parents, we knew what that scholarship meant for you. We know how important is it to be able to start your own life without the debt of school hanging over your head. We wanted you to enjoy college and not have to work full time and study just to feel like you were keeping your head above water."

"You said it was best to let Dylan go," I remind him.

Dad nods. "I did say that. It wasn't until you were gone that I could see the error in my ways. That boy loves you, Avery. He's worked hard to be the man he feels like you deserve."

"That's not his choice!" I scream. "I loved him for who he was, not who he could be for me. For him, just Dylan."

"We know that, Avery."

"Then explain to me why. You knew he was what I wanted. From the day he ended us, you all encouraged me to go to Western. I was planning to stay here anyway, hoping he would see that it could all work out. You and Alan, you all convinced me it was best." I'm crying now.

"Avery—" Dad stands from the couch.

"Don't!" I jump from my seat and hold my hand up. "I need to be alone." I turn and stomp up the stairs like a teenager. I can't help it. It's like I'm living this all over again, and my heart is breaking once more.

Then there's Dylan. He's the same Dylan, my Dylan, and he's saying all the right things, doing all the right things. I feel like I'm in the fucking twilight zone.

Slamming my bedroom door, I turn the lock and fall onto my bed. My phone beeps in my pocket but I ignore it. I don't want to talk to anyone; I just need to process this. Curling up with a stuffed bear Dylan won me at the county fair, which I refused to get rid of, I cry myself to sleep.

Hours later, there's a knock at my bedroom door, waking me. I see it's dusk outside. "Avery," Mom calls out. "Honey, can you open the door?"

With a heavy sigh, I climb out of bed and twist the lock, opening the door. My mom stands there, Dylan behind her.

"Aves," he says, relief in his voice.

"What are you doing here?" I ask him.

"You didn't answer my messages and I was worried."

"Why didn't you just call my parents? I hear the three of you are well acquainted these days."

"I wanted to see you."

"I said slow, Dylan. This is not slow."

"Slow gets thrown out the damn window if I think something's happened to you."

"Four years, Dylan." I hold up four fingers. "I was gone for four years and you weren't there to look out for me."

He opens his mouth to speak, then slams it shut.

"Nothing to say to that?" I taunt him.

"Avery," Mom scolds.

"I'm fine, Dylan. You can go."

"Avery," he pleads.

"Look, I have a lot to think about. I'll talk to you soon."

He nods, then slowly turns and walks away.

"Avery, what has gotten into you?" Mom asks.

"Let's see. I lost the love of my life, and then I find out my parents encouraged me to do something they knew I didn't want, and now they admit they were wrong for doing so. Oh, and said love bought my dream house and refuses to live in it without me. That's just the top of the list—should I keep going?"

"Let's sit." Mom walks into my room and sits on the edge of the bed, tapping the spot next to her. "When you're a parent, you'll realize there is no rule book. You do what you think is best for your kids, give them advice that you think is the best. People change and so do opinions. Your dad and I thought you leaving was best. We didn't want to see you give up what you had worked so hard for. It's not until we saw the light leave your eyes that we realized we'd made a mistake. We just want you happy. Dylan lost his light too. We watched both of you mourn the loss of the other."

"I love him." My voice breaks as the words leave my lips. Mom wraps me in a hug and I let the tears fall. It's been a while since I've had a good cry.

"Honey, take it slow. Get to know him again. See if these feelings are still there. The only advice I'm going to give you is to follow your heart. I should've said those exact words four years ago. I'm sorry I didn't."

"Me too," Dad says from the doorway. "We just want you happy."

I scoff. "That's what Dylan said too, but he still ended us."

"Honey, he didn't want to. He wanted to stay together, remember? He only ended things because he didn't want to be the reason you gave up your dream of Western."

"People change, dreams change. All I wanted was Dylan."

"Come on, let's get you some dinner."

"I'm not hungry."

"Okay. We'll let you be." They both give me a hug and leave me alone to my thoughts.

I'm more confused now than I was this morning. Can Dylan and I really make this work after all this time?

Chapter 32

Dylan

It's been three days since I've heard from Avery and I'm ready to lose my mind. I've been trying to give her space, but I'm done with that. Grabbing my phone from my back pocket, I send her a quick text.

Me: Hey, are you busy Saturday night?

I wait for her to reply. I'm staring at the screen, willing her to reach out to me. Just as I'm about to slide my phone back in my pocket, she replies.

Avery: We agreed to go slow, Dylan.

Me: I miss you.

Avery: I just need some time.

Me: I'll be on my best behavior. I just want to see you. Saturday night?

Avery: What did you have in mind?

Me: Dinner and a movie?

Avery: Where should I meet you?

Me: I'll pick you up. I get more time with you that way.

I know I'm pushing my luck, but that's how we used to do it. It's my job to remind her of that, of what we were, and show her what we can be.

> **Avery:** I can drive, Dylan. What time should I meet you?

> **Me:** How am I going to woo you if you won't let me pick you up?

> **Avery:** Fine. Seven?

> **Me:** I'll see you then.

I can hardly focus the rest of the day as I plan our date. The rest of the week drags on. I did an oil change on a car that was here for new brakes and put water in a radiator instead of coolant. All things that can be fixed, and one customer got a free oil change. Dad finally told me to go home.

I spent all day yesterday making sure I have everything I need for the date tonight. I picked up the movie, I know where we're eating, and I have flowers. I washed our blanket, the one we always used either in my truck or up on the roof. I have it all planned out; now I just need to execute it.

At ten till seven, I pull into her driveway. I grab the flowers sitting in the passenger seat and climb out of the truck. Before I can get to the door, she's there, standing before me.

"Avery," I greet her.

"Hi." She raises her hand in a wave. *Cute as hell, this one.*

"These are for you." I hand her the flowers.

She brings them to her nose and sniffs. "Thank you, Dylan. Let me put them in some water and we can go. Am I dressed okay?"

"You're prefect."

She gives me a look that tells me she thinks I'm laying it on too thick and heads into the house. When she emerges, I hold my arm out for her just like I did at the wedding. She rolls her eyes but takes my arm and allows me to lead her to my truck. I open the door for her and wait for her to buckle up before closing it.

"Where are we going?"

"Well, I kind of like our version of dinner and a movie, so I thought we would do us."

"Do us?" she asks.

"Yeah, you know, on the roof of the shop. That was our first date."

"I remember. Dylan, I don't think that's such a great idea."

"That's our spot, Aves. I was just—"

"It's our spot all right," she laughs humorlessly. "That's where you ended us, Dylan."

Fuck. "I know that, but it's also where we had our first date. I just thought… we have a lot of good memories up on that roof."

"The bad sometimes outweigh the good," she says softly.

"One day, the one I will regret for the rest of my life. I didn't know that living without you would be as hard as it was. Can we just… remember the good times we had here?" I reach out as if to take her hand but think better of it, placing it back on the steering wheel, gripping it tightly. "Just try, Aves. If you don't want to stay, if it's too painful, we can leave. Just try." My voice is pleading.

"Fine," she grumbles.

I sigh with relief. I almost told her we could change plans, but I really don't want to. I want her to remember us together, the love we shared. I pull into the back of the shop and ask her to wait for me to get her door. Of course, she doesn't. My hand on her back, I lead her into the shop, locking the door behind me.

"You know the way," I say, holding my arm out and stepping to the side so she can pass me to go up the steps. Cautiously she opens the door that leads to the roof. I know what she's seeing. I made sure everything was as close to the same as I could. The TV is now a flat-screen and it's a little bigger, but the couch, the pizza, the movie, the blanket, everything else is exactly as it was the first night I brought her here.

"You've been busy," she says, walking toward the couch.

"Hungry?" I ask, avoiding her comment.

"Sure." She takes a seat on the couch, kicking off her flip-flops. "What movie are we watching?"

"*Hunger Games*," I answer, not looking at her. I make us both a plate and then take my seat beside her. Grabbing the remote, I hit Play and we settle into the couch, eating our pizza.

"You want more?" I ask once she finishes hers.

"No, I'm stuffed."

I take her plate and mine and set them on the table. Reaching behind us, I grab the blanket and cover her legs with it. She just smiles and goes back to the movie. Not ten minutes later, I feel her hand wrap around mine. I don't look at her, just open my palm and allow her to lace her fingers with mine. That's how we finish the movie—hand in hand, sitting side by side.

"Thank you for tonight." She pulls her hand from mine and stands.

"It's still early." I'm not ready for her to go.

"You work tomorrow?"

"Doesn't matter. I want to see you."

"Dylan, I'm still trying to process all of this. I want to jump back into us more than you could ever know, but is that just the eighteen-year-old me talking? How do I know? I need time."

"Okay," I concede, because pushing her too far too fast will not end in my favor. "I'll take you home."

Picking up the blanket, she starts to fold it.

"I can get that."

"It's not a problem." She makes the final two folds. "See, I'm already done."

I wait for her to place it on the back of the couch, then hold my hand out for her. She takes it and we head back downstairs to my truck. The drive back to her place is quiet and I hate it. Before I even have the truck in Park, I reach over and grab her hand.

"Dylan?"

"Avery." I turn to face her. I can see from the way she scrunches her eyebrows that she's confused. "I just need to do this." Cupping her face, I lean in and press my lips to hers. She's still until I trace her bottom lip with my tongue; then she opens for me and kisses me back. I don't think about where we are, who might catch us, not like when we were kids. I couldn't give a fuck less who sees us. This is my Avery.

"Dylan, we should stop."

I still, my lips hovering over hers. "Do you want me to stop, Aves?"

"No," she whispers.

I trail my lips across her cheek and down her neck. She moans, which spurs me on. Sliding my hand behind her neck, I hold her to me while my other hand rests on her thigh, moving higher and higher. My index finger slides under the hem of her jean shorts that have been driving me mad all damn night. I seek out her panties and my finger traces under the hem.

"Dylan." It's a plea.

"Tell me, Aves. Tell me what you want."

"We shouldn't be doing this."

"This is all about you, Avery. You tell me what you want." I kiss the spot on her neck, right under her ear, that always used to drive her crazy. From the way she tilts her head, giving me full access, I know it still does. My index finger is stroking just under the edge of her panties. I'm pushing my luck, but at the same time I'm letting her call the shots. She's scared, but I know my girl. She wants this just as much as I do.

"More." She lifts her hips.

"Like this?" Going a little farther, I run my finger through her folds. She's wet. Bringing her lips back to mine, I kiss her slow and deep, keeping my tongue and finger in sync. She breaks away from the kiss, her head resting sideways on the seat as I bring her closer to the edge. "Tell me what you need, Aves."

"Don't move." She grabs my hands and holds it in place while my finger slides inside of her. "That. So much yes… that," she pants.

It only takes a few thrusts from my hand and I feel her start to quiver from the inside. "I got you, baby. Just let go."

She grips my arm, nails digging into the skin. I don't stop; I can't. It only takes one more time before I feel her falling over the edge. I slow down but don't stop, not until she opens her eyes.

"What happened to slow?" she whispers. Her eyes are glassy and she looks as though she's coming off a major high.

"I love you, Avery. I know I agreed to slow, but I don't know how I'm going to do it. I can promise you this: no sex until you've decided we can give this another shot. A real shot, Avery."

"What do you call what just happened?"

"Foreplay. Sex is when I get to slide home for the first time in four years. Sex is where I get you naked in a bed for hours—*hours*, Aves. I've missed the hell out of you. I'm not certain it won't be days." Leaning in, I kiss her. "Stay put, I'll get your door."

This time she actually listens.

"What am I going to do with you, Dylan Knight?" she asks, taking my hand and hopping out of the truck.

I pull her into my arms, her head resting on my chest. "Just love me, Avery. I promise you, if you let me back in, you will never forget it." I kiss the top of her head before grabbing her hand and leading her to the front door. "One more," I say, leaning in and kissing her lips. "Night, beautiful."

Still looking dazed, she turns the knob and disappears inside.

Chapter 33

Avery

Harley and Brad come home today. It's been three days since my date with Dylan, and even though I've not seen him, he texts me every day. Harley and I have so much to catch up on since I didn't want to bother her on her honeymoon. I already know how she feels about Dylan and me, but I need to talk to someone about all of this.

We agreed to meet at the park today; I need to have her undivided attention and no witnesses. Pulling in, I see her already sitting at the picnic table, Subway bag in front of her.

"Well hello there, Mrs. Harris," I say, walking up behind her. She's beaming when I sit down. "Looks like the honeymoon was a success."

"It was amazing," she gushes. "So what's up? You sounded a little stressed on the phone."

"Not stressed exactly, confused is more like it. I have so much to tell you."

"You talk, I'll eat. I'm starving." She opens her sandwich and takes a big bite. She offered to grab me one as well, but I had a late breakfast.

"Okay, so the night of your wedding…" I spend the next twenty minutes catching her up on everything that's happened with Dylan since that night. She's surprisingly quiet as I give her all the juicy details. When I finish, she doesn't say anything at first, just studies me.

"You want my opinion on what you should do? Or do you want to know what I think about everything that's happened up to this point?"

"Both?" I need to be able to see this from all angles.

"Okay, but I'm going to be honest with you. You might not like it, and he might not either, but I think it's time."

"What are you talking about?"

She stands, gathers her trash, and tosses it in a nearby can. "Let's take a walk." I stand and follow her. We walk for several minutes in silence. "You know I think you're hiding behind the pain, that you're not taking the time to see Dylan's side of things."

"Yeah, I've actually thought a lot about that the past week."

"Good. There's more to it than that." She takes a deep breath. "So what I'm about to tell you is probably going to piss you off, but you need to know that we did it because we love you. He loves you."

"You're really starting to freak me out."

"Dylan loves you, Avery. I know that because he checked up on you."

"What do you mean he checked up on me?"

"At school. He would be in the shadows, but always looking out for you."

"How?" *What the hell is she talking about?* "I left town when he came to visit."

She nods. "You did, but there were other times. Like the time you were in that play sophomore year. He was there."

"How did he…? You told him?" I'm not sure how I'm feeling right now.

"Not that time. That was your parents, or maybe it was Alan."

"What?" I grab her arm and pull her to a stop. "Dumb this down for me, Harley. It sounds like you're trying to tell me that my family, you, and Brad gave Dylan a play-by-play of my life."

"We kind of did. Just big things, like the play or when you were honored for your volunteer work with that inner-city school. He was there for that too."

"Is that it?"

"No. When Brad and I came home that week, junior year, he went to Western, stayed at Brad's apartment, and kept an eye on you."

"What do you mean kept an eye on me?"

"I mean I told him where you would be each night after I would talk to you, and Dylan was there to keep you safe."

"Are you fucking crazy? Why would you do that? Keep me safe? He fucking broke me, Harley."

"You had a hand in that too, Avery. It wasn't just Dylan. You refused to see any other option except for the one you had in your head."

"Oh, so now it's my fault. What about Dylan? He wanted it to be his way or the highway. Guess what? I got the fucking highway. He dumped me."

"He did. You were both scared and so in love that you didn't know how to handle it."

"Look at you. Now that you're married, you're an expert on relationships?"

"I know you're upset, but we did it because we care about you."

"Yeah," I scoff. "Leave my safety in the hands of the one guy who single-handedly tore my heart to shreds."

"He loves you and you love him. Why are you fighting it?"

"I'm not. That's not love, it's an obsession."

"Come on now, you're overreacting just a tad, don't you think?

"What's it matter what I think? Everyone else always fucking decides for me." I turn to head back to my car.

"Where are you going?"

"Away."

"Avery!" she yells as she runs to catch up with me, reaching out for my arm.

"Don't," I say through gritted teeth. "I can't be around you right now." I take off running and when I get to my car, she's not following me. With shaking hands, I manage to dial the one person who hasn't betrayed me, at least not that I know of.

"Kara." I begin to cry as soon as she answers.

"Avery, are you okay? Are you hurt? What's wrong?"

"Are you with Alan?"

"No, he's meeting with the coaching staff. What's going on?"

"I need a place to stay just for a night or two. Can I stay with you?"

"Of course you can. Where are you? Do I need to come and get you?" I can hear the worry in her voice. She's going to think I'm a nutcase.

"I'm fine. Yes, I can drive. I'll be there soon." I toss my phone in the cup holder. As soon as I pull into Kara's driveway, my phone rings. Looking down at the screen, I see Harley's name. I send it straight to voice mail. Phone, keys, and purse in hand, I make my way to the front door. Kara is there, arms open wide. I fall into them and let the tears fall.

"Let's get you inside."

I blindly follow her inside through the tears. She guides me to the couch and I fall into the soft cushions. My phone rings but I don't bother looking at the screen from where it's clutched in my hand.

"It's Dylan," she says softly.

I laugh humorlessly. "I'm sure it is. Harley more than likely called him. I'm sure she's going to call my parents and Alan too. They're all traitors."

"That doesn't sound good. You want something to drink?" she asks, handing me a box of tissues.

"No, thanks." I grab a handful of tissues and dry my face.

"You want to talk about it?"

I spill the story, what little of it I actually know. I was so angry, I'm a little fuzzy on some of the details.

"How could they do that to me?" My phone rings—it's Mom. I send it to voice mail.

"They're going to worry about you."

"I know, but I don't want to talk to any of them right now."

"How about I call your parents and let them know you're here and you just need some time. I'll send Alan a text, and you can handle Dylan and Harley."

"They can suffer through it. But yeah, calling Mom and Dad's fine. Tell them not to come here. I just... need a minute to process." Silent tears roll down my cheeks as Kara calls my parents and then my brother. I listen as she assures them that I'm okay and that they need to just give me some time.

"Thank you, Kara. I'm so sorry to barge in on you like this."

"You're fine. It'll be good to have a girls' night."

"I'm not much for good company," I say, grabbing another tissue from the box.

"Everyone needs a good cry now and then. You hungry? I just finished some spaghetti for dinner. Join me?"

"I'm not that hungry, but thank you."

"Nope. You're staying here, you eat with me. I hate to eat alone, and since I just told my date for the night to stay home, you're next in line."

"I'm sorry." I hang my head. *How did everything get so screwed up?*

"Eat. That's the only apology I need."

Nodding, I stand and follow her into the kitchen. "You know, I don't agree with them keeping that from you all these years, but I really do believe their hearts were in the right place."

"They lied to me."

"Did they? I mean, it seems to me they cared so much about you that they wanted you to be happy. They all know that you two being together is what's going to make you both happy."

"And you know this how?"

She shrugs. "Dylan, mostly."

"Dylan? Not you too."

She holds her hands up in surrender. "No, but I've spent some time with him, when he and Alan are going over plays."

"Plays?"

"Shit," she whispers.

"What else am I missing?" I close my eyes and wait for the blow.

"Dylan is your brother's assistant coach."

"How did I not know this?"

"My guess is everyone thought they were protecting you."

"By lying?"

"Not lying, withholding information. None of them have actually lied to you, at least not from the details I've been given."

My phone vibrates with a text. Glancing down at the screen, I see it's from Dylan. I ignore it and go back to my plate of spaghetti.

"You're not going to answer him?"

"Why should I?"

"Let me ask you this. What if the roles were reversed? What if Dylan had the full ride and wanted to give it up for you? What if you found out he was just given information about how you kept up with his football career and even went to a few games when he thought you ended things and never looked back?"

"That's not what happened."

"Humor me. What if?"

"It's a free country. I can go see a football game," I say stubbornly.

"It is," she agrees. "Same goes for plays, right?"

Shit. "They kept it from me."

"Look, Avery. I've been through some things." She pauses taking a deep breath. "I was almost raped my freshman year of college. It was just me and my grandfather, who didn't get around real well. I didn't have a Dylan or an Alan." She smiles softly. "I had no one to turn to. No one who was worried enough about me to watch over me. No one who was physically able, anyway."

"Kara, oh my God. Are you okay?" I look over her like I'll be able to see physical signs of her abuse.

"I'm fine. A janitor for the school heard a noise and decided to check it out. He saved me. I didn't tell you this so you would feel sorry for me. That's the hand I was dealt, and it could've been so much worse than what it was. I still have a hard time sleeping, and I don't like being out at dark on my own. Alan has been amazingly patient with me. I just want you to know that there are worse things, you know? Yeah, Dylan kept tabs on you with the help of your friends and family, but think about that for a minute. Look past the anger and the betrayal that you're feeling and really think about it. That's a love so deep it never fades, Avery. Sometimes in life you have to let go of the past in order to see the future clearly."

I close my eyes and let her words sink in.

"When you see your future, not the one you've planned the last four years but the future you see when you close your eyes and dream of happiness, what do you see?"

"Dylan." I don't even hesitate. "I've always seen Dylan."

"I think you have your answer."

"I agreed to take it slow, you know. Just one day at a time. We even went out on Saturday, but then today…"

"Today, your world tilted a little, but it's up to you to put it back right. You choose, Avery. You say Dylan is what you see. Are you willing to put in the time and the work to see if you two have what it takes?"

"I still love him," I confess. Admitting it out loud seems to bring clarity to the situation.

"Then fight for him. Fight for love. Stick with the plan and see where it takes you."

Standing from my chair, I walk to the other side of the table and give her a hug. "Thank you, Kara. I needed to hear all of that."

"Kind of my job." She smiles.

My face falls. Of course. She's a social worker.

"Not what I mean, Avery. I love your brother. He's my only family at this point, though I hope one day that changes and I can add you and your parents to that list. Maybe even Dylan?" she winks.

I can't help but smile at her. She's right. I need to let the anger go and move forward.

I want Dylan. I need to keep an open mind and see where our love can take us.

Chapter 34

Dylan

It's almost midnight and I still haven't heard from her. Alan called me about an hour ago and told me that she's staying at Kara's. I had my keys in hand and one foot out the door when he specifically told me not to go over there. Avery just requested some time. I know she deserves that much, but this is not how I wanted her to find out. I should be pissed at Harley, but I can't be. I was going to tell her, I just wanted us to be on a little more solid ground before I did. I decide to send her one more text for the night, then leave her alone until tomorrow.

> **Me:** Hey, Aves. I'm sorry I didn't tell you. I couldn't let you go. I love you.
>
> Please call me.

I hit Send and wait. I stare at the screen, willing her to reply, but nothing happens. I toss my phone beside me on the bed and close my eyes. All I can see is her. She's all I've ever seen, and now I may lose her all over again before I even really get her back.

Just as I start to drift off to sleep, my phone alerts me to a message. I pat the bed until I find it. Tapping the screen, I see it's after two in the morning and the message is from Avery.

Avery: We'll talk soon.

I stare at the screen. The message is cryptic, and I have no way of knowing what she's thinking or how she's feeling.

Me: Good night, beautiful.

I can see that she read the message, but there's no reply. Plugging my phone in, I set it on the nightstand to be sure not to miss her when she does call or text. I'll be ready for her.

I toss and turn all night, restless sleep. I checked my phone at least twenty times just to make sure I didn't miss a message from her. I have this sick feeling in the pit of my stomach that this is the end for us. I can't deal with even the idea of that. I can only hope she hears me out.

After a quick shower and a bowl of cereal, I head to the shop. We have a busy day today and I'm grateful; I need something to keep my mind occupied. Before I get started, I pull out my phone and send her another text.

Me: Good morning. Can we get together and talk sometime today?

I don't wait for a reply before sliding the phone back in my pocket and getting to work. The morning creeps by as thoughts of what I should've done drift through my mind. The first time I lost her, that was me giving her every opportunity she deserves. This time, if I lose her, I have no one to blame but myself.

It's a little after eleven and I just finished pulling the engine from the Camaro we're doing a swap on when Dad calls my name.

Looking up, I see him smiling. "You have a visitor." I don't see her at first, not until she steps out from behind my dad. "You finished there?" He points to the Camaro.

"Yeah."

"Why don't you kids take the rest of the day? New engine won't be here until tomorrow," he says over his shoulder as he heads to his office.

I slowly make my way toward her. "I'm sorry."

"You think we could go somewhere and talk?"

"The roof?"

"No."

"Okay, I know a place. You want to ride with me?"

"I'll follow you."

It's not what I wanted her to say, but I'll take baby steps. She's at least going to talk to me. She's either willing to listen to what I have to say or she's going to tell me to stay away from her. Let's hope for option number one. "Okay. Let me go clean up. Give me five minutes?"

"Yeah." She points to the parking lot. "I'll just be out in my car."

I reach out to touch her and she steps back. My heart drops. "I'll be quick." I drop my hand and head to the bathroom to wash off the grease and grab a new shop shirt from dad's office. At least I won't be covered in grease.

It takes longer than I thought to scrub off all the grease, and then I had to dig through a box of Knight Automotive shirts to find my size. Dad sits quietly and watches me.

"Dylan," he calls out, stopping me as I reach the door.

Turning, I release a sigh of frustration. He could've said what he had to say while I was digging in the damn box. "What?"

"If you want any kind of future with that girl, you need to come clean about all of it. Don't hold back, son, or you're going to lose her for good."

"Noted," I say, turning and walking out the door. Avery is sitting in her SUV, which is parked next to my truck. I stop next to her window. "I was thinking we could go to the house." I hold my breath as I wait for her reaction. She doesn't respond. "It's quiet and will be just the two of us."

"I don't think that's a good idea. I'll meet you at the park." She doesn't wait for me to reply before she backs out of the lot.

"Fuck!" I scream, kicking the tire of my truck. I rest my elbows on the bedrail and run my fingers through my hair. That sick feeling is even more prominent now. I've lost her. "Fucking jackass," I mutter to myself.

Pushing off the bed, I climb into the truck and head toward the park, the entire time saying a silent prayer that this isn't the end of us.

She's parked under a shade tree, a picnic table in front of her SUV. I park my truck next to her and take my time climbing out. I take a seat across from her and fight the urge to grab her hands and hold them, to hold her. My heart is breaking from the sad look on her face. The tables are turned; now I know how she felt.

"Dylan—"

"Wait. Just… Can I go first?" I ask, panicked that I won't get to explain before she tells me to never contact her again.

"Okay."

I swallow hard. "That day, when I told you that we had to end, that was the worst day of my life. I tore my own heart out. I held strong all summer, keeping up with you through Brad and your brother. You see, I went to him that day. I knew you would need someone and that I couldn't be that someone. All I ever wanted was for you to live the life you dreamed of, to be roommates with your best friend, go to the college of your dreams. It killed me to think that you might give any of that up for me. I'm just this regular guy who already has his future planned out as a mechanic in this small town. I was never good enough for you."

"Do you hear what you're saying, Dylan? Do you actually hear yourself? You think I cared what your career was going to be? No, I cared that you had one, one you loved and were passionate about. Dreams change, Dylan. Mine changed the minute you told me you loved me for the first time." She wipes a tear from her eye.

I don't acknowledge that. I don't know how much time I have and I have to get through this. "That summer, I did okay. I knew you were here in town and I was able to catch glimpses of you here and there. I was coping, or so I thought. The day you left, it took me about ten minutes to panic. My heart was gone. I called Alan and begged him to keep me posted on how you were doing. He must've been worried, because he convinced me to go fishing with him and your dad. That day they assured me they would let me know how you were, and we sort of started making it a tradition. We've done that several times over the last four years. My dad would even come with when he could."

"Wow." She shakes her head. "How did I never find out?"

"I didn't want you to know. You see, I pushed you to go to Western, but then I was the one who couldn't deal with the choice I made. I would like to think that if I knew we were still together, I would've handled it a little better, but I don't really know."

"So, what? You came to Western to spy on me? Is that what happened?"

"Not to spy on you, Aves. Just to see you. Seeing you living your dream, it helped the ache in my chest. It only happened a few times each year. Freshman year, I would go to Brad's games and I would see you there. I stayed in the shadows, but it was easy to spot you. With your golden blonde hair, I could pick you out of a crowd of a million. Sophomore year, it was more football home games and then that play you were in. I swear I cheered so loud for you, I couldn't talk the next day."

"So you caught a glimpse of me at a few football games and a play? Harley said you were there for the teaching award ceremony."

"Yeah, I was so fucking proud of you. I told everyone around me who would listen too."

"Thanks," she whispers.

She's not running away, so I push on. I plan to tell her everything right here so we can move forward. "Then your junior year, Brad and Harley came home for a week and you stayed behind. I almost lost my shit on Brad, and then he told me if I was so damn worried, I could stay at his place and keep lookout. Of course, I readily agreed, but I had to get Harley on board. I begged her to tell me where you were each night. She agreed as long as it was within reason. I also had to agree that if you were with another guy I couldn't interfere. I had to leave you be, as long as you were safe."

"You kept your distance." I'm not sure if this is her theory or if she's asking a question.

"I did, until the last night. You were at a bar with a group of friends, at least that's what Harley told me. I stayed hidden at a back booth, never taking my eyes off you. I watched you down drink after drink. I wanted to stop you, cut you off, but I promised Harley that I wouldn't interfere. You were stumbling, and I knew you were way past your limit of being able to make clear decisions, but I sat back and watched. You disappeared into the hallway with a few of the girls you were with. I watched, waited, but you never came out. When they finally emerged without you, I sprang into action. There was a guy with a girl pressed against the wall at the back end of the hallway. I knew it was you without even seeing you. I felt it here." I place my hand over my heart. "He was kissing your neck, his hand resting on the waistband of your shorts. As I got closer, I could see your eyes were closed and you were just kind of there. I knew it was the alcohol. You hadn't given him permission to touch you—he was taking it."

"I don't remember," she says sadly.

"You were gone, Aves. I mean, you were practically comatose. I pulled the guy off you. He raised his fist, but I was faster. His drunk ass fell to the floor. I picked you up and carried you out. Luckily, Brad had a key to your place on his key ring. I took you home, made you drink some water and take some headache medicine." I take a break before I tell her the rest. "You thought you were dreaming, Aves. You told me that dream Dylan was so much like the real thing, you begged me to stay. You told me you loved me and that the only time you could see me was in your dreams."

"I dreamed about you all the time," she confesses.

"I was torn. I made a promise to Harley and to you. I stayed just long enough to know you were going to be okay. That you were going to be able to sleep it off. I knew you had one more year left, and I hoped that you would come home after. I told myself that I would be ready to fight for you when you came back." Reaching out, I take her hands in mine. She lets me. "I came home and the next week the house came up for sale. I didn't hesitate to put in an offer. I put the rest of my focus on finishing up my degree, wanting to be someone you could be proud of. I wanted to build you a life to come home to."

Chapter 35

Avery

My mind is racing as I try to process everything he's told me. He took care of me, saved me. When I think of it like that, it's hard to stay mad. His love for me protected me, even if I didn't know it.

"Are you ready?" I ask him.

"For what?" He keeps his head down.

"The fight."

His head shoots up. "For the rest of my life, Avery. I will fight with you, because of you, for you."

"Is there anything else?"

"No, that's it." He pauses. "Wait! I'm the assistant football coach at the high school."

"Kara might have mentioned that."

"Alan, he kept me in line and when the position came open, he insisted I was the best man for the job."

"I agree with him."

"Yeah?"

I nod. We're both silent. I'm sure he's thinking the worst after all of that, so I decide to put it out there and see what he thinks. "I still like the plan of taking things slow. I like the idea of getting to know each other. Of falling in love with you all over again."

He stands and leans over the picnic table, takes my face in his hands, and kisses me. "I love you, Avery Stanton. I want to spend my life falling in love with you every single fucking day."

"The past is the past. Today we're moving forward."

"I'll never forget the past because it brought us to this point. I've loved you for every minute of the last five years."

My heart swells with his confession. I love him now—I never stopped—but I'm not ready to tell him that yet. I want to see if this love is as strong or, if we're lucky, stronger than it was back then. We need time to let that happen. "I should let you get back to work."

"I'm off the rest of the day, remember?"

"That's right." I laugh.

"How about dinner and a movie?"

I smile. "Yeah, I think that sounds great."

"I'll pick you up at seven?"

"That works. I stayed at Kara's last night, so I need to grab my things and then head back to Mom and Dad's."

"I've got a date to plan." He stands and offers me his hand.

This time I take it with zero hesitation. I feel lighter somehow. "I'll see you soon?"

"Be safe, babe." He opens the door and waits for me to buckle up before closing me in and tapping the roof.

I pull away with a smile on my face. Glancing in my rearview mirror, I see him watching me, wearing a matching grin.

I take the long route to Kara's and drive past Brad's parents.' When I see Harley's car in the drive, I take that as a sign and stop. She meets me at the door, a look of sorrow on her face. "You got a minute?"

"Always," she says, taking a seat on the porch swing.

"I'm sorry I ran like that yesterday. I was… a little of everything. Mad, hurt, sad… I just didn't know how to process it all."

"And today?"

"Today is a new day. I talked to Kara last night and she helped me see a few things. I just left Dylan a few minutes ago. We talked about everything." I take a seat next to her on the swing.

"How did that go?" she asks hesitantly.

"It's hard to stay mad at a guy who saves you like that."

"I would say it would be. I can still remember that night, Av. He called us at three in the morning and he was freaking out. He was pissed, wanted to go hunt the guy down, but even he knew he was just some drunken frat boy. He insisted we get home ASAP to check on you. Not that he needed to, because as soon as we heard, we were making plans to come back early. We were all three worried sick about you." She pauses to collect her thoughts. "I'm sorry too. I shouldn't have helped him, but Avery, if you had seen him you would've done the same thing. Selfishly, I wanted you to stay at school. I needed my best friend. It wasn't until that night, the fear in his voice, that I knew I should come clean. Brad convinced me to let it ride another year. I did, but now with you both back in the same town, I know how you each feel for the other and I just want you to be happy."

"We're working on it."

"What does that mean?" She turns to face me on the swing.

"It means that Dylan and I are dating. We're moving forward to see if what we think we feel is still there, if that love is just as strong."

She laughs. "You both know it is."

I smile. "Maybe, but we need this time. Time to grow and get to know each other again. A lot changes in four years."

"It's a good plan, but you need to hurry. I want our babies to grow up together."

"Wait, are you…?"

"No. But we don't want to wait a long time. Brad started at the bank last week, and we're going to start looking for a house. We want to be young parents."

"I can't even think about that right now."

"Sure you can. You know you're going to have fun practicing."

"Baby steps," I tell her.

"Exactly!" she says, and we both laugh. "I'm sorry, Av."

"Me too." I reach over and give her a hug. "Okay, I'm off to Kara's to get my stuff and then to Mom and Dad's. That reminds me." I pull out my phone and text Alan, asking him to meet me there. "I have to make this quick, I have a date tonight."

"Does this mean we can double?"

"You're an old married woman now, you date?" I tease her.

"You got jokes." She grins. "I'll have the guys set it up."

"Sounds good." I stand and give her one more hug before saying goodbye.

I swing by Kara's and gather my stuff, leaving her a note thanking her and promising to return her clothes. I leave the key she gave me this morning sitting beside the letter, then send her a text when I get in the car.

> **Me:** Thank you for a place to stay and the talk. You helped me so much.
>
> **Kara:** You're welcome. Stay as long as you want.
>
> **Me:** I'm going back to Mom and Dads.' A lot has happened today. Alan can fill you in or we can catch up tomorrow when you get off work. I have a date tonight.
>
> **Kara:** Dylan?
>
> **Me:** Yep!
>
> **Kara:** I'm happy for you, and yes, we need to catch up. Alan will leave out the important stuff.
>
> **Me:** LOL. Sounds good. Thanks again.

When I get to my parents,' Alan's truck is in the driveway. *Good, I get three for one.* Walking through the door, I find the three of them sitting at the dining room table. I take a seat at the opposite end of the table and wait. No one says a word.

"Look. I talked to Dylan today and he filled me in. I get why you did it, but I still think it was wrong."

"Av," my dad starts, but I hold up my hand to stop him.

"Let me finish." I look at Alan. "Kara and I talked a lot last night." I can tell he knows what I mean. "She helped me understand that, although it was wrong to keep me in the dark, I'm lucky to have all of you. Then today, Dylan and I talked, and we're moving forward."

"What does that mean exactly?" Mom asks.

"We're dating. Taking it slow." All three of them audibly sigh and relax in their seats. "What?"

"You two…" Dad shakes his head.

"What your father is trying to say is we're happy for you and we'll stay out of it from here on out."

Dad turns to look at her and she gives him a pointed look. He nods in defeat. I have to bite my lip to keep from laughing. "No more secrets, with any of us." I make eye contact with each of them as they nod their agreement. "Now if you'll excuse me, I'm wearing Kara's clothes. I need a hot shower and my own wardrobe to get ready for my date tonight."

Chapter 36

Dylan

"Dinner and a movie." Avery smiles when we pull into the back of the shop.

"That's how we do it." I smile back at her. Reaching over and grabbing her hand, threading our fingers together, I pull her into the middle of the seat. She laughs and I close my eyes, just soaking up the sound. "Missed this."

"Me too."

Keeping her hand in mine, I climb out of the truck, guiding her to follow me. She climbs out of my side and I push her up against the truck. "I need some help," I tell her.

"Oh yeah?"

"Uh-huh." I lean in closer. "You said slow. I can do slow, but I need to know, can I kiss you? Can I hold you? What's off-limits, Aves? I don't want to chance screwing this up.

Standing on her tiptoes, she presses a kiss to my lips. "Yes to kissing," she says, dropping back to her feet. She wraps her arms around my waist and hugs me tight. "Yes to holding."

I bury my face in her hair and breathe her in. "Deal. When you're ready for more, you let me know."

"You sound awful sure of yourself."

"The one thing in this world that I'm sure of is how much I love you. Everything else will just fall into place."

"So cocky," she teases.

"Come on, you." I pull on her hand and lead us into the shop, then up to the roof.

"No pizza?" She smirks.

"I thought maybe we've graduated from that. I was thinking we could order Chinese."

"Perfect." A smile lights up her face when she spots the DVD lying on the table. She picks it up and shows it to me, like I didn't already know it was there.

"Sticking with the tradition, huh?"

I shrug. "I've never seen it." I'm referring to the second *Hunger Games* movie. "I bought them all if we decide to make it a late night."

"You've never seen it?"

"No. I didn't want to watch it without you."

"Dylan." She shakes her head in amazement.

Pulling out my phone, I dial the new Chinese restaurant in town, then hand it to her. "Just order two of whatever you want and give them the shop name. They deliver our lunch frequently."

She takes the phone and orders for us. "How will we know when they're here?"

"Good point. We should probably go downstairs and wait on them." I offer her my hand, which she takes, making me feel ten feet tall and bulletproof.

I decide to use this time to show her a little about the shop; I never thought to do that when we were kids. "Let me give you the tour." I lead her to the front of the building. "This is what I guess you could call reception. People can wait if it's a simple fix, like tires or an oil change." We take a few more steps. "Out there is the garage. That's where all the magic happens." I wag my eyebrows at her, making her laugh. "Down this hall are the offices, the bathroom, and the break room."

"So how many people do you have working for you?"

"Six not counting Dad and me."

"That's great, Dylan. I'm so proud of you," she says, placing her hand on the arm that's already holding her other hand and leaning in to me. "Can I see your office?"

I lead her down the hall and push open the door. For a mechanic shop, it's pretty clean. My associate's degree hangs proudly behind my desk. I watch as she walks around the desk and takes a seat in my chair. I know the minute she sees them, the pictures of her, of us.

"How long have these been here?"

"Since the day I pushed you away."

I watch her reaction. She smiles, the corner of her lip tipping up in a shy smile as she stands from the chair. "Come here." She waves me over, and like a moth to a flame, I follow her. She pushes me toward the chair and I fall willingly. "We're alone, right?"

"Just us." The next thing I know she's climbing on my lap, straddling my hips. Reaching out, I rest my hands on her waist to steady her. "How many women have you brought back here?"

"None."

She raises her eyebrows. "You can tell me."

"I just did. None. I'm not going to lie and say there was no one else. I've had my drunken regrets when the sorrow of missing you got too bad, but no one has been here, or in my bed. Hell, not even at my house."

That must be what she wants to hear because she leans in and kisses me. I let her set the pace—I'm good with any pace, actually. Her lips are on mine, and she's on my lap. I'm pretty much in heaven right now. "What about you?" I ask once she pulls away for air.

"There were a few, and alcohol was involved, but I knew what I was doing. I was trying to get over you."

"How did that work out for you?"

"It did the opposite, really. I compared them to you."

Tilting my head up, I kiss her. "I don't want to hear anymore," I say against her lips. "You're here, you're mine, and that's all that matters."

"Yours, huh?" she asks, wearing a flirty grin.

"Mine." I kiss her hard. She rocks her hips against me and I moan at the contact just as there's a loud knock at the outside door.

"Food's here." She laughs, hops off my lap, and runs to the front door.

I adjust my hard cock that can't be hidden and rush after her to pay the bill.

Once we've stuffed our faces, we head back up to the roof for our movie. Avery is standing beside the couch with our blanket. "You first," she says. I take a seat on the couch. "Can we lie down?" Her question is almost shy.

Doesn't she know yet? I would give her anything. I stretch out on my side and pat the spot in front of me. Avery lowers her body next to mine and curls up with the blanket in her arms. Resting my hand on her hip, I pull her close. "This okay?" I ask, snuggling into her.

"Yeah, it's not as hot now that the sun has gone down."

"You might actually need that blanket depending on how long we stay out here."

"I thought that's what I had you for?" she asks, not taking her eyes off the TV.

"You have me, Aves. Any way you want me, you have me." I kiss the back of her head and settle in.

It's not lost on me that I've waited to watch part two of this movie with her and that we're now getting our part two. I can only hope that ours never ends.

Chapter 37

Avery

"Look at us, all grown up." Harley laughs. The four of us are sitting in a booth at the local steakhouse for group date night. "Oh, did we tell you we found a house?"

"Really? That's great." Dylan places his hand on my leg and gives it a gentle squeeze. I can only assume it's because we have our house. Well he has a house. My dream house.

"Where is it?" Dylan asks, taking a sip of water.

"Not far from your shop. You know that two-story green one, burgundy shutters?" Brad asks Dylan.

"I do. Nice place. Have you looked at it?"

"We did." Harley practically squeals with excitement.

"I take it that went well?" I laugh.

"You have to see it." She turns to Brad. "Babe, can we take them to see it?"

"Did you put in an offer?" Dylan asks.

Brad grins. "Yeah, we're just waiting to hear back." He turns to his wife. "Call the realtor and see if she can get us in to look at it again."

"Can you do it tomorrow?" she asks, already pulling out her phone, fingers flying across the keys.

"Harls, it's Friday night," Brad reminds her.

"She's in real estate. You work when the buyers are available." He just smiles and shakes his head. I can see he's just as excited as she is.

"It's pretty similar to yours. Full basement, four bedrooms. I think your detached garage and yard are a little bigger," Brad tells Dylan.

"You've seen it?" I ask him.

He looks at Dylan for guidance. Dylan nods. "Yeah, he showed it to us after he bought it."

I look over at Harley and she looks guilty. "If it's any consolation, you're going to love it."

I let that sink in. Dylan bought a house, for us. He's paying for this beautiful home that he refuses to live in or even change until I put my two cents in. It's been a month since we had our heart-to-heart and put everything out on the table. It took me until the end of that first movie night to know I still love him just as strongly as I ever did. The heart knows no distance.

I knew when I suggested it that I loved him wholeheartedly. I just wanted some time to reassure myself. I haven't told him yet. Things are great between us and I don't want to ruin it by going too fast. This time, I want us to be forever.

"She said tomorrow works. How's noon?" Harley asks us.

"Babe?" Dylan turns to me.

"It's your day off," I tell him.

Leaning in, he whispers just for me, "As long as I'm with you, we could be watching paint dry."

The melting, tingling feeling I get when he says things like that rushes through me. "Yeah, that works for us," I tell Harley.

"Where to now?" I ask Dylan as we pull out of the restaurant after saying goodbye to Brad and Harley.

"I told Brad we would come back to their place. You okay with that?"

"I am. I'm surprised Harley didn't mention it."

"I don't think she knows," he says cryptically.

"What are you up to?" I turn in my seat to face him. It's dark, but the low glow from the dashboard illuminates his features just enough. He's grinning.

"Nostalgia."

I don't push him for more, just reach over and rest my hand on his lap. He threads his fingers through mine and we drive the rest of the way in comfortable silence. When we reach Brad's and we keep driving, I know what we're doing. I don't speak until we round the corner of the tree line hiding the big open field. I see Brad's truck parked in the back corner and can't contain the grin that crosses my face. Dylan parks in the opposite corner from Brad and kills the engine.

"Hold tight." He leans in for a quick kiss and climbs out of the truck. Turning in my seat, I watch as he grabs blankets from the back seat and lays them out in the bed of the truck.

Opening the driver door, he motions for me to come to him. I do without hesitation. "You look beautiful in the moonlight." He presses a gentle kiss to my lips.

"Aren't we a little old for this?" I tease him.

"Hey, they're"—he points over my shoulder—"the old married couple."

"True story." I wrap my legs around his waist and my arms around his neck, and he lifts me from the truck. "Well, you got me here, Dylan Knight. What are you going to do with me?"

He squeezes my thighs and I squeal, the sound echoing into the night. I clamp my mouth shut, afraid of getting caught.

"We're not kids anymore, Aves." He sits me on the tailgate and kisses me breathless. "Crawl on back." He motions with his head to the makeshift bed behind us. Kicking off my shoes, I set them off to the side and settle back on the soft bed of blankets and pillows.

"Let's see, what am I going to do with you?" His hand trails up my bare leg, stopping at my shorts. He pulls away, then makes the same slow ascent up the other. "I could slide under here." The top of his finger runs under the hem of my shorts. "What do you think, Aves?"

"Hmm." I'm lying back, hands in his hair while he begins his slow torture that I've come to love over the past month of us being back together.

Dylan removes his hand from my shorts. I'm just about to protest when I feel his callused fingers on my belly. Slowly, at a speed only Dylan can master, he traces up my left side, running his finger under the swell of my breast within my bra.

"We should take that off," I say, my voice husky with want for him.

"You think so?"

"Definitely."

He chuckles softly but helps me sit up. I perform a magician act, removing my bra but leaving my shirt on. I toss it beside us and lie back on the pillows. "I think you should rewind and repeat."

"I like the way you think." His hand snakes under my shirt with the same slow, torturous ascent until he reaches my now bare breasts, running his index finger under one and then the other. "So soft," he murmurs.

Closing my eyes, I just feel. I enjoy his hands on me, the spark that seems to zip between us every time we touch. It's just like I remember.

"Need to see you, all of you, in the moonlight."

"Anything," I whisper, my eyes still closed as I focus on his touch.

I feel his weight shift and then both hands are on my ribs as he slides my shirt up and over my head. "Fuck," he hisses. His lips close over a nipple while he pinches and rolls the other at the same time. The act sends warmth rushing through me. "Dylan." His name is a plea falling from my lips. It doesn't seem to faze him as he sucks and nips, driving me wild.

"What, baby?" he asks, lifting his head.

"You know what." I grin at him.

"This?" He switches sides and sucks my other nipple into his mouth, giving it equal attention as his fingers play with the one his mouth was just on.

"That works," I pant.

He chuckles, my nipple still in his mouth. "What about this?" He lifts his eyes to meet mine. Propping himself up on one elbow, the other hand unsnaps my shorts. Deftly his large hand slides under my panties. "For me?" he asks when he feels how wet I am.

I don't respond, too lost in the feel of his fingers driving me wild. When his mouth latches onto a nipple, I raise my hips trying to get closer. The sensation of him sucking my sensitive nipple and the rhythm he's set with his fingers as he pushes in and out is almost too much. Grabbing his arm, I hold on tight. "Don't stop," I plead.

He hums against my breast, causing an all-new sensation to rush through me, pushing me over the edge of orgasmic bliss.

"Welcome back," he says, leaning in for a kiss.

I have no idea how long I checked out, but I feel relaxed. Relaxed, happy, and in love. Only Dylan has ever made me feel this way. One hand in his hair, I run my fingers through it. He drops his head, making it easier for me to reach; he claims to love it when I run my fingers through his hair. My other hand sneaks down to the waist of his cargo shorts. I get the button undone before he stops me.

"Not tonight."

"I want to," I tell him honestly.

"Tonight is about you."

"Dylan, it's been all about me the last month. The last time I looked, there were two of us in this relationship."

"There are, but I can't feel your lips on my cock, Aves."

I must look confused as hell because he releases a heavy sigh, then explains.

"Avery, I ache for you. My cock goes hard as stone just from the sound of your voice."

"All the more reason you should let me." I try again, but he grabs my arm to stop me.

"The next time I come, I'm going to be inside you. I've used my hand for four years with the memories I have of us. I want to know the next time my cock gets relief, it's because you love me again. I want to know that from that day forward, it's only ever going to be you."

I try hard to stop the tears but they seem to fall anyway. "Dylan, I—"

Leaning in, he kisses me softly. "Shh, not tonight. Not because of what we've shared or words I've said. I want it to be on your terms. I'm not going anywhere, Avery." With one more soft kiss, he rolls over on his back and tugs me into his arms, pulling one of the blankets over me to ward off the chill of the late-night air. We lie there looking up at the night sky, just enjoying being in each other's arms.

"Are they leaving?" I see headlights coming toward us. I squirm, needing to at least put my shirt back on, but Dylan tightens his hold on me.

"The old married couple can't hang." He laughs. "We're good here. They're not going to stop."

"We can't stay here, what about his parents?" I ask panic in my voice.

"Aves, baby, we're adults now. Nothing to be worried about."

I let his words sink in and relax against him. "This feels so much like then, you know?"

"I do, but this time it's better. This time, no matter what you throw at me, I'm never leaving your side."

He kisses the top of my head. Closing my eyes tight, I fight tears for the second time tonight.

Chapter 38

Dylan

Tonight's the first home game of the season. Alan and I have been working with the team since early July, memorizing plays and strategy. We're ready; we have a great team this year, good group of kids. Reminds me a lot of when Brad and I played. This is my third season with the team and I'm amped up about the fact that my girl will be in the stands. Takes me back.

"Coach, hottie, five o'clock," Cody, our quarterback says.

"Dude, Ms. Stanton is—" Brian doesn't get to finish that sentence because I slap him on the back of the head.

"That's Coach Stanton's little sister, asswipe." Cody shakes his head like he himself didn't just refer to her at a hottie.

"She's more than that, boys," I tell them. Their eyes lock on me, waiting to hear my remark about how fucking gorgeous she is. "She's mine."

At first they look as though I've lost my mind. When Avery steps beside me, she links her arm with mine and rests her head on my shoulder.

"Good luck, babe," she says. Her voice is soft but Cody and Brian hear her.

"Coach Knight, give me some." Brian holds up his hand for a high five.

As their coach, I have to be a professional role model, so I bring it in for five and a fist bump with Cody.

Avery chuckles beside me. "I'm going to say hello to Alan and then head up to the stands. I'll see you after. Gentlemen," she addresses my two players, her students who are still drooling over her. "Good luck tonight. Let's bring home a win."

I hold back my laughter as the two of them fall all over themselves to promise her a win. My girl has that effect on people.

Avery untangles her arm from mine, but I stop her. Bending down, I give her a chaste kiss. "Love you, Aves."

Her face lights up just like it does every time I tell her. I started telling her as often as I could a couple of weeks ago. I couldn't hold it in anymore. I can tell she wants to say it but she's scared. I get that, and I'm good with it. As long as she knows how much I love her, that's all that matters. I know where her heart is. She'll tell me when she's ready.

"All right, fellas, let's do this," I rally the troops. Alan joins us a few minutes later, gives his pregame speech, and we hit the field. The stands are packed and the student body—hell, the entire town—came out to support the team. I only care about one spectator. Avery. I smile up at her and she waves. Win or lose the game, I got the girl.

"Good game, Coach," I tell Alan a few hours later as we sit in his office. We took home the win, 32–7. The last player just left, so we can finally lock up. "You and Kara going to celebrate?" He winks. "Right." I laugh. "You going to dust the cobwebs off the diamond tonight?" He confessed several months ago that he bought a ring for Kara. I've been waiting for the announcement that has yet to come about their engagement.

"Me? What about you? You bought a house and she was back in town, what, a week or two before you bought a ring?"

"Three weeks. It was after Brad and Harley's wedding."

"I think yours has more cobwebs than mine."

"You got me there," I concede.

"So?"

"When she's ready."

"Exactly. I keep it close so when the moment happens, I'll be ready."

"You don't have some big elaborate plans?"

"Damn it, if you tell her," he warns me.

I throw my head back in laughter. "Why would I tell her?"

He runs his hands through his hair. "Fuck, I'm nervous as hell. I know she's ready, but what if I'm wrong and she says no."

"Does she tell you she loves you?"

He gives me an "are you crazy" look. "Yes."

"Do you believe her? Do you love her."

"Yes, more than anything."

"Then do it. You can bet your ass, the day I know your sister's ready, I'm dropping to one knee."

"She's ready," he tells me.

"She's getting there. I'm not pushing her. I know where I stand."

"Where's that?"

"Beside her. Always."

"I approve." He laughs.

"You coming?" I ask, standing from the chair across from his desk. "They're waiting."

"Finally. I didn't think you'd ever shut the hell up. I'm starving." He slaps me on the shoulder, laughing as he walks ahead of me.

Alan and I have become close the last four years. I look to him as an older brother. One day soon, he will be. Makes me sound like a chick, but I couldn't care less. I consider myself lucky that we have her family's support as well as my father's. Makes life easier, although she's it for me regardless of what they think.

I follow Alan out of the locker room and sure enough, his family and Kara are standing on the sidewalk waiting for us. In years past, this was always how it happened, unless Aves was home. We would all go out together. Tonight, it's different. Better. She's here and she's smiling at me. I keep my eyes locked on hers as I step in front of her.

"Woo-hoo!" she cheers, throwing her arms around my neck. I bury my face in hers and wrap my arms around her. Tonight it's better. Everything is better with Avery back in my life.

"I love you," I whisper, kissing her neck before lifting my head and helping her settle back onto her feet, on solid ground. I keep my arm wrapped tight around her waist.

"You hungry?" She looks up at me.

"For you," I mouth. Even in the dim lighting of the streetlamps from the parking lot I can see her blush.

"Come on, you." She takes me by the hand and leads me to her car. "Good game, Coach," she says once we're on our way to the restaurant.

"Thanks, babe. I'm glad you were there," I say, resting my hand on her thigh. Her lips tilt up in a smile. She's happy that's all I've ever wanted.

"So I think Alan is going to propose," she blurts when we pull into the parking lot of the local steakhouse.

"Oh yeah? What makes you think that?"

"I asked him the other day and he just grinned."

"So you think that means yes?"

"Of course it does."

"You think she'll say yes?"

"She loves him. She had it rough growing up. I'm glad she's going to be a part of our family."

Our family. I know she's not referring to me. Not yet anyway. "What about you? You think about marriage?"

That has her full attention. Pulling the keys from the ignition, she turns to face me. "Recently or in the past?"

"Both." I want to know it all.

"Yeah, I mean, back then I thought that would be our endgame, you know? After I finished college."

"And now?"

"Now? Now I'm still trying to process the fact that we're here sitting in this car together. It's as though I'm living a dream. So many times I wished for this, for you."

"And here we are." I bring her hand to my lips and kiss her knuckles.

"Here we are."

A loud knock comes at her window, causing us both to jump. Alan roars with laughter as he walks by. "Come on, you too!" he yells for us.

"I swear most of the time I feel like the oldest child." Avery shakes her head.

"Girls mature faster."

"Of course, take his side." She laughs as we climb out of the car.

"Who's taking sides?" Kara asks.

"No one." I laugh and pull Avery to me side.

"Where are you parents?" I ask Alan.

"They had to stop for gas. They'll be here." He gives me an odd look. I want to call him out on it, but that would be a dick move, so instead I hold my girl's hand while the hostess leads us to a very large table in the back.

"Seating for six," she says sweetly. We all take our seats. I pick up the menu and start looking it over.

"Can you believe her?" Kara asks.

"Right?" Avery agrees.

"What did I miss?" I ask them.

Avery just smiles and leans her head against my shoulder. "She was totally checking you both out with us right here."

"Baby, I don't see anyone but you." I kiss the top of her head.

"What he said," Alan tells Kara.

I study him and he seems nervous as hell. That's when it hits me— he's going to do it tonight. I sit up a little straighter in my chair. I need to take notes if he does it here.

The rest of the night, I keep a close eye on the situation without trying to be obvious. When Avery's dad pays the bill, even though I try to grab it first. Still no proposal. Maybe I was wrong.

"Alan was off all night. Has he said anything to you?" Avery asks in the car.

"Probably just thinking about the next game. Coach's job never ends."

"What about you? You seem fine."

"I'm the assistant coach, not as much pressure." I wait for her reply but it never comes. Her wheels are turning.

"You staying with me tonight?" I lean in for a kiss. I ask her all the time and she's yet to take me up on it. She doesn't want to stay under Dad's roof or her parents either. I've offered for us to go to our house, but she refuses. I've yet to get her there.

"We've talked about this."

"I know." I don't want to pressure her, but damn it's hard to leave her every night. "When is your first break from school?"

"Uh, Labor Day, I guess." She picks up her phone and scrolls through her calendar. "Yeah, we get a three-day weekend."

"Don't make plans."

"Oo-kay."

"You and me, three days." I kiss her again. "You good with that?" I ask, my lips hovering over hers.

"More than you know."

That gives me around three weeks to plan something. I need to get my ass in gear and make some calls.

Chapter
39

Avery

It's Friday afternoon and the bell just rang announcing the end of the school day. It's also the beginning of the three-day holiday weekend.

Dylan has plans for us. He's reminded me often over the last three weeks, not giving any hints. Well, I guess there is one hint—it's just going to be the two of us. When you think about it, that's not much of a hint, considering he told me that was his goal when we talked about it that first night.

"Hey, girl, you excited for this weekend?" Harley asks, stepping into my classroom.

"I am. I wish I knew what we were doing, but I'm excited to just spend some time with him."

"You're going to love it." She beams.

"He told you?"

She shrugs. "He told, Brad. That's telling me by association."

I laugh at her explanation. "I'll have to remember that in the future."

"While you're having this romantic getaway, I'll be painting." She says it likes it's going to be a pain in her ass, but the smile on her face tells me otherwise.

"You love it and you know it. When are you guys going to start moving in?"

"Hopefully after this. The closing took forever, and then they requested an extra thirty days to move. I didn't think we would ever get the keys."

"I'm excited for you. As soon as we get back, any help you need, just let me know."

"I will, thank you. This could be you, you know?"

"What? Staying home to paint your house?" I know what she means, but I like getting her worked up.

"Avery," she scolds me. "Dylan bought you your dream house and you have yet to step foot in it."

"I know." I sit down in my chair and sigh. "I just can't go in there and see the future I've always planned with him and then not get it. That would break me."

"Have you been sleepwalking through the past couple of months?" She's completely serious.

"No."

"Then you're an idiot. I love you, Aves, you know I do, but come on. He loves you. Dylan has never given up on you or his feelings for you. You know he's not going anywhere, unless you plan on leaving him?"

"No," I say firmly. "I love him. I admit that, at first, I was afraid it was all too good to be true and I wanted to wait and see how things went. Now it just feels like I should wait until we make things official, you know? Wait until we've made the decision to move in together."

"Are you mad that he bought it?"

"Not at all. I've always loved that house and he knew it. It's still hard for me to process it and believe it's real, Harls. Everything I ever wanted, or talked about wanting, he's making it happen. Every day he reminds me of something that we said or did back then, and I fall in love with him all over again."

"Have you told him?"

"Not yet. I'm going to do that this weekend."

"How have you held out for," she lowers her voice, "sex this long?"

I laugh. "It's been a struggle, for sure, but I'm also glad we waited, that we worked on us before adding in sex."

"So, this weekend?" She wags her eyebrows.

"God, I hope so," I admit.

She throws her head back and laughs. "Have fun, and be safe. I need to get going. I'm hoping we can knock out these couple of rooms we have to paint and then maybe move our bed and some clothes in so we can start staying there."

"You should go pick up an air mattress and surprise him. Have a little sleepover."

"I knew there was a reason I liked to keep you around."

"Good luck," I say, standing to give her a hug.

"You too." She waves over her shoulder.

I finish packing my bag after she leaves. I have a few tests to grade that will have to wait until Monday night. I'll have to make sure we're back in time; no way am I taking them with us wherever it is we're going.

"Ms. Stanton," I hear from my doorway. Looking up, I see Cody, one of my students and a player on the football team.

"Hi, Cody, what can I do for you?"

He pulls his hands from behind his back and hands me a single red rose. The other hand is holding an envelope. "Delivery from Coach." He grins.

"Thank you, Cody." I take them from him, sniffing the rose. "Where is he?"

He shrugs. "Don't know, he just told me to make sure you got these right after the last bell rang."

I just shake my head. "Well thank you. Enjoy your long weekend."

"Yep," he says before turning and walking away.

Carefully, I open the envelope.

Aves,

I can't wait to spend three entire nights with you in my arms. I'll be there to pick you up at four. I'll be the one in white.

I love you,

Dylan

I can't seem to help smiling when it comes to Dylan. He makes my heart happy. I think it's time I tell him. I grab my things and head home. I'm already packed for the weekend, so after a quick shower to wash away the day, I'll be ready to go. I might have an ulterior motive to shave every inch of skin. I need to be ready for him.

I'm sitting on the front porch like a teenager, just waiting on Dylan to show up. I'm the only one home, and I was going crazy watching through the window, so I brought my Kindle out to the porch swing. When a new white SUV pulls into the drive, I stand to greet whoever it is and tell them Mom and Dad aren't home. I stop in my tracks when I see Dylan climb out of the driver side.

"Dylan?" I say, surprised. "Did you rent a car for the trip?"

"Hey, baby." He snakes an arm around my waist, pulling me into him. "You ready?" he asks, pressing a kiss to my lips.

"Yes."

"I like that word from your lips." He kisses me again before releasing me and grabbing my bag. "Is this all you have?"

"Yes."

He grins. "Let's get this show on the road."

"You going to tell me where we're going?"

"Nope. Not yet. You'll know when we get there." He loads my bag in the back before opening my door for me. Leaning in, he steals another kiss before shutting my door.

"I love this car," I say as soon as he climbs in the passenger seat. "How long is this road trip?"

"Couple of hours."

I mess with the radio and find a country station, putting it on low. "How was your day?"

"Long as hell. All I could think about was getting to you to start our weekend together."

"Thank you for the rose, and the note." It hits me. "I guess you really did show up in white," I laugh at his description of the rental car.

"What's this button?" I ask as Dylan stops at the light in the center of town. I push it and the bumper of the car in front of us pops up on the screen. "No way, how cool is that?" That little discovery spurs me on push all the buttons and mess with all the gadgets. "We could've taken my car, saved the money on the rental, but this is pretty sweet. This is my dream car."

"About that," Dylan says.

"Uh-oh, that doesn't sound good."

"This isn't a rental."

I let his words sink in. "You bought this?"

"I did."

"Dylan, that's awesome. It was time for you to have a new vehicle. Although, I see you as more of a truck guy, not the SUV type."

"I am," he agrees.

"Then why did you buy a Tahoe? I mean, yeah, it's a truck, kind of, but you should've bought an actual truck."

"I'm going to. I actually found one that I like when I was there buying this one."

"Why do you need two vehicles? New ones, at that?"

"I don't. I bought this one for you."

"What? Dylan, that's crazy. You can't buy me a new car."

"Too late." He glances over at me and grins.

"I don't even know what to say right now."

"Say 'thank you, Dylan.'"

"Dylan, I can't accept this."

"Sure you can. I wanted you to have it. Besides, our last road trip, we took Brad's mom's and you said you wanted one, remember?"

"I do. Just because I said I wanted one years ago doesn't mean you go and buy me one. Who does that?"

"The man who loves you. I want you to have everything you've ever wanted, Avery. You're just going to have to accept that."

My mind is racing with this new discovery. He bought me a new fucking car! I remember every detail of that trip; it was where we had sex for the first time. Then it hits me. Turning in my seat as much as my seat belt allows, I look at him. "I know where we're going."

"You think so?"

"The cabin."

"That place holds good memories for us."

"I love you," I say with conviction. Not the most romantic place but it's the truth. "Not because of—what are you doing?" I ask as he signals and pulls off onto the side of the road. Once the car is in Park, he turns on the flashers, takes off his seat belt, and leans over the console.

His strong hands cup my face. "Say it again." His eyes are dark as they bore into mine.

"I love you."

He crashes his lips to mine, sucking on the bottom one. "Again," he says between kisses.

"I love you."

He kisses me hard before pulling away and resting his forehead against mine. "Avery." His voice cracks with emotion. "I wish…" He swallows hard. "I wish I could find the words to tell you how much I love you. I can't breathe without you."

"You just did," I say softly.

He kisses me again before sitting back in his seat. I don't take my eyes off him as he closes his eyes and slowly exhales. "I wasn't sure. I mean,

I knew you cared about me, but I wasn't sure I would ever hear those three words pass your lips when it comes to me."

That's when I take off my seat belt and mimic his earlier actions. I take it a step further and do what his big body isn't capable of, climbing over the console and straddling his lap as I cup his face. His eyes are locked on mine. "I love you." His big hands grip my hips. "I've always loved you, Dylan. You were my first and only love. I don't ever want that to change."

"Not as long as I'm breathing." Bringing my lips to his, I kiss him, slowly, only to be interrupted by the honking horn of a passing car. "We definitely need to get these front two windows tinted." He laughs.

"Agreed." Awkwardly I climb over the console and back into my seat. Dylan waits for me to get buckled back in before he pulls back on the highway. The rest of the drive is quiet, but comfortably so. I think we're both lost in our thoughts and feelings and the question of what it all means.

Chapter 40

Dylan

"I think we should stop for supplies now so we don't have to come back out if we don't want to."

I don't want to. I don't want to leave the bedroom once we reach the cabin. Sex or not, I need to feel her skin against mine. It's been too damn long.

"Definitely."

I pull into the local general store just about a mile from the cabin. As soon as I take the keys from the ignition, I lean over and kiss her. "Ready?" I ask, forcing myself to pull away.

"Yes." She grins.

"You know, I'm liking that word from your lips today."

She laughs. "Come on, you." She climbs out of the car.

I meet her in front. She links her arm through mine and we head inside. I grab a cart and push while she holds on to me. We grab more food than we'll need while we're here, but like I said before, I don't want to have to come back out. I couldn't care less if we see the outside of that cabin until Monday when we have to leave.

Outside, I toss her the keys. She catches them and then stops. "I can't drive that huge thing, Dylan. What if I wreck it."

"You'll be fine. I'll be right there with you. Besides, you need to get used to it if you're going to be driving it every day."

"I'm not."

"You are. I bought it for you. I already have the dealership working on my truck. I'll pick it up when we get back."

"How can you afford this? Sorry, I know that's none of my business, but the house, the Tahoe, your truck?"

"Pop the gate." I motion to the keys in her hands. She hits the button and the rear gate lifts. I toss the groceries in the back and put the cart in the corral. "Hop in, Aves. We can talk on the way."

She hesitates before conceding and climbing into the driver side. I wait while she adjusts the seat to her height and messes with the mirrors. "You've driven my truck before. This is just like it."

She nods, starts the engine, and slowly backs out of the space. "That camera makes that less stressful." She laughs. I can tell she's nervous.

"It does. Just remember to always still look beside you as well."

"Got it."

I wait until she's on the road that leads to the cabin before I address her concerns. "Avery, I worked every day for the last four years, barely spending a dime of any of my paychecks. Dad refused to let me pay rent and he had savings for college, insisted I use it. That first year, I worked as many hours as I could, trying to work away the pain. The second year, Dad increased my pay. Said I was putting just as much into the business as he was and should be compensated as such. We do really well, Avery."

"I understand that, but you're doing all of this for me and I feel guilty. I don't love you for what you can give me, Dylan. I love you for who you are. For the way you love me."

"I know that. That's all the more reason for me to spoil you. That's all I've ever wanted, baby. Just to love you and make you happy. I'm in this, us. I want to spend forever with you. The house, it's an investment in our future. This car is the same thing. I want you and our kids to be safe when you're out driving around."

"Kids?" she sputters.

"Yeah, you always said you wanted at least two, if not more."

"I do."

"Turn here," I tell her. She takes the long dirt road, and just past the tree line is our cabin. She turns off the car and pulls the keys from the ignition.

"I want that with you, Avery. I want every fucking second of the life we used to talk about. I want that for us."

"This place hasn't changed a bit," she says, taking in the cabin before us.

"Did you hear me, Aves?" I'm not going to let her hide from this.

She turns to face me and there are tears in her eyes. "I heard every word. I don't know what I did in this life to deserve you, Dylan. All I know is that I'm holding on tight. I want it all as long as you're by my side."

I'm not gonna lie, I have to swallow back the emotion that's welling in my throat.

"Let's go check it out." She's out of the truck and racing to the front door before I can protest. I race after her and catch her, one arm locked tight around her waist from behind as I lift her off the ground and twirl her around. When I set her back on her feet, she turns in my arms. "Thank you for bringing me here."

"This is our place." That's how I'll always see it. Our place.

"We better get the groceries inside."

"Party pooper." I give her a quick peck on the lips. "Here." I pull the cabin key out of my pocket.

"How did you get that already?"

"They mailed it to me. You go on in. I'll get our bags and the groceries."

"I can help," she protests.

"I'm good, babe. Go ahead and get the place opened up. I'll be right there." With one more parting kiss, I rush back to get our bags and the groceries. The sooner this is done, the sooner I get to be with my girl. Just us.

It only takes two trips to bring it all in. I grabbed the bags from the store first so she could start putting them away. She's pretty much done by the time I bring in the final few bags and our luggage.

"Now what?" she asks once everything is stored.

"Hold that thought." I make sure the front door is locked before turning back to her. "Now, I hold you. No expectations, Aves, but I need you in my arms, especially after the drive here."

"Can you give me a few minutes first?" she asks shyly.

I kiss the top of her head; I can't keep my hands and mouth off her. "Sure. If you can do one thing for me?"

"Anything."

I hold my hand out for her. "Cell phone. I don't want anyone here with us this weekend."

She smiles softly and pulls her phone out of her back pocket. I watch as she turns it off before placing it in my hand. "Five minutes." She raises on her toes, kisses me too damn quickly, and then she's racing toward the bedroom.

Turning my phone off as well, I place them on the living room table, then walk around the cabin and let the memories of being here with her wash over me. I was hoping this place would remind her of all that we shared here, I could tell by her smile I was right.

I check the patio door and make sure it's locked as well, then go through and turn out all the lights. Glancing at the clock on the stove, I see that it's been ten minutes. I promised her five.

I head toward the bedroom. Pushing open the door, I stop at what I see. My beautiful Avery is lying on the bed, her hair feathered out on the pillowcase. Her arms and shoulders are bare. Her hand is clutched to her chest, holding the white cotton sheet.

I can't speak. Literally, words won't form. On trembling legs, I walk into the room, shutting the door behind me. When I reach the side of the bed, she turns to face me. Her blue eyes tell me a story, a story of love and a future that only we can have. It's in this moment that I know—she's ready. My hand shakes when I push it into my front pocket and pull out the ring I placed there just before I reached her place today. I guess you could say I was hopeful.

Keeping the ring closed in my left hand, I push her hair out of her eyes with my right. "No matter how many times I see you like this, it will never be enough." Leaning in, I softly kiss her lips. "No matter how many times I kiss you, it will never be enough." Snaking my hand under the cotton sheet, I run my fingers up and down her bare thigh. "No matter how many times I feel your soft skin against mine, it will never be enough." I rest my head on the bed in front of her and feel her hands run through my hair. "Every touch, every kiss has me craving more." Lifting my head, I look at her. "I loved you since that first night at the bonfire. In here." I place my hand over my heart. "This is where you've been since that day. Never a minute passed that I didn't think about you, that I didn't love you."

"Dylan," she whispers as a tear falls from her cheek.

"I never want to be away from you again. I want to be your shoulder, your rock. I want the good times and the bad. I want to make babies with you. I want to grow old with you sitting on the front porch swing as we watch our kids and grandkids fall in love like we did." Lifting my left hand, I open my palm and show her the ring. She gasps as more tears fall. Holding the ring up, I lock eyes with her. "Avery, you're my dream. A life with you would make that dream come true. Will you do me the incredible honor of becoming my wife?" My voice is strong and certain. On the outside, I appear to be holding my shit together, but on the inside, I'm freaking the fuck out. Grabbing her hand, I place the ring at the tip of her finger.

"Yes," she whispers through her tears. "Yes, yes, yes!" she says, laughing as a watery smile covers her face.

Relief rushes through me. I slip the ring on her finger and then kiss it. Standing, I pull my shirt over my head and toss it on the floor. My jeans and boxer briefs are next. Avery lifts the sheet, allowing me to slide in as close as I can and wrap my arms around her. The sensation of her soft skin pressed against mine is one I will forever crave.

"I love you, Dylan."

I close my eyes and savor her words. *She's mine, she said yes. We're getting married.* "I love you, Aves." She's lying in front of me, her back to my front. I watch as she holds her hand out, admiring her ring.

"You remembered," she says softly.

"Every word, Aves. You said you liked the idea of a heart-shaped diamond. You said it signifies the guy giving the girl his heart." She nods. "I gave you mine years ago, but this one? This one shows the world that you own my heart and soul."

"It's beautiful."

"You're beautiful."

She rolls over so her head is resting on my chest. "How long have you been planning this?"

"I bought the ring the week after Brad and Harley's wedding."

"Wow," she whispers. "And this, was proposing a part of this weekend's plans?"

"No. I've been packing this ring around with me for months, just waiting for the right time. Waiting for you to give me the sign that you were ready for us to take the next step in our lives together."

"You're an amazing man, Dylan Knight."

"Because of you."

She snuggles into me and when her breathing becomes slow, I know she's fallen asleep. Making sure she's covered by the sheet, I close my eyes and allow sleep to claim me as well.

Chapter
41

Avery

When I wake up, I immediately raise my hand and look for the ring. It's there.

It wasn't a dream.

Dylan has his arms wrapped around me; my head is still on his chest. Looking at the window, I see it's now dark outside. My hand is resting on his abs, and I can't help but run my hands over the ripples and ridges. Eighteen-year-old Dylan was always in good shape; twenty-three-year-old Dylan is a new playing field.

I can't help myself, moving my hand lower, and suddenly I get an idea. For months he's been putting me off, not letting me really touch him. That changes tonight. Slowly, as to not wake him, I slide under the sheet and down to the foot of the bed. He's hard. I know that happens naturally, but I would like to think it's from sleeping next to me. I take his cock in my hand and lightly run my fingers up and down. Unable to resist, I take him in my mouth.

"Mmm," he moans at the contact.

If my mouth weren't full of him I'd be smiling right now. I take my time, just enjoying being able to do this for him. I'm turned on from the noises he's making. Feeling brave that he's still sleeping, I take all of him, and I know immediately that he's awake. His hand rests gently on the back of my head, and he raises his hips as if he's trying to get deeper.

"You're cheating," his deep sleep-laced voice rumbles.

Letting him fall out of my mouth, I take him back in my hand while pulling the sheet back with the other. I look up and our eyes connect. "Can't a girl make her fiancé feel good?"

His eyes darken. "I told you, Aves, the next time you make me come, I'll be inside of you."

Well all right, then. On my knees, I straddle his hips, his hard length beneath me. I swirl my hips in a slow rhythm that's driving me insane. From the growl that comes from him, I'd say it's doing the same to him. "Avery." My name is a warning.

"What, babe?" I ask, my voice full of want for him.

"Condom."

"I'm on the pill." His eyes shoot open. I hold up my hand and wiggle my ring finger where my engagement ring sparkles. "There's nothing between us now. We're forever, right?" I ask innocently.

"Damn right," he says, placing me on my back with him resting his weight between my thighs. Cock in hand, he guides himself to my entrance. "You sure?"

"Make love to me, Dylan. With nothing between us but love."

He bows his head and slowly pushes into me. Never taking his eyes off of our joined bodies. "Fuck me, why didn't we do this years ago?" he asks as he rocks into me.

"We were kids," I force out through the pleasure coursing through me.

A few more pumps and a swivel of his hips and he pulls out of me. "I just... fuck, Avery, you feel too good, baby. I'm ready to blow."

"I want that. I want to feel you come inside me."

I watch as he bites down on his bottom lip. "You first, beautiful." Before I can stop him, he has his face buried between my legs, rushing me to the finish line with his tongue.

"Dylan," I pant. He doesn't stop. This has been our thing over the past few months, and he can take me there from zero to sixty in no time flat. He plays my body like an instrument. I bury my fingers in his hair and hold on for the ride. "There." I'm so close. He doesn't stop as I fall over the edge. My body is humming from my orgasm when he slides back inside me.

"Fuck, that feels incredible. I can feel you pulsing around my cock."

I don't bother replying, not that I could if I wanted to. Instead I place my hands under his arms and grab his back, digging my nails in as he thrusts inside of me. It's a feeling like nothing I've ever experienced. I wish I could say it's because we're bare, but even more so it's because it's Dylan. The love we share shines through with everything we do, hence the reason they call it making love.

"I'm close, baby," he says, never losing his rhythm. I hold on tighter, just enjoying the feel of him. "Avery!" he screams and I can feel him release inside of me, which sends me into another blissful orgasm.

"Shower," he says a few minutes later. Still inside me, he lifts me to where I'm sitting on his lap. With his long legs stretched out, he climbs off the bed, never losing our connection.

"Ohh," I moan at the sensation as we walk toward the bathroom.

"You're good for my ego, future Mrs. Knight."

"You're just good," I reply.

He smacks my ass. "Shower, then food. Then I'm staying inside you for the rest of the night."

"I like this plan."

"Hold on, babe." Slowly, he pulls out and helps me stand on my own two feet in the shower. Once I'm steady, he cups my face in his hands. "I love you, Avery Knight."

The sound of his name with mine from his lips has me melting into a puddle of love for him. "I love you too."

That's how the rest of our weekend goes. We make love, shower, eat, and repeat, never leaving the cabin once.

We're both smiling like fools even though it's now Monday morning and we're packing up to leave.

"You about ready?" Dylan asks, coming up behind me and wrapping me in his arms.

"Yes, I just have to do one more walk-through. Did you leave the key on the counter?"

"Yes, dear," he teases. I smack his arm.

I go back inside, making sure we didn't forget anything. "Did you take the trash to the dumpster?"

"I did."

"Okay, I guess we're ready."

He reaches out for me and I take his hand. In the Tahoe, we both turn our phones on and leave them in the cup holders. They both start beeping like crazy with everything we've missed the past few days. Whatever it is, it was worth it. I'll always remember this time here with him.

Picking up my phone, I scroll through my messages. "Oh my God!" I scream.

"What? What happened?" Dylan asks, a little panicked.

"Alan and Kara got engaged!"

"Figures he'd pick the same damn weekend as me."

"Wait a minute? You knew?"

He shrugs. "We talk."

"Does he know?"

"He knows I have a ring, but he doesn't know that I asked you this weekend. Your parents know as well. I asked them for their blessing. Not that I needed it, of course. I would've done it without it, but it helps knowing they gave it to me. The wedding will be a lot smoother that way." He laughs.

"Wow, you've really put some thought into this."

"I have. Now all I need for you to do is tell me what kind of wedding you want and to pick a date."

I think about what he's asking, and the only thing I do know is that I don't want to wait. The sooner we start our lives together, the better. "Soon," I say, feeling him out.

"You tell me when, Aves, and I'll make it happen."

"I don't want anything big. Just small, our closest family and friends."

"Okay. We can do that. Where?"

I bite my bottom lip and decide to just go for it. "Our house," I say softly.

He turns to look at me before putting his eyes back on the road. "Our house?"

"Yeah, it's where we're going to start our lives together."

"We can do that. Can I ask you a question?"

"Anything."

"Will you move in with me?" He's grinning.

"Uh, we're getting married. That's kind of how it works."

"No, I mean now. I want to show you the house."

"I thought we agreed to go there today."

"We did." He nods. "But I want to live there with you now. I don't want to wait. Avery, I don't think I'll be able to sleep without you."

For a man who claims to not have the words, he melts my heart when he says things like that. "Okay," I agree. I don't have to think about it. I want to curl up beside him every night for the rest of our lives.

Reaching over, he holds his hand out, palm up. I place mine in his and he squeezes gently. "So the date?" he asks.

"We don't have a huge guest list. Mom, Dad, your dad, Alan, Kara, Brad and Harley. Anyone else?"

"As long as you're there, I don't care who else is."

"I'll make some calls. I'm thinking I can get it all together in a few weeks."

"Dress, preacher, all that?"

"Yeah, Mom and Harls will help."

"What can I do? Name it."

"I mean, you've already given me this ring and your heart. I don't know what else there could be… Oh wait, one more thing I need from you."

Another gentle squeeze of my hand, "Name it."

"I'm gonna need your last name."

"Fuck, you don't know how long I've wanted to give you that."

I giggle like the teenage me. "Then we're good. I'll make some calls, and once I know we can get it all worked out, I'll set a date. I'd like it to be a couple of weeks, a month at the longest."

"Are you sure this is what you want? Baby, we can have it as big or small, destination, whatever you want."

"I just want to be your wife, Dylan. I don't need all that other stuff. A wedding is for us, not them."

"Honeymoon?" he asks.

"The cabin."

"Aves—"

I stop him. "It's our place, Dylan. I just want time with my husband at our place. It's where we made love for the first time, and it'll be the first place we do as husband and wife. It's fitting."

"Done. You tell me when and I'll make it happen."

Dylan drives us straight to our house. "Home sweet home," he says, pulling into the driveway.

"I can't believe it's ours."

Pulling the keys from the ignition, he climbs out of the Tahoe and I follow him. We make it to the front porch and Dylan unlocks the door. Before I know what's happening, he bends and lifts me into his arms.

"What are you doing?" I laugh, holding on to his neck.

"Carrying you over the threshold."

"We're not married yet, Dylan."

"In my heart, you've always been mine. Now hush and let me show you our home." He carries me through every room no matter how much I protest.

"Now we have some people to visit. What if we call my dad and have him meet us at your parents'? We can tell them together," he suggests.

"Perfect. No, wait. I don't want to take away from Kara and Alan's news."

"They've already told everyone. The picture they sent was on your parents' back deck."

"Right, okay."

"Go ahead and call them. Harls and Brad too. Might as well tell them all." He winks, then sits me on the kitchen counter and stands between my legs as we make our calls, asking everyone if they can meet us in an hour. "Now we have one hour for you to tell me what you want to change. I'm getting that done so we can move in."

"Nothing, Dylan. I don't want to change anything."

"Paint?"

"Nothing. I mean, when we have kids, we'll have to paint one of the bedrooms for a nursery, but I love everything about it."

"Okay. So tonight? We're staying here?"

"Where are we going to sleep?"

"Air mattress? We can go tomorrow when you get off work and buy a bed."

"Okay."

"Okay?" he asks like he can't believe I agreed.

"Yes," I say, pulling him into a kiss.

When we get to my parents' thirty minutes later, everyone is already there.

"Nice ride," Alan calls out from the front porch where everyone is sitting.

"Thanks, my fiancé bought it for me," I fire back.

It takes them a few seconds to process what I've said. Harley screams and comes barreling at us. She wraps us both in a hug before pulling my hand from Dylan's to see the ring.

"He remembered." She looks at me and smiles.

"I got one too," Kara says, wearing a beaming smile.

We're both hugged and congratulated by those who mean the most to us.

"Let's go out back. I'll grab some drinks," Mom tells us.

The crowd fades away and I start to follow, but Dylan stops me. I turn to face him and he pulls me close, wrapping his arms around me.

"Come on, you two, what are you waiting for." Brad laughs, knowing he's interrupting what was I'm sure was about to be another epic kiss from my fiancé.

"I'm reminding Avery," Dylan yells back.

I look up at him in question. "About?"

"How much I love you." And he gives me that epic kiss I was hoping for.

Epilogue

2 years later

Avery

Trying to surprise my husband is a chore. He's so in tune with me he knows I'm hiding something. I hate lying to him, but telling him the truth would ruin the surprise. It's all going to be worth it in the end.

It took me a few days to decide how I want to do this, but once I figured it out, I knew it was perfect. I've been planning and sneaking and I'm glad tonight is finally the night. My husband is ready to stage an intervention at any minute. I wouldn't put it past him to lock me in our room, maybe even tie me to the bed until I tell him what's been going on. He has this need to protect me, to fix what might be wrong. I love him for it, but he can't always fix it.

Lucky for me, my father-in-law is amazing. When I told him I wanted to plan a surprise for Dylan and use the rooftop of the shop he smiled and asked what he could do to help. Together we came up with a plan for Dylan to run errands this afternoon so I could access the roof without him seeing me. Everything is set up, so now all I have to do is call him. I know he's almost back to the shop.

"Hey," he says after the first ring. "Dad has me running errands, why he couldn't get one of the guys to do it I don't know. I'm almost back at the shop, should be home in like a half hour or so." He rambles on.

"Dylan." I laugh. "Take a breath, babe. I'm actually at the shop now. I stopped by to see what time you were getting off and your dad told me you were running errands." *Just a little white lie.* "I decided we should do date night on the roof."

"Perfect. I'll be there in about five minutes."

"Drive safe. I'm heading on up to the roof."

"Love you, Aves."

"Love you, too." I end the call and place my phone on the table next to the pizza box that is our dinner. I'm nervous, but I know I shouldn't be. It's just an all new experience for both of us. The unknown, I guess is what has my stomach feeling like a thousand butterflies are dancing around, flapping their wings.

"Aves," Dylan calls out for me as he pushes through the door to the roof.

"Hello husband," I say with a smile standing to greet him.

His eyes darken at me calling him husband. He loves it. We've been married for two years now and he still uses wife in as many sentences as he can. He says it's just a daily reminder that our life is real, not a dream. We've been through a lot, but it's only made us stronger.

"Best idea ever," he says placing a kiss on my lips.

"Good. I just ordered pizza and then some dessert."

"Perfect." He grabs my hand and leads me over to the worn our patio couch and we both sit. This couch has been here for years, our first date and I'm sure many more before that. It's old and faded but still in good condition. This old thing holds a lot of memories for us.

"How was your day?" he asks before taking a large bite from his pizza.

"Good. I went to the store, post office, bank, got all my errands caught up. I'm not sure what I'll do the rest of the week," I laugh. I'm a school teacher and summer break just started.

"Take a break, baby. You deserve it. Besides, once we have kids your summers will be full of activities." He winks.

"In the meantime, I might just go crazy."

"So what brought all this on?" he waves his hand at the pizza box and the box of dessert sitting on the table in front of us.

"It's been a while since we've been up here. I just thought it would be nice." I shrug as if it's no big deal. I'm a terrible liar and we both know it.

"Uh huh, what else you got for me?" he asks sitting his plate on the table.

"Dessert," I say pointing to the white box.

"Aves, come on babe, something has been up with you. I was hoping this was your way of finally opening up and telling me what's going on. I'm worried about you," his voice trails off. I can see that me trying to surprise him really has had him worried.

"Dylan, I'm fine. I promise. Let's eat dessert, then we can go home and I'll show you how fine I really am."

He studies me, not moving.

"Really. It's just an adjustment. Last summer I was helping Harley with the baby and that took up a lot of my time. I'm just trying to get in the groove." I'm going to hell for lying to my husband. "Here," I pick up the white box filled with brownies and hand it to him. "Eat up."

Reaching in the box, he doesn't take his eyes off of me. Grabbing a brownie, he takes a bite. *Shit. He was supposed to open the box all the way.* "Good?"

He nods. "Talk, Aves. I've had dinner, I've had my first round of dessert," he winks, "now talk."

"One more, I bought an entire dozen." I hold the box up as if I'm presenting evidence, in a way I am.

Not one to ever deny me, he reaches for the box, again not taking his eyes off of mine. I pull the box away and he raises an eyebrow. "Look at them, don't they look yummy?" I open the lid, like he was supposed to and hold the box out toward him.

"Avery, what's going on?"

"Just look, come on, Dylan. I worked really hard to plan all of this. The least you could do is look." I'm laying on the guilt but I'm getting desperate. My plan is about to fail epically.

He sighs, but turns to look at the box. I watch his face as he furrows his brow. I wait giving him time to read what's written on the lid.

"Babe?" There is question and awe in his voice.

"Read it to me," I prompt him.

"Eat up. My mommy doesn't want to be the only one with a belly, Love, Baby Knight." The last words are chocked out.

"Congrats, Daddy," I say sitting the box on the table.

"Aves." My name is a plea on his lips. "Are we?"

I smile and nod. "Yeah, we're pregnant." Dylan drops to his knees and buries his head in my lap. His large hands cover my still flat belly. I run my fingers through his hair giving him time to process the news. I've had a few weeks to come to terms with it.

"How are you? How is the baby?" he whispers lifting his head.

"Good and good. I went to the doctor two weeks ago and confirmed it. We're due in seven months."

He lifts my shirt and places his warm lips against my skin. "I love you, baby Knight." Looking up his eyes find mine. "You." He shakes his head. "I didn't think it was possible to fall even more in love with you." His hand gently caresses my belly. "You and this baby, you're everything, Avery. I love you." he leans down and kisses my belly. "I love you, too."

I don't even try to fight the tears. I knew he would be excited, but in typical Dylan fashion he melts my heart. "I love you, too."

"We made a baby," he says reverently. "Part of me is growing inside of you. Holy shit, we're having a baby." His smile is blinding. With one last kiss to my belly and one to my lips, he lowers my shirt and stands, offering me his hand.

"Where are we going?"

"Home. I need you in our bed. I need to make love to you."

"That's kind of what got us in this situation."

He winks. "I know and we need to celebrate." He gently tugs on my arm until I stand and follow him downstairs.

Epilogue

2 more years later

Dylan

I left the shop early today. It's our four-year wedding anniversary, and if I have my way, I'm going to convince my wife to stop taking her birth control. My little princess needs a little brother or sister—I'll take either.

I pull into my in-laws and leave the truck running. "Dadda," Katie says from her pop's lap on the front porch.

Walking up the steps, I stoop down and hold my arms out for her. My father-in-law places her on her feet and she races toward me. "Dadda," she cheers, then gives me a big sloppy kiss on the cheek. It's hard to believe she's two. We just celebrated her second birthday last month.

Katelynn Hope. I never thought I could love anyone as much as I love Avery. I was wrong. My daughter and my wife, they hold my heart.

"Hey, princess, you ready to go home?"

She nods, resting her head on my shoulder. This kid, I'm telling you she has me wrapped around that little pinky of hers. "We have to go get Mommy some flowers."

"Flowers," she says sleepily.

"We were working on swinging our way to a nap," he tells me.

"You sleepy?" I ask, rubbing her back.

Of course, she replies, "No." That seems to be her go-to word these days. Aves says it's because that's all she hears. The little bugger is into everything.

After gathering her bag, I get her strapped into her seat and we head to the flower shop. Of course, she's asleep by the time we get there; she's doesn't move a muscle as I get her out of her seat. I called ahead and paid over the phone, so all I have to do is pick up the flowers I ordered.

"Let me carry these out for you," the lady behind the counter offers. "Looks like you have your hands full."

"Thank you." I lead the way out to my truck and open the back door. She places the flowers in their box on the floorboard while I get Katie strapped back into her seat. With a thank you and a wave, we're off to pick up dinner. I called ahead for Chinese and told them what time to have it ready. I'm a little early, so I sit in the truck and text Aves.

> **Me:** How's your day?

> **My wife:** Good, the day's almost over. Chinese for dinner?"

I text her a picture of the restaurant.

> **My wife:** You're off work early.

I text her a picture of Katie sleeping in her seat, careful not to get the flowers.

> **My wife:** She looks like her daddy.

She does. She has my same dark hair and facial features, but she has her momma's eyes.

> **Me:** See you at home.

> **My wife:** Love you.

Climbing out of the truck, I unstrap my daughter from her seat again and this time she rubs her eyes, slowly waking up. With her head nestled on my shoulder, we make our way into the restaurant.

"Bite," Katie says.

I laugh. "Are you hungry?" She nods sleepily. I kiss the top of her head. "We need to wait on Mommy. She should be home when we get there."

"Mommy," she agrees.

After paying for the food and managing to get Katie into her seat without dropping it, I buckle her in. "Today is Mommy and Daddy's anniversary," I tell her on the way to our house. I catch a glimpse of her in my rearview mirror and she's looking out the window. I guess I can't expect a reply from a two-year-old.

Avery is waiting for us on the front porch when we pull in. "Hey," she greets me at the truck. "I could've gone to pick her up or the food."

I bend down and kiss her. "Happy anniversary, baby."

"Happy anniversary."

"Momma," Katie calls out.

"I'll get her. Can you take the food?" I reach into the back seat and grab the takeout bag. I make quick work of getting Katie unbuckled and carry her into the house.

"Babe," I call out.

"In the kitchen."

"Katie's in here. I'm running back out to the truck."

"What did you forget?" she asks, coming around the corner with Katie on her hip.

"Don't you worry about it." I tap the end of her nose, then run out to get the flowers. She sees me and the flowers as soon as I enter the house.

"What am I going to do with you?" She smiles.

"I have an idea," I say, leaning in for a kiss.

"Oh yeah, and what might that be?"

"Make a baby with me." My voice is even, no laughter. I want her to know how serious I am.

"This again?" she asks.

"Avery, come on, Katie just turned two. She'll be three by the time the new baby gets here. You even said you don't want there to be years between them like with you and Alan."

"Can we talk about this after we eat?"

"Yes, as long as we talk about it. Tonight. And maybe even get started tonight." I smack her ass, passing her to go to the kitchen. I sit her flowers on the counter and make Katie a plate. She loves Chinese just as much as her momma.

"How was your day? Did that new sales rep fix the shipping issue?" Avery asks. We spend the next hour talking about our days and laughing at Katie. She's such a ham, my little girl.

"Baby duty or kitchen duty?" she asks me.

"I'll take whatever you don't want."

"I want baby duty." She grabs Katie from her high chair and heads upstairs.

I take in the cleanup—the worst part is the floor. We let Katie feed herself and she's a little messy. I get to work and have the mess cleaned up in record time. Sprinting up the steps, I find my girls in Katie's room. Avery is sitting in the rocking chair, reading her a story. Katie is sound asleep.

"She's out," I whisper when Aves catches me standing there.

She smiles, stands slowly, and places Katie in her crib. I join her, bending down to kiss my princess good night.

"Now we celebrate," I say softly, leading Avery to our room. She makes sure the baby monitor is on, then sets on the bed.

"You ready for your present?" she asks me.

I pull my shirt over my head and grin at her. She throws her head back, laughing. "Not that one, this one." She reaches into the nightstand, pulls out a small white box, and hands it to me.

"We still get the other one, right? You said we would talk about it, Aves."

"Yes, I know I said we would talk about it, and we will. I just want to give my husband his anniversary present first."

"Whatever it is, I'll love it. It came from you." I pull the lid from the box and search through the tissue paper. It takes some digging, but I finally feel a piece of long, thin plastic. Pulling it out of the bag, I see what it is. "Are you...? It says positive," I tell her, even though I'm sure she already knows.

She laughs. "Yes, Dylan, I know it's positive."

"How? I mean, you said..." I'm holding a positive pregnancy test. We're having another baby.

"I didn't want you to get your hopes up. Mom had trouble after Alan, and I just didn't want you to have to worry. I stopped taking my pills about three months ago."

"So how are you feeling?" I sit on the bed next to her, placing my hand on her belly. "Have you been sick like before? How far along are you?" I fire off questions.

"No sickness this time, and I'm guessing not far, maybe four or five weeks. I have an appointment next week to see the doctor." She runs her fingers through my hair where my head now rests on her belly, next to our baby. "Good surprise?"

"The best, but I don't want you keeping things from me, Aves. We're in this together. If we struggle with the next one, we go through it together. All of it."

"The next one?" she asks, trying to hide her smile.

"We make cute babies."

She laughs. "Katie is your only reference."

"Have you seen that kid? Her daddy's hair and her mommy's eyes. We do good work," I tell her, making her belly and my head shake.

"Let's get baby number two here before we start thinking about three."

"Deal." Sitting up, I cup her face. "I love you, Mrs. Knight."

"Remind me."

And I do.

Epilogue
4 years later

Brad

"There's my princess," I bend down to catch my niece as she flies into my arms. "I need some lovin,'" I tap my cheek with my finger.

Katie doesn't hesitate to give me what I'm asking for. She giggles as her lips connect with my cheek just where I told her to. "Hi Uncle Brad." She gives me one of her toothless grins.

"Where is everyone? Are your cousins being good to you?"

She nods. "In the living room. Aunt Harley is tired and she's hot."

I hold back a retort of telling just how hot I know my wife is. But I know what she's trying to say. Harley is pregnant with our third child.

"That's your new baby cousin, cooking." I tickle her sides. I expect her giggles, but she just squirms and lays her head on my shoulder. "What's up princess?" It's a name that Dylan gave her, and I can still remember the day that she told me she was a princess and that's what I should call her. We all laughed but I haven't referred to her as Katie since, well not to her face anyway.

"I'm sad," she whispers.

Immediately I think that her younger brother, DJ or one of my boys Collin or Corey did something to upset her. It may be wrong but with her being the only girl, Dylan and I both dote on her. "Why are you sad, Princess?"

"Cause I'm not gonna be your princess anymore."

What is she talking about? "Of course you are. What make you think that?"

"Aunt Harley says the baby is a girl and I won't be the only little girl anymore."

She sticks her bottom lip and it breaks my heart. I don't know how Dylan ever tells her no. I'm so fucked when it comes to my little girl. "Not true. You see you're going to need to show your new baby cousin how to be a princess. She needs to learn everything she knows from you."

Her eyes light up. "You can have more than one princess?" Her voice is full of awe and wonder.

I love this kid. "Absolutely. You see we're family. We love each other the same no matter what. Just because you're my niece doesn't mean you won't still be my princess because I'm going to have a daughter." I watch as she thinks that over. "Your daddy is going to have niece, that's what the baby will be to him."

She furrows her brow. "So my daddy is going to have two princesses too?" she asks hesitantly.

"He is. Since you're older you need to show her how it's done. How to stick up to the boys." She giggles. "How to dress up, how to play Barbies, and a whole bunch of other stuff. You think you can handle that?" She bobs her little head up and down as fast as she can.

"I can," she whispers.

"Good. I'm counting on you to teach her how it's done," I say hugging her tight.

"I will, Uncle Brad. I promise." She looks over my shoulder and a grin splits her face. "Daddy!" She holds her arms out and Dylan catches her with ease.

"What's up Princess?" He kisses her cheek.

"I'm gonna be a princess teacher. Uncle Brad says I have to teach the new baby how it's done. Aaannnd," she grins, "I get to tell her how to stick up to the boys." She curls up her nose.

"Wow, sounds like you're going to have your hands full," Dylan says.

"Yeah and you know what else?"

"What's that, baby?" he asks. She has his full attention.

"I'm still gonna be his princess too. Just cause there's another girl we can both be Princess's."

Dylan looks over at me and I shrug. "Really?" he asks her.

She nods. "Yep and you will have two princesses too daddy." She gives him a booth toothy smile and I can visibly see him melt for her. "I gotta go tell mommy and Aunt Harley." She wiggles out of his hold and he lets her go.

"She's a fireball, that one," I say once she's out of earshot.

"Man, you have no idea."

"I'm in for it huh?"

"Yep. Avery and Katie know how to work me. DJ he's easy, goes with the flow, we throw the football around and he's golden. Katie, she wants tea parties and to play Barbies."

I laugh. "Yeah, she's roped me in a time or two."

"Yeah, but man, I'm telling you when it's your daughter, when she looks up at you with your features and your wife's eyes." He shakes his head. "With one look I'd give her the world."

I follow him into the living room where Avery and Harley are sitting. Katie is already back in the playroom with the boys. I sit down beside Harls and rub her belly. Leaning down, I kiss her and speak softly. "You're not dating until you're thirty."

Harley laughs. "She's not even born yet and your making threats."

"Promises." I kiss her swollen belly again. "Daddy loves you, Princess."

Contact

Kaylee Ryan

Facebook:
www.facebook.com/pages/Kaylee-Ryan-Author

Goodreads:
www.goodreads.com/book/show/17838885-anywhere-with-you

Twitter:
@author_k_ryan

Instagram:
Kaylee_ryan_author

Website:
www.kayleeryan.com

Other works by
Kaylee Ryan

With You Series
Anywhere With You
More With You
Everything With You

Stand Alone Titles
Tempting Tatum
Unwrapping Tatum
Levitate
Just Say When
Unexpected Reality
I Just Want You

Soul Serenade Series
Emphatic
Assured

Southern Heart Series
Southern Pleasure
Southern Desire

Acknowledgments

To my readers, I appreciate each and every one of you. This journey has been amazing and I am honored to have you along for the ride. Thank you for spending your hard earned money on my words. From the messages, e-mails, posts, tags, all of it. Your support pushes me through. I will forever be grateful. #myreadersrock

My family. I love you. You continue to stand beside me during this journey. Your love and support keeps me going. Thank you.

Sara Eirew, thank you so much for an amazing photo and cover design. You've made Dylan and Avery come to life.

Tami Integrity Formatting, you never let me down. You make my words come together in a pretty little package. Thank you so much for always taking the time to work me in. I would be lost without you.

My beta team: Kaylee 2, Jamie, Stacy and Lauren I love you! From day one you all have been there and I cannot tell you how much that means to me. You take time away from your lives to read for me and then read it again and again. I don't know what I would do without the four of you.

Give Me Books, thank you for hosting and organizing the cover reveal and release of Reminding Avery. I appreciate all of your hard work getting this book out there.

To all of the bloggers out there...Thank you so much. Your continued never-ending support of myself, and the entire indie community is greatly appreciated. I know that you don't hear it enough so hear me now. ***I appreciate each and every one of you and the***

support that you have given me. Thank you to all of you! There are way too many of you to list…

To my Kick Ass Crew, you ladies know who you are. I will never be able to tell you how much your support means. You all have truly earned your name. Thank you!

S. Moose, thank you for taking the time out of your busy writing schedule to beta for me. It's nice to have another authors opinion. I know I can always trust that you give me your honesty. I could not ask for more.

With Love,